UNEXPECTED DEATH

Dell Shannon

UNEXPECTED DEATH

DEATH

William Morrow and Company, Inc., New York

Wonders are many, and none is more wonderful than man.
—*Sophocles*, ANTIGONE

UNEXPECTED DEATH

ONE

Lieutenant Luis Mendoza, L.A.P.D., Homicide, came into the office
a little late that Tuesday morning in late March. They had this and
that on hand, and nobody else was there but Sergeant Lake at the
switchboard and Glasser typing a report in the big detective-office.

"George and Art went out to see that Donovan," said Lake.

"*Dios*, I'd forgotten about him," said Mendoza. Donovan they'd
just picked up yesterday afternoon. He and his pal Roderick
Dover had had some boyish fun last week sniping at an innocent
driver—probably while high on something. But it was just as Hackett had brought Donovan in yesterday that the other case had
broken, the funny one that had had them talking to themselves, that
Edward Holly, and they'd never questioned Donovan at all; they
had booked him straight into jail.

"New report on your desk," added Lake.

Mendoza went on into his office, sat at the desk and looked at
the report. It was signed by Schenke. And it was a curious enough
little thing that Mendoza's eyebrows shot up and he said to himself, "*Extraño*. I do wonder."

At half-past eleven last night a Mr. and Mrs. John Hurley had
come prosaically home from the movies. They lived in a four-family
place on Elmyra Street, the other side of the railroad yards, and
the garages were in the rear along a little alley. As Hurley had
turned the car into the alley, his headlights had showed them a body
up there. About, Hurley had told Schenke, in front of Hurley's own
garage. The Hurleys had called for cops, and first of course they got
a patrol car and then Bob Schenke. The body, said Schenke, was
interesting. The body of a very pretty young woman, early twenties
at most, in a green lace evening gown. Hardly a mark on her: no
jewelry: no purse. Just the beautiful blonde, dead in the alley. The

9

interns said her neck was broken. "The body," wrote Schenke, "obviously not local. Dress looks like Beverly Hills," and that was in a note to Mendoza. "Hurleys ordinary citizens—middle-aged, he works for the city. N.G. Looks like a real mystery—have fun with it."

Mendoza's curiosity took him down to the morgue.

The blonde had been a good-looker all right. About twenty, twenty-two, fine small features, very white skin, big blue eyes, and her naturally blonde, shoulder-length hair looked to have been professionally cared for. Not, as the report said, a mark on her but for a couple of dark bruises on her slender throat.

"Let's have a look at her clothes," said Mendoza interestedly. The attendant brought them out for him. Schenke's instinct had been quite right: the green lace formal bore the label of Gina, a shop in Beverly Hills—a very expensive shop. The underclothes— white lace bra, nylon lace panties, garterbelt and very sheer nylon stockings—were all of expensive quality. The high-heeled black patent pumps likewise wore an expensive label; they were size four and a half. She'd been a small girl: five feet, one hundred pounds. And no indication on her hands that she'd fought back when she was attacked: her nails were pristine, freshly manicured, painted a modest iridescent pink.

"*Muy extraño*," said Mendoza. "Now who is she and how did she end up on Elmyra Street?"

"I'm just paid to keep track of 'em until the funeral," said the morgue attendant gloomily. "Seen all you want?"

"For the moment," said Mendoza. He went back to his office and told Lake to connect him with Missing Persons. "Carey? Mendoza. Our latest corpse—" He described her minutely. "Ring any bells?"

"Nary a bell," said Lieutenant Carey. "I'd have remembered one like that. Nobody's reported her."

"Also funny," said Mendoza. "She looks like somebody who'd be missed right off. She'd been—mmh—taken care of. Pampered. Somebody's darling."

"Well, I'll let you know if we hear anything about her," said Carey.

"Yes, thanks." Mendoza put the phone down, smoothing his moustache absently.

"Oh, I didn't say," said Lake, looking into the office, "but Tom went out on a tip—that Milner, one of the pigeons called in, said he was at a greasy spoon over on the Row."

"Um," said Mendoza. That one. A longtime hood with a long

pedigree, who had for pretty sure shot the part-time liquor store clerk last month. Nice to catch up to him.

"And Matt went out on a new call."

"Um," said Mendoza again. "What?"

"Old woman dead in her own kitchen—Cortez Street in Boyle Heights. Daughter-in-law found her."

Which didn't sound like much, of course. Wait and see. The blonde was a good deal more interesting. The night men had, of course, taken her prints, and passed them on to the Feds in Washington as well as Records here. The Feds had a lot of prints of quite respectable citizens as well as the pros; maybe they had hers.

Maybe the little mystery would clear itself up in short order; but Mendoza had a small hunch that also maybe it wouldn't.

Both Palliser and Grace were off on Tuesdays.

Mendoza's mind strayed momentarily to the offbeat one they'd just cleared up yesterday: that had been something, all right. Now they had something else coming along; they usually did. Central Homicide, L.A.P.D., got kept busy.

Lake looked in again. "I've got that John Holly," he said. "Wants to see you."

"Who's—oh," said Mendoza. "Oh, well, we haven't even got the autopsy report yet—Bainbridge is busy—I don't know anything to tell him." John Holly's father—that was another queer little thing, of course. Edward Holly, in his fifties, market-manager at a supermart, but rapidly going blind. Who never went out at night. Rented a small rear apartment on Crosby Lane. Found dead a block over on Crosby Place, Sunday morning, on the front porch of an elderly widow who hadn't known him. "Oh, well, I'll see him," said Mendoza. "Shove him in, Jimmy."

John Holly was a thin, rather shabbily dressed young man. He was an accountant at one of the smaller brokerages on Spring. He looked at Mendoza drearily and said, "But I just can't figure it. I just can't. Dad was so—so regular about everything. I mean, following routine and all. He never went out after dark, since his sight had been going so fast. He wasn't going to be able to work much longer —I told the other detective about that. And I—"

"You said there wasn't anything missing from his apartment? Detective Landers asked you to look."

"Yes. I know. There isn't. He was going—going to move in with us—Bonnie and me—Bonnie, that's my wife, she thought an awful lot of Dad—we were going to look after him—get a bigger apartment—he'd sold some of his furniture already. See, my mother died about ten years back and Dad—but it wasn't as if he'd had a lot of money or anything valuable—and if it was just a burglar, how come Dad was way a block away from home? I—"

It was, when you thought about it, a teasing little problem. Why had he been? Even stranger, of course, the fact that his wallet had still been on him, with fifty-six dollars in it.

"We ought to get the autopsy report some time today, Mr. Holly," said Mendoza. "That will tell us something more."

"I just can't figure it," said Holly miserably. "I just wondered if you'd found out anything. Well, thanks." He stood up.

As he went out Hackett and Higgins came in, the two big men dwarfing the office as usual. "So Donovan's a carbon copy of Dover," said Hackett, sounding exasperated, "except that he wasn't high when we brought him in. The damn fuzz interfering with his fun. But of course Dover ties him in, what we got there, and his prints'll probably be in the car."

"Yes," said Mendoza. "Is that so? Sit down and hear about our newest mystery." He handed over Schenke's report. Higgins read it over Hackett's shoulder. "I went and had a look at her. She was, surely to God, irrelevant—that's a word for it—irrelevant to Elmyra Street," said Mendoza. "No missing report on her."

"That's a funny one all right," said Higgins, his rough-hewn face thoughtful. "Wait to see if she's in Records, or Washington knows her."

"Sí. How's the family?" asked Mendoza.

Higgins smiled. "Fine. Just fine." The men at Central Homicide had all been wishing Higgins luck in his humble pursuit of Bert Dwyer's widow, and had been pleased when she married him six months back, to give him his ready-made family of Dwyer's good kids, Steve and Laura; and now she was going to have a new baby, and Higgins as foolish and fond over that as any prospective parent —Higgins the longtime bachelor.

Landers looked in and said, "That Milner. He was there—I picked him up. Somebody want to sit in on the questioning?" He was rubbing his shoulder; Landers was just back on the job the last month since getting shot up by a sniper. "You know," he said now, "I think that Chalmers guy did me a favor. This damn shoulder. I've kind of tested it, and I'll be damned but it's made a weather prophet out of me. Starts to ache the day before it rains."

Hackett sighed and stood up. "As if we haven't had enough of that." It had been the wettest winter, so the papers said, in seventy years. "I'll sit in. Always the routine. He give you any trouble?"

"Nope. He was too surprised."

At about the same time Bertha Hoffman was feeling surprised and asking, "Off on a trip?"

"Yeah, that's right," said the boy. "Mom said I was to tell you not to come for a while. She'll let you know. When they get back."

"How come you kids didn't go along?"

"Oh, Mom and Dad, they had to go back east, take care of my grandma—she's sick. Besides, we got to go to school. I'll be late for first class—I just stayed to tell you, Mom said you needn't bother to come."

Mrs. Hoffman was annoyed. She earned her living cleaning other people's houses for them, and the loss of a weekly half day's revenue was irritating. This particular employer had usually paid on the dot too. "Well," she said. "Well, all right."

"I just stayed to tell you," said the boy. "I got to go—I'll be late." He banged the front door behind him and came past her down the front steps.

Mrs. Hoffman hesitated. She always spent Tuesday mornings here, and Tuesday afternoons at a house across the street, the house of another old and prompt-paying employer. It seemed a waste of time to go all the way home—perhaps she could work over there this morning instead.

She crossed the street to ask.

"Now, Mrs. Darley," said Piggott, "I realize you're upset, but if you'd just—"

"Upset!" exclaimed Rose Darley. "Upset! That's a funny sort of word for it—finding my own mother-in-law *murdered!* Upset! And what Charley'll say—my goodness, it's just awful, what's happening these days—and old people alone—but none of us had the room for her and besides she owned this place—and my goodness, I got to call Charley and tell him—"

"The patrol-car men have gone to get your husband," said Piggott patiently. He'd put in a call for the mobile lab and the men were at work here now. Piggott looked around the place and suppressed a sigh. Cops saw the bottom of things, inevitably.

This was an old, small, shabby house on Cortez Street, not far from headquarters. It was a sagging frame house, unpainted for

13

years, and at least for the years in which Mrs. Marion Darley had owned it, it had not been a house well cared-for. Piggott and young-ish Mrs. Rose Darley were in the living room now, but he remembered the kitchen vividly, where the lab men were busy now—a dim hole of a room, with a stack of dirty dishes in the sink, something gone bad in the ancient refrigerator, and the rather ghastly corpse of Marion Darley on the floor—a grossly fat old woman in a tattered flannel bathrobe over a worn flannel nightdress. The living room was, in some ways, just as bad. It was sparsely furnished with aged, falling-apart furniture—a sagging couch, two upholstered chairs, no carpet: and against the walls were stacked literally thousands and thousands of old magazines—old movie magazines, *True Love, True Romance*. The whole place was dirty and dusty.

"Mrs. Darley, if you'd just—"

"Well, I told you how I found her. I usually stop by on my way to market two or three times a week—see, we live up on Bixel, only a couple of blocks—ask if she wants anything at the market, like that. And I usually come in the back door, because she usually sits in the kitchen, if you get me. And so I walk in and there she was. Dead. *Murdered.* Well, my goodness—"

Looking, Piggott reflected, very thoroughly beaten up. Not a very nice corpse. "Mrs. Darley, was your mother-in-law in good health? Able to get around? Do any of her own shopping, or did you—"

"Well, sure. Sure she was. I just stopped by, maybe save her the walk, that's all." Rose Darley stared at him. She was about thirty, a little too plump, and darkhaired. Her husband Charley had a job at a service station somewhere down here. Mrs. Darley's other two sons were both currently on Welfare. She'd had the state old-age pension.

"How long had she lived here? Do you know whether anyone around here might have had a reason to do this to her?"

"Anybody around here? How the hell should *I* know? She'd lived here maybe thirty years, I guess—they just got the house paid for when her husband died. Charley's father. He worked for the railroad. I don't know anything about it, except I walked in and found her. How would I? It must've been a burglar breaking in— my God, the things that happen nowadays! Just last week it was the Harts only four doors up from us got robbed—"

"Would you know if anything's missing? If you'd look around—"

"Yeah, I guess I would. But she didn't have much of anything—

14

I mean, she was just on the pension, that's all she had. I can't see as anything's gone."

"Did she have a TV?" Most people did, even the ones on Welfare and the pension. Piggott amended that thought to, especially those.

"No, she didn't. She used to come watch ours—and Bill's and Joe's." Her other two sons. "And other people's around. You know."

One of the lab men, Duke, looked in and caught Piggott's eye. Piggott went out to him, in the tiny square passage just inside the front door. "So?"

"So, a lot of prints," said Duke, and grimaced. "Hell of a dirty, dusty old place—hasn't been cleaned in years. So what's to say any latents we pick up mean anything? As for anything else, the interns say she's been dead since some time last night—maybe around midnight. You saw the setup in the kitchen—evidently she'd got undressed and was sitting at the table there having a glass of beer, when in comes X. Just walked in—the back door wasn't locked."

"Helpful," said Piggott. Piggott tended to be a pessimist. "So, ask the neighbors if anybody saw or heard anything. The routine. It might bave been anybody—and anybody living alone, even in neighborhoods like this, the gossip gets round about the cash stashed away, it could have been something like that. But the place hasn't been ransacked, of course. Which it probably would have been if— Well, thanks for nothing."

"Something may show—we'll have a look at her clothes and so on. I want to get her daughter-in-law's prints for comparison," said Duke. "She walked in the back door too, and all too likely messed up any X might have left."

The front door burst open, shuddering on its ancient hinges, and a stocky dark man rushed in. The uniformed men were behind him. "What the hell is this all about?—Ma?—these guys said—"

"Mr. Darley? I'm Detective Piggott of Homicide." Piggott hauled out the badge. "I'm afraid your mother is dead. I know you're upset to hear—"

"Upset!" said Mrs. Darley behind him. "For God's sake, *upset!*"

It went on being a usual day for Central Homicide. Landers and Hackett spent a while questioning the hood Milner, and got exactly nothing. They already had, of course, some beautiful latent prints of Milner's off the cash register at that liquor store where the clerk had been shot. They had thought the clerk had nicked Milner some-where—blood found in the street—and interestingly enough there was a nearly-healed scar of some sort of wound on Milner's left upper arm. It was a gamble whether they'd be able to nail him for it, but they booked him in and asked for a warrant to look at his rented room—they might come across the gun.

Piggott came back to type up a preliminary report on the new one, and Mendoza heard about that.

"Another mystery," he said. "Probably not a very big one. The routine may turn up something."

There was another anonymous corpse over on the Row, prob-ably dead of an overdose of alcohol. Higgins went out on that. There was a suicide found in an old hotel out on Olive: a middle-aged woman, note left, so just the paperwork on that. There was a hit-run with the victim D.O.A., over on Wilshire: a ten-year-old boy. Hackett went to look at that.

And Mendoza continued to wonder about the blonde in green lace. When he came back from lunch he asked Sergeant Lake to get him Beverly Hills headquarters, was passed around a little, and finally described the blonde to a Sergeant Macy. "She looks like Beverly Hills, if you get me. The labels in the clothes and so on. Our Missing Persons hasn't had a report on her. Just occurred to me maybe yours has. Depending on where she's missing from."

"We aren't divided up into neat departments like the big-city fuzz," said Macy dryly. "So I can tell you right off, we've heard nothing about your fancy lady in green lace. If we ever do, I'll let you know."

"You do that," said Mendoza. "It's strange—one like that, I'd have thought she'd have been missed by now."

He called Sergeant Barth at the Wilcox Street precinct in Holly-wood, but Wilcox Street hadn't heard anything about the blonde either.

Piggott and Landers had gone back to Cortez Street to start the routine on Marion Darley. Talk to the neighbors, had anyone seen or heard anything suspicious. The routine so often did pay off.

Everybody was out except Mendoza when the General Hospital called at three-forty. The doctor reporting was apologetic; the Gen-eral tried to be careful about these things, but there it was. Roderick Dover had succeeded in slashing his wrists a couple of hours ago.

"*¡Por vida!*" said Mendoza. "*Eso sí que está bueno.* And it doesn't even save the taxpayers the trial expenses, because there's Donovan. Damnation, yes, and it makes it all the more likely that Donovan'll get off clear—we know it was Dover who fired the gun. Or are you going to pull him through?"

The doctor said he doubted it. "He'd been on the acid, LSD, hadn't he, as well as heroin? Well, they will do the most fantastic—naturally we'd taken everything potentially dangerous away from him. His belt, pocketknife, etcetera. That's routine. He—"

"So how did he manage it?"

"There wasn't even a drinking glass in the room. He used the bulb from the ceiling fixture. Evidently stood on the bed—he was six-two, of course—and unscrewed the bulb, and smashed it. Used the biggest piece to— Well, he's all but dead now. He'd just been given sedation, and nobody checked on him for about an hour, and he was pretty far gone then. Evidently did it before the shot reached him."

"*Vaya.*" So, more paperwork. And very likely now Donovan would be let loose on probation, thought Mendoza, annoyed. One just as potentially dangerous as Dover, but he'd only been driving the car on that caper.

Well. Better inform the father. Derek Dover: that sad man washing his hands of a son so unexpectedly gone to the dogs. And then type a report.

Hackett came back as he was finishing the report, and said, "Do I have to tell you? That hit-run. About forty witnesses, and so forty different descriptions of the car. We might as well throw it in Pending right now."

"Work it a little first," said Mendoza. "It's part of the job to make bricks without straw, Arturo. Something may show. Oh, by the way, we've lost Dover." He enlarged on that and Hackett swore.

"Not that he's any loss, but now the other one'll get off with a slap on the wrist."

"Way the cards fall." Mendoza signed the typed report on Dover, sat back and lit a cigarette. "That beautiful blonde is still intriguing me. Just on the looks of the thing, she should have been missed. I wonder—"

"Don't," said Hackett, "borrow trouble. One thing at a time."

"That's just what we never get, of course," said Mendoza. The words were not out of his mouth when Sergeant Lake came in.

"Traffic," he said tersely. "A 187 over on Westmoreland. A woman."

"What did I tell you?" said Mendoza. One eighty-seven was the number of the penal code which translated to murder. Not just a plain homicide. He got up, automatically yanked down his cuffs and reached for his hat.

"There's an ambulance on the way," said Lake, "and a lab truck."

"*Bueno.* Come on, Art."

"I've got this damned report to— Damn it, if it isn't one thing it's seven," complained Hackett.

They drove over to Westmoreland Avenue in Mendoza's Ferrari. It was shabby middle-class along there, small apartments, old courts, a few single houses, many with smaller houses built at the rear of the lots. The address the squad-car had called in was that of an eight-family apartment, an old brown stucco place needing paint. It was an upstairs apartment, at the rear. The neighbors downstairs were out in the hall, curious and gabbling—a fat woman in a pink cotton housecoat, a pretty dark young woman looking frightened, clutching a yelling red-faced baby, an elderly man with a hearing aid, asking each other questions in the front hall, staring up the stairs at the cops as they came and went.

The ambulance had arrived, stood empty at the curb. Mendoza and Hackett climbed uncarpeted stairs, and as they climbed listened to the voice from above: a man's voice, hysterical, loud, out-of-control. Both of them had been cops for a long time, and they were from experience shrewd evaluators of the truth. And hearing that voice, both of them knew instantly that they were hearing the truth. More painfully, hearing a man bare his soul in agony.

"But Kitty—my Kitty—no, no, it's not true, it's not true, oh, sweet Jesus Christ, no, no, no, no, no—Oh, Kitty, Kitty, Kitty—not Kitty—"

They came to the landing and the hallway. Down there at the end of the hall, at the door of the right rear apartment, was a little knot of struggling men: the two interns in white, a civilian, one of the uniformed men. The civilian was sobbing, trying to get away from them back into the apartment. "Kitty Kitty Kitty—my own darling—no no no no no no—"

As Mendoza and Hackett came up the hall, the interns had closed with him; one of them had a hypodermic needle ready as the uniformed man and the first intern held him. The needle went in even as the man struggled and sobbed; they held him, and he started to go limp.

"The poor devil," said the intern with the needle, sounding shaken. "All to pieces. Well, he'll be out a few hours now." He looked up and saw the men from Homicide. "Came home from work, found his wife— He was rational enough up to about ten minutes ago, delayed shock I guess. The body's in the bedroom."

Mendoza and Hackett went into the apartment. The living room was ordinary: old furniture, but everything clean and neat. On the coffee table before the couch was a tray, with three plastic coffee cups on it, cream and sugar, a decanter. A door to the left led into a little kitchen; a door to the right led into a bedroom. The other squad-car man was in there.

An ordinary bedroom: double bed made up with a white chenille bedspread, a straight chair, a double dresser, door to a closet, another door open on the bathroom. And on the bed the body. The body of a young, darkhaired woman—naked, legs sprawling, bruised and beaten and dead. Maybe raped? The doctor would say.

TWO

In another thirty seconds the shot had put the husband right out: the interns brought up a stretcher and took him away. "Name's Robert Durand, sir," said one of the squad-car men, Bartlett. "We got a little out of him before he broke up. He's a waiter at the Ambassador Hotel. Home early because he'd done overtime last night."

The lab men arrived. "Damn it," said Mendoza, "we didn't hear anything from those interns about times—" but they'd be back for the body. He and ·Hackett went back to the living room while the lab men started to take photographs, and he eyed the coffee table. "Say something to you?"

"Two things," said Hackett. "Considering that Durand wasn't doing any acting. One time we can count out the spouse, *¿cómo no?* Oh, we'll check on him, but for my money Durand's out. And— somebody she, they, knew?" He nodded at the coffee table. "The door wasn't forced."

"So she let X in. Two X's, Art?" There were three cups—green and yellow daisies in a pretty pattern on the plastic. Tray to match. The decanter was green· plastic, insulated. The cream and sugar jugs matched the cups. Three stainless steel spoons in the saucers, used. Apparently coffee had been drunk, poured from the decanter.

"That's what it looks like," agreed Hackett. "I know, funny. Looked as if she'd been raped. Well, all right, that's happened before too."

"*Como sí.* I suppose we'd better talk to some of the neighbors out there, find out what they knew about the Durands. The interns'll be back—"

There were now a couple of women out on this floor—a Mrs. Gentry and a Mrs. Otten, both youngish housewives. They told Mendoza, almost in chorus, that the third apartment up here was occupied by the Woosters, who both worked and weren't home. Yes, they'd known Mrs. Durand. They exclaimed and asked questions: he gave them a minimum of information, and asked more. Yes, the Durands were nice people, they said, quiet people. Neither of them knew Kitty Durand very well; she'd been working too, up to last week, so they hadn't seen much of her. She'd been a salesclerk at a dress shop out on Wilshire. No, never any wild parties or noise. They didn't think the Durands had been married long: youngest people living here. It just didn't seem possible—a nice quiet young girl like that, right in her own home—

Yes, they'd both been right in their own apartments all afternoon, and hadn't heard a thing. No screams or anything at all. Naturally, if they had—what time since they'd been out? Well, Mrs. Otten had gone to the market between eleven and twelve, and Mrs. Gentry had got up with a migraine headache at six this morning and gone back to bed after taking some codeine tablets, but she'd been awake since noon and right here, and hadn't heard a thing.

The interns came back to see if they could take the body; the lab men were finished with it now. Mendoza asked for an estimate of how long she'd been dead.

"At a very rough guess, call it five to seven hours," said the older one. "Can we have it?"

Mendoza waved a dismissal, glancing at his watch. Five-forty. So, possibly while Mrs. Gentry was still asleep and Mrs. Otten out at the market?

Downstairs, Hackett was hearing more of the same. The landlord, who turned out to be the elderly man with the hearing aid, gave him something else. The Durands had always been prompt with the rent, he said, and had lived here just short of two years. Nice quiet young people, he said.

They compared notes on the steps outside. The end of a working day; pick up the threads tomorrow. "You can check at the Ambassador, Art," said Mendoza, lighting a cigarette. "On the face of it, X an acquaintance at least, and she opened the door to him. We probably can't talk to Durand until tomorrow anyway."

"No." Hackett yawned.

As they started back for the headquarters lot and Hackett's car, Mendoza said, "Another odd one. In a way. Once in a while we get a spate of them. But it's that blonde who worries me. Just as I said, somebody's darling. She should have been reported—she really should."

21

"Take it as it comes, boy," said Hackett. And as Mendoza pulled into the lot, the first few drops of rain pattered on the windshield. "Just like Tom said, damn it. More rain. I'll be damned. They say it's been the wettest winter in—"

"Yes, I heard that too."

Hackett drove home in the Barracuda through an increasing downpour. He thought the blonde was rather funny too—in the sense of funny-peculiar—but she wasn't worrying him as, apparently, she was bugging Luis. But then, he reflected, Luis was prone to read in the complexities where they weren't. To be hoped, what he was doing here.

When he came in the back door, dripping from the dash from the garage, Angel said, "Honestly! *More* rain. I'll be going stir-crazy with these offspring of ours cooped up here. Dinner in ten minutes."

Sheila, uncertain on her fifteen-month-old feet, tottered up to him; he bent and picked her up. "How's my Sheila-girl?" Mark Christopher arrived at a run.

"Interesting day?" asked Angel, dropping a chunk of butter into the asparagus.

"So-so," said Hackett. "The routine. There's Luis' blonde, of course." He paused. "I do wonder if he's having a hunch about that blonde," he said thoughtfully.

Higgins got home to the house on Silver Lake Boulevard through a downpour. His house—even after six months he was still feeling surprised to realize that he had a house, and a family—if a second-hand family, soon to have added to it a first-hand family, and he was still feeling incredulous about that—was warm and peaceful, Mary busy setting the table in the dinette. Laura was practising her piano lesson.

"You O.K.?"

"Fine," said Mary, smiling at him. "Dinner in ten minutes. . . . Don't fuss, George. It's not my first attempt at it, after all. Which makes me feel all the—the funnier about it—with Laura ten. And it's a little embarrassing, both of them so interested—" She laughed. "I know one thing. It is going to take all my time and brains to keep this baby from being the most rottenly spoiled brat in the country. Especially if it turns out to be a girl."

"Now, Mary—"

"I know you. And Steve!" said Mary, laughing. "You might go and tell him to get washed up for dinner."

Higgins, grinning somewhat foolishly, went to find Steve brooding over his homework, and told him. "O.K.," said Steve, scrambling up off the floor. "George, I just can't hardly wait for the baby, you know? Gee, October, that's an awful long time. Gee, I hope it's a girl, don't you?"

"Well, I guess we wait and see. You see the doctor this afternoon? What'd he say about the brace?" After the hit-run accident last fall, Stevie having to wear the brace.

"Oh, he said it can come off next month. I mean, a baby brother'd be sort of nice, but I sure hope it's a girl," said Steve earnestly.

Mendoza came home in time to witness the twins' baths, and hear a disjointed account about *el pájaro* and the cats. Joining Alison at the dining table, he said, "Don't tell me that damn-fool bird is back, *amante?*"

"He never went away," said Alison. "He's nesting. Or rather, apparently, had nested—in the alder tree in the back yard—and I can just imagine what his wife said to him when he came back after nearly a week's disappearance." The mockingbird, which had apparently had a losing encounter with a tar-spraying machine, getting his wings stuck tight, had been brought home by Bast, rescued by Alison and Mrs. MacTaggart, and had spent some perilous days in a box in the house while they labored over him freeing his tarred wings. "Máiri spotted the nest, and evidently the eggs are hatched because both of them are foraging like mad—*el pájaro* and his wife —when he isn't dive-bombing the cats. The twins are fascinated."

"*Caray*," said Mendoza. "He'd better watch his step."

Alison poured coffee. "Bertha did a wonderful job on the table— I like that new wax," she said, regarding the shining mahogany pleasedly. "But she was annoyed at the Spencers—how she does hate her routine to get upset. They've gone off on a trip somewhere and don't want her for a while. And it seems last week Mrs. Spencer had run out of checks and hadn't enough cash, so she owes her. It's funny—"

"Mmh?" Mendoza had exchanged perhaps six words with Mrs. Spencer across the street, in the time they'd lived here.

"*¡Cuidado!*" said Alison, and Sheba landed lightly on the table beside Mendoza's cup. She slid on the new wax and knocked the bowl of peas off its trivet. "No—*bad cat! Not* on the table, *mon-*

struoso!" Alison got up to lift her off, and Sheba swore at her loudly. "You're looking preoccupied," she added as she sat down again. "Tough new case?"

"There's always a new case," said Mendoza. "Isn't there? But that blonde—she worries me. Why hasn't somebody reported her? It's the kind of curious thing I don't like."

"So tell me about it," said Alison dutifully. And very fetching she looked, her shoulder-length copper hair shining, her hazel-green eyes smiling at him.

"Well—"

And doubtless something would show on the blonde sooner or later; ask at that dress-shop in Beverly Hills? But it was the kind of offbeat little thing that annoyed him, and his large bump of curiosity was aching. Luis Mendoza, who had come into a fortune from that old ogre-on-the-hearth his crooked-gambler grandfather, needn't work at all; but his insatiable curiosity kept him holding down the desk at Homicide.

After dinner, with Alison writing letters in the den, Bast and Sheba coiled together on the sectional, Nefertite on his lap, and El Señor probably playing watch-cat in the nursery, he sat with *Traffics and Discoveries* open on top of Nefertite, and his mind kept drifting briefly back to the blonde. Presently Nefertite hissed in a halfhearted way, and a heavy warm something was laid on Mendoza's knees. He opened his eyes: their recently-acquired shaggy dog Cedric. Mendoza roughed his head and pulled his ears. "And what the hell I am still doing down there at the thankless job," he told Cedric, "only God knows." Cedric smiled at him and offered a large hairy paw.

Wednesday morning, Higgins off, and it was still raining—a gentle dispirited drizzle. To balance Higgins, John Palliser and Jason Grace were back. They took off with Piggott down to Cortez Street to start the routine of questioning Marion Darley's neighbors. Glasser began to type up an initial report on the unidentified body from Skid Row.

When Mendoza came in at eight o'clock, he asked, "Anything in from Missing Persons, Jimmy?"

"Not a thing, why? Oh, that blonde. No, nothing," said Lake. He looked glum, but Mendoza was aware of the reason. The sedentary job had caught up with Lake at last and he was on a diet. After a few months of trying to take up smoking, on the reverse principle that smokers who stopped generally gained weight, he had unwillingly accepted the diet-list from the doctor and these days was probably breakfasting on dry toast and black coffee.

"That is very funny," said Mendoza. "Indeed. Dead since Monday night. Any autopsy report in on her?"

"Not on the blonde, no. Not yet. There's—"

"Well. Get me the General." Mendoza went into his office. He was passed around at the General Hospital, finally got hold of a doctor who told him yes, he could come talk to Durand: Durand was awake and, in fact, very anxious to talk to the police. He'd be released today. Mendoza thanked him and picked up his hat again. "I'm going over to the General to see Durand," he told Lake. "Hold the fort."

"What else do I ever do?" said Lake. "I wonder if I got a transfer back to the street again—"

"Riding a patrol car's just as sedentary," said Mendoza, grinning at him.

"You can talk!" said Lake balefully. "You damn guys who never gain a pound! I've got a lot more sympathy for Art Hackett than I had before, I tell you. Cottage cheese! Black coffee! Lamb chops! I swear to God—"

"You just don't live right," said Mendoza.

Landers came in late, having overslept after watching a late movie on TV. Everybody was out, and Lake was brooding over a report of some kind.

"This just came in. Cleans one up for you—or at least halfway. I suppose you'll still want to do some legwork on it. Funny, too. You thought it was a mugging, didn't you? Looked that way."

"What?" Landers took the report. It was a belated autopsy report on Edward Holly. And what it said, in a sense cleaned that up, and another way made it look all the queerer.

Nobody had attacked Edward Holly. He had been drunk. Blood-alcohol count well above the legal rate of drunkenness. What injuries he had sustained—skull-fracture and bruises—had in all probability been sustained in a fall, or several falls. After receiving the skull-fracture, which had been the cause of death, he might have lived an hour or two, managed to crawl some distance.

"What the hell!" said Landers blankly. They had been so sure he'd been attacked. Of course, his billfold still on him, but—and by

25

what the son said— "That is a queer one all right. I'd better go see the son again."

He went out into the rain and drove up to the brokerage on Spring where John Holly worked. He talked to Holly in his little cubicle of an office. And when he broke the news to him, Holly just stared at him and said flatly, "That's impossible. That's just impossible, Mr. Landers. Dad didn't drink. It's im—"

"He was a teetotaller, Mr. Holly?"

Holly shook his head. "Not that, but—it's *impossible!* No, but he never—he'd never—look, if he had a glass of wine before dinner once a year on his birthday, that was about it. Like that. For one thing, it's expensive. Any of it. And he was a—a responsible man." He made a vague gesture. "I just can't figure any of this. It doesn't make sense. Saying Dad was *drunk*—it's crazy! Why, the only time I remember ever seeing him take even two drinks in succession—it was when Mom died—right after, he was shook up and the doctor advised—but this is crazy!"

"Well, you know, Mr. Holly," said Landers slowly—it had only just occurred to him—"he was in a kind of crisis, wasn't he? Having to retire early, and losing his sight—it just could be—"

Holly shook his head. "I just don't understand it. . . . What about the funeral? Can we—"

"You can claim the body any time," said Landers. "I'm sorry, Mr. Holly. These things happen." He came out and sat in his car and opened a County Guide. Both Crosby Lane—where possibly Holly had been heading, home—and Crosby Place, were only two short blocks down from Echo Park Avenue. About the same distance from Sunset Boulevard which crossed Echo Park. There would probably be bars along there somewhere. Bars, and the respectable, responsible Edward Holly? Landers shrugged and started the engine.

After hitting every place with a liquor license along Sunset— he'd soon discovered that for several blocks Echo Park was all residential—across from the lake—he began to feel discouraged. He'd found only one place technically open, the owner there doing some painting; most of these places wouldn't open until ten, noon, or even later. He got three bartenders out of bed to question, after ferreting around for names and addresses at stores near the bars; there were four possible other bars which were closed and anonymous; he couldn't even find out who owned them.

The bartenders all told him, with varying degrees of annoyance, that aside from regulars they couldn't say who had been in last

Saturday night, how could they? A middle-aged man, thus-and-such description, very thick glasses, maybe a little liquor affecting him a lot? They just couldn't say, didn't remember anybody like that.

Annoyed, Landers thought he'd have to wait until the other possible places were open, try there. But as he started back for his car parked on a side street, he saw that since he'd passed the Wiki-Wiki Grill on Sunset down from Echo Park, it had opened. At least the door was open. He went in. "Anybody here?"

A stocky balding man turned from the bar-flap. "We're not open, sir."

"I'm Detective Landers, Homicide." Landers produced the badge. "Are you the owner here, sir? Work here? Could you tell me who was tending bar here last Saturday night?"

The stocky man was interested. "A cop? You are? You don't look old enough, mister. You *are*? Well, anything I can tell you—Saturday night? At the bar? Well, I was. I'm not here on Saturdays usually—I'm half-owner, and my partner, Kev McCleery, he takes Saturday nights usually, but he's got the flu. All this rain. It was me. Why?"

"Well, Mr.—"

"Moynihan. Robert Emmett Moynihan."

"Mr. Moynihan, do you remember this man coming in?" Landers described Holly. "It's possible that a rather small amount of liquor affected him—" On the other hand, of course, the blood-alcohol count—

Moynihan grabbed his arm excitedly. "Somethin' happened to that poor guy! It did, didn't it? You comin'—a cop. That poor guy! I never saw him before but I tried to stop him— His name was somethin' like Christmas, mistletoe, damn it, he told me—Ivy—"

"Holly."

"*Holly*. Sure, sure, that one. Somethin' happened to him? The poor guy. He had three straight Scotches, see, and I could tell he wasn't noways used to it. At all. See? When I gave him the second one, he wanted to talk, like it takes some, you know?" Landers nodded. "He told me his name, and he said—for God's sake, he said he'd never been in a bar before! He said—lemme think now—he said, maybe he oughta get in the habit. He said he never realized before why people liked a little drink. I see he wasn't used to it, and—oh, another thing he told me, he was goin' blind. The poor *guy*. Well, after he got the third one down, I wouldn't serve him any more, see. One like that. I tell him to go home, he's had enough.

It's reached him like maybe seven or eight'd reach somebody else. He wants to buy a bottle. I tell him no. Not that I'd do that anyways, it's not legal, like, you know. I shepherd him out, I ask can he get home O.K., and he's acting some steadier then when the air gets to him, see, and off he goes. That was maybe nine o'clock, around there. But somethin' happened to him later on?" Moynihan shook his head. "That poor damned guy."

"I guess we can figure out what happened," said Landers, thinking. "You were the Good Samaritan, Mr. Moynihan. Tried to send him home. But—so he wanted to buy a bottle—"

"I wouldn't do that. I told him—"

"Yes. But maybe somebody else—" said Landers. You could work it out. Holly, the very sometime drinker, feeling depressed; going out again after his landlady had heard him come in; going into a bar for a little drink. Unprecedented, sure, but they knew that's what he had done. Picked up by the drink—feeling better. Happier. Suddenly realizing why some people took more than one drink. And probably—though they might never uncover who—at some other bar along here, somebody had sold him the bottle. There wasn't a liquor store here for several blocks, and anyway liquor store owners were generally chary of selling to obvious drunks; their licenses could get lifted so easily. And Holly would still have been showing it. Anyway, Holly making for home with the bottle. Drinking from the bottle? And eventually falling, possibly more than once, eventually falling on his head as he made erratically for home. Losing the bottle. Managing to crawl up onto that porch—

It was way out of character. But if there was one thing that cops learned, dealing with the human nature, it was that people did all sorts of surprising, sudden, unexpected, uncharacteristic and foolish things.

Do a little follow-up on it? Have a look for the bottle around where he'd been found? Anyway, they could mark the case closed. Explained. If only in terms of foolish human nature.

"Thanks very much," he said to Moynihan.

"The poor guy," said Moynihan, shaking his head. "What happened to him?"

Down on Cortez Street, the plodding routine wasn't turning up much. Jason Grace was listening to Mr. Fred Dawson, four doors down from Marion Darley's house. Dawson was middle-aged, nondescript and rather dirty, and he didn't like cops overmuch. There was a Mrs. Dawson and four children from seventeen on down: the seventeen-year-old a gangling lout of a six-footer who didn't like cops either. Dawson worked at a shoe-repair shop on Broadway, was at home with a cold. All this damned rain, he said.

"Sure we knew Mrs. Darley," he said. "So what? Most people around knew her—knew who she was. Which don't say we know anything about who killed her, for God's sake. What? No, I don't recall seein' her, last couple days, at all." The wife and kids all said the same thing. Grace, reflecting that the kids shouldn't be at home on a weekday—all drop-outs?—came out and met Piggott just leaving the house next door.

"Nobody knows nothin'," said Grace, smoothing his moustache, his chocolate-brown face wearing its usual cynically amused expression.

"Satan traveling up and down, Jase," said Piggott. "But—a neighborhood like this—they could be telling us the simple truth. I haven't found anybody on Welfare on the block, they all seem to be holding jobs of some kind. So they're away from home—days or nights. If I was a swearing man—" Piggott, of course, the devout Free Methodist—"I'd swear about that. The woman who lives nearest to Darley's back door, in the rear house on the next lot, cleans offices at night and never gets home before two-thirty A.M. If she'd been home, she might have heard something."

"Frustrating," agreed Grace.

Sergeant John Palliser came up in time to hear that. "I think it's just the crude anonymous thing. We'll never get anybody for it, unless the lab turns up something. The daughter-in-law finally told us Darley's handbag was missing—one she always carried. Wouldn't have had more than a few bucks in it. So, X breaks in after the loot, puts Darley out, grabs the bag, looks around and sees there's nothing else of any value, and vamooses. Leaving us no leads at all."

Piggott said, "I wouldn't take a bet. I did hear something from that Mrs. Lampowski who lives next door on the other side. She said Mrs. Darley had just lately had a big fight with Mr. Felker—he owns the place next door, where the office-cleaner lives in back—because of all those old magazines Darley kept around. He said it was a fire hazard and they had quite a fight."

"Well," said Palliser. "Big deal. Enough to—"

"You just never do know," said Grace, "what people are going to

29

get up to, John. Over what little reason. Maybe we'd better tackle Mr. Felker sort of en masse. Prod at him some."

"Oh, it's possible, I suppose," said Palliser. "I wonder if the lab's turned up anything on it. Early to ask, of course." The lab so thorough and cautious.

Hackett had spent the morning at the Ambassador Hotel, asking questions about Robert Durand. He had heard nothing but praise for Durand, from the supervisor of the hotel kitchens, from the maître-d' of the principal dining room. Durand was regularly on the day shift, Room Service and afternoons in the dining room and cocktail bar. He had worked there for three years and was a very steady, reliable man. His regular shift was nine to six, but occasionally he stayed overtime. He had done so on Monday night, to help serve at a convention banquet—a national convention of dentists. Consequently he had left about two hours early on Tuesday.

Everybody apparently liked Durand. A very nice young fellow, was the consensus. In any event he was alibied: very demonstrably visible at the Ambassador between nine and four on Tuesday. And the murder probably committed sometime between eleven and one. Which was all, or nearly all, Hackett was interested in. But with the indication that Kitty Durand had known X, had admitted him to the apartment and served him (them?) coffee, he asked other questions too, and drew blank.

A lot of other waiters and kitchen help—it was a big hotel—but everybody said no, they hadn't fraternized socially with the Durands. Had never met Mrs. Durand. Had never so much as been in their apartment; in fact, nobody but the kitchen-supervisor knew Durand's address. They had never seen Durand outside of working hours. Several people—the maître-d', the assistant chef and two waiters who seemed to know Durand best—had volunteered that Durand was just crazy about his wife, and hadn't been shy of saying so.

And of course, with this breakdown, that looked quite kosher.

Whom had the Durands known socially? Well enough that Kitty Durand had trustingly opened her door to the rapist-killer? They didn't know yet that it was rape, but it had looked like that.

Hackett went back to the apartment on Westmoreland and asked around, without result. Apartment-dwellers tended not to mingle, in working-class neighborhoods.

There had been an address-book in the rickety little desk in the

Durands' apartment. Mendoza had got it from the lab men after they'd printed it, and passed it over to Hackett last night. Hackett got it out and looked at it now, sitting in the Barracuda with the rain pattering down. Not many names in it. Addresses in Chicago, Rockford, Illinois, Long Beach, Hollywood, Lakewood. They'd have to be checked out.

Before he set out for the nearest one, one Janet Nutting on Cahuenga Boulevard in Hollywood, he dropped back to the office to see if anything new had come in.

Mendoza was on the phone as he came in. "Nothing? *¡Qué demonio!* Well, thanks." He put the phone down, looking dissatisfied. "I just say it's odd," he said to Hackett. "Very damned odd, that that blonde hasn't been missed. From somewhere. By somebody. What have you got, on what?"

"*Nada,*" said Hackett. "Durand is a paragon of virtue, hard work and respectability. Also he is alibied. He was at work when Kitty got murdered."

Mendoza swiveled around in his desk-chair to look out at the gray veil of gentle rain over the city. He said after a pause, "So cynical we get—the first place to look, at the husband or wife. Yes, so he wasn't X. We had guessed that, hadn't we?"

"By intuition," agreed Hackett. "I'm just about to start tracing the names in that address-book. Jimmy said you went to question him. Durand. Get anything useful?"

"Not much," said Mendoza. He swiveled back to face Hackett. "The routine should turn up something eventually. On this one. But—"

"But, the blonde," said Hackett amusedly.

"She worries me," said Mendoza, frowning.

THREE

Robert Durand had looked very young and forlorn, sitting on the side of the hospital bed. They were letting him go; he was rational, he was dressed, but still shocked and shaken. He was only twenty-four. Mendoza had reflected that it was probably another sign of advancing age when the young began to look so damned young.

Durand was more than willing to talk to him. "Just so you find out who—who did that to my Kitty. Somebody breaking in—somebody—" He put his hands over his face. Rather a goodlooking young fellow, Durand, middle-sized and slender, dark, with regular features, dark eyes. "I—I'm sorry I went to pieces like that, but I just—*Kitty*—I—she was going to have a baby, you know, we'd just found out and we were both so happy—that was the reason she'd quit her job, the doctor said she shouldn't be on her feet so much. She was going to get a part-time job, she'd heard of one addressing envelopes—my Kitty—" But he straightened up; he said, "I want to help you—you've got to find out who."

Mendoza gave him time; let him talk, before he asked questions. "I'm—I didn't mean to go on waiting table all my life—we had plans, you know. I'd—kind of drifted around since high school, but I wanted to get places for Kitty, make better money. I go to night school at Hollywood High—I was always interested in photography, that's what I'm taking. We thought, have our own studio, you know. Now I don't know. I don't know. Oh, God, she was only twenty-two. Why did it have to happen to Kitty? So good—so innocent—my Kitty."

But when Mendoza began to ask about their friends, he was surprised. "Do the police think—somebody we *know*? Why, that's—I thought—"

"The coffee cups, Mr. Durand. Evidently she'd had visitors, served coffee. To two people. She might have done that?"

"Why, sure," said Durand. "Sure, if somebody she knew—but it wouldn't be anybody like that who—"

"Well, we don't know, do we?" said Mendoza. "We have to start somewhere. And the door hadn't been forced, you know. She let in whoever it was. I'd just like to hear who your friends were— people you knew, invited to the apartment."

Durand put a hand to his temple as though his head ached. "That's —crazy," he muttered. "Nobody we knew would—and it's not—not as if we knew many people—neither of us much for parties or—that's wild." After a moment he reached into his hip pocket, brought out his billfold. "I—she used to pose for me," he said painfully. "For practise. I did some art study shots once—of course I wouldn't show those in class. You know, nudes—but—I guess I took a thousand pictures of Kitty—" his shaky hands sorted out from one slot a wallet-sized print in color; he handed it reverently to Mendoza. "My Kitty —you can see how beautiful she was—anybody might, you know, notice her on the street, maybe follow her home—one of these wild men around these days—I always told her to be careful, about locking the door and so on, and she *was*. But—"

Mendoza looked at the photograph. Kitty Durand had indeed been a beautiful and photogenic girl. Irish? he wondered. The very white skin, the black hair curling in a short cut, the gray eyes and black lashes. A real beauty. Just looking at the picture, he felt abstract regret that anything so beautiful had been destroyed. "Yes, Mr. Durand," he said gently. "She was very lovely. What I want to ask you—"

"Whatever I can tell you," said Durand drearily.

He couldn't tell Mendoza much. Kitty had gone to a convent school, and hadn't any close friends here; she was from Chicago. They'd met three years ago when she came out to visit an aunt. The aunt was since deceased. Neither she nor Durand was much for entertaining, socializing. Kitty did have one pretty good girlfriend here, a Janet Nutting; had met her at the first job she'd held here when she decided to stay awhile. Janet was engaged but Durand had never met her fiancé. Of course they knew the other people in the apartment, but just casually—there wasn't any fraternizing. Kitty had friends, her parents, in Chicago—"Oh, God, I'll have to call her mother and father—"

There was a couple about their own age, Jeff and Sharon Lyman, who both attended the night photography class. Durand had got acquainted with them there, had invited them to the apartment a couple of times. "Jeff was new at it, he was interested to know how to fix up the kitchen to use as a darkroom, you know." And there was a Denis Daley, fellow he'd gone to high school with; he'd just got married this last year and sometimes the Durands had gone out to a movie with them, something like that. They lived up on Normandie. Denis was a mechanic at a Chrysler agency.

"I guess you could say the best friends we had. Closest, I mean. I never got so very chummy with any of the other fellows at the hotel." Durand flushed a little. "I don't mean, as if I thought they weren't good enough—but—well, my dad was a C.P.A., his own business, but he hadn't saved any and when he and Mother were killed in that accident just after I got out of high school, I—sort of drifted. There wasn't anything left, only about three thousand insurance. It wasn't till I met Kitty I—started to fly right. I wanted to get places —for Kitty." There was a long pause. "Now, I don't know."

Mendoza stood up. "Don't you think she'd want you to do that—for her now, Mr. Durand?"

Durand looked at him blindly. "Maybe so. Yes. But—right now —it just doesn't seem worth the effort. Why it had to be my Kitty—" Another pause. Then he said, "But—I told you—she went to that convent school. She was—sort of innocent—even when she was a city girl, and I'd told her to be careful. She'd have opened the door to anybody who sounded all right—a salesman—"

But not, thought Mendoza, served the salesman coffee.

He passed that on to Hackett now, and Hackett said, "Well. You never know what turn it might take. She was a raving beauty by the photo, hah?"

"And by what we saw of the corpse, had a very good figure," said Mendoza.

"Yeah. So this girlfriend Janet's boyfriend was maddened by her charms," said Hackett. "One like him she'd have let in. Served coffee to. Or the new acquaintance from night school. Or any of the men in the apartment building."

"Yes, we'd better look at them too," said Mendoza. "You're right. But two people, Art?"

"The couple from night school," said Hackett promptly. "Calling on her. The coffee. They leave. Wife has some shopping to do, says

34

she'll meet hubby later. He goes back, rings the bell and says wife left her gloves."

"This is off the top of your mind? It could have been something like that. Anyway, go and have a look at these people." Mendoza regarded him sardonically. "For what, in the pro slang, is known as a ton of law, you do sometimes get the nuances from people."

"I did major in psychology," said Hackett mildly. "I'm going." He went.

Mendoza brooded awhile, swiveled around in his chair looking out at the rain, and finally got up to seek an early lunch. Everybody was out of the office on something; eventually he'd hear what. It was Glasser's day off. As he came out to the anteroom, Lake handed him a teletype and a lab report. "Just came in at the same time." Mendoza put his hat down and looked them over.

The blonde in green lace was not known, by her fingerprints, to L.A.P.D.'s records: that they had known. Now Washington was saying they didn't know her either. "*¡Condenación!*" said Mendoza.

The other was the autopsy report on the blonde. A very simple one. It was, by the formal description, a very anonymous body: five feet, one hundred pounds, natural blonde hair, blue eyes, no birthmarks, very little dental work: she had one filling in a lower molar. "Talk about frustrating," muttered Mendoza. She had been *virgo intacto*. A respectable blonde. Estimated age, twenty to twenty-one. And her neck was broken. Very likely, said Bainbridge, by manual force. A slight, small girl, slender neck; possibly somebody started to strangle her, or just shut off a scream. If the somebody had been a strong man it could have been done without intent to kill. Or it could have been deliberate.

"A handful of nothing!" said Mendoza bitterly. "And I doubt whether the lab could get anything useful from her clothes. They looked very damn clean. She was just dropped there—anything on her pretty green lace dress would be from that alley, tell us nothing."

"The tough ones come along," said Lake inattentively; he was studying a calorie list.

"I am going out for a leisurely lunch," said Mendoza, and picked up his hat.

Alison called Angel at noon. "I know it's too early, the baby isn't due till October, but I thought we ought to think about a shower for Mary Higgins. Maybe in May sometime?"

"And I'd thought of it too," said Angel briskly. "Of course. *Isn't* it nice about the baby? But I'll tell you one thing, Alison—I've only met George Higgins a couple of times, but men I know—if it's a girl, heaven help her. What with him being a bachelor so long, and those big tough men, the very worst—you know—soft and sentimental as —as melted butter."

Alison laughed. "You could be right. And coming so late. But I thought we ought to plan for it. Ask Roberta Palliser, and Virginia Grace, and—I must ask Luis if his Piggott is officially engaged to that girl. And probably Mary's got unpolice friends too—"

"Yes."

"Better have it here? You can make that mousse—the out-of-this-world one with the whipped cream—it'll be hot enough weather by then. In the afternoon. We can shut the cats and Cedric out—"

"Not my adorable lamb Cedric," said Angel. "He'd be an asset to any party, Alison. Cedric comes to the party."

"Oh, well—let's set a definite date, then—"

When Alison hung up, she became aware that Angel's adorable lamb Cedric was creating quite a disturbance in the back yard. She went out to the kitchen door.

Sheba, Bast and Nefertite were crouched in the porch, using it as an impromptu air-raid shelter. El Señor was in the middle of the yard, making futile if savage passes at the mockingbird who was enthusiastically dive-bombing him. Both of them were swearing heartily at each other, and Cedric was emitting a steady salvo of thunderous barks at the mockingbird. The twins were watching entranced.

"See el pájaro, Mamacíta! El Señor bad, try to bite el pájaro—" Johnny ran up to her excitedly.

"Don't let Cedric hurt el pájaro, Mama—you said el pájaro got los niños to take care of—Mama—"

"El pájaro," said Alison, "isn't in any danger at all, Terry. He can take quite good care of himself."

As if to prove the point, the mockingbird hurled himself at El Señor and zeroed in for a hard peck on El Señor's bottom. He then swirled up to a limb of the alder tree and uttered his war cry, the first four bars of "Yankee Doodle."

"Honestly!" said Alison. "If we acquire any more livestock around here—"

"And I think," said Palliser, finishing his steak sandwich and groping for a cigarette, "that wandering around questioning the neighbors is a waste of time. It was the crude thing, just as I said before Matt heard about that Felker. That's N.G."

"Well, you've got a nose too," said Mendoza. Palliser, Piggott and Grace had come into Federico's to find him here just relaxing after his early lunch, and had given him an account of their unproductive morning down on Cortez Street. "What about Felker?"

Palliser shrugged. "Ordinary citizen. Maybe a slightly more productive citizen then anybody else down there. He looks very unlikely."

"He had a fight with Mrs. Darley?"

Grace smiled and finished his coffee. "He owns the house next door—"

"Where," said Piggott sadly, "the office-cleaner lives in the rear. If that one had only been home—"

"And he was concerned with the fire hazard the Darley woman was creating—all those stacks of old magazines. Not," said Grace, "unnaturally. He warned her he'd inform the Fire Department if she didn't get rid of them. She said she wouldn't. But Mr. Felker doesn't strike me as having a hot enough temper to go and murder her over it. All he had to do was call the firemen—they'd have got an injunction against her and made her get rid of 'em. Which Felker knew."

"Tempest in a teapot," said Palliser. "It's just what I said—either somebody thought she had loot stashed away, or just walked in after her pension money. It was the crude anonymous thing. Any lab report on it yet?"

"No," said Mendoza. "State the place was apparently in, they might get nothing useful anyway. I'm inclined to think you're right, John. But we have to work them—routine may turn up something yet." He looked at his watch. "*Caray,* one-twenty, we'd all better get back on the job." He beckoned the waiter for their bills.

They came out to North Broadway and the parking lot at the side of the restaurant. "Hey," said Palliser suddenly. "What—" And a heavy gun spoke somewhere nearby.

"The squad-car—" said Piggott, and they all ran.

Out there in the street, at the intersection of North Broadway and a side street, was a black-and-white patrol car. The two men in blue were out of it, beside a dilapidated-looking old Ford sedan, and two civilians were struggling with them. One had broken away and was running up toward the side street; one uniformed man was after him, firing more warning shots, shouting. The other civilian

37

had just, by a lucky chance, knocked the other man down and was plunging behind the wheel of the Ford when Palliser grabbed him and pulled him out again. Piggott and Grace ran after the other one, but the uniformed man had already tackled him and had him down. He was led back to the cars swearing, the uniformed man hauling out the handcuffs—"All right, hands behind your head!"

"What goes on?" asked Mendoza. The other man, getting up fast, was frisking the second civilian. His partner yanked the other man away from Palliser and applied cuffs to him. They looked at the men in civilian clothes with polite, cold eyes, and one of them said, "Police business, sir," with obvious dismissal in his tone. Mendoza grinned, surveying the prisoners.

"The thought has crossed my mind before," he said, "that the born cop is the man who jumps toward trouble instead of the other way. Relax, boy. We're all out of Central Homicide, just back on the job after Code Seven."

"Oh!" said the uniformed man. He looked confused for a moment. "Oh, I'm sorry, sir, I didn't know. Well, we just curbed the Ford for an illegal left turn, and they put up a fight like you see."

"I wonder why," said Mendoza. Neither of the men was drunk. They were both young, and fairly well dressed. They stood sullen and silent in cuffs, heads down. "Take a look at the car. Yes, I know you'd do that anyway."

There were odds and ends of clothing in the car, a six-pack of beer, a new bottle of vodka. Then they opened the trunk.

"My good God Almighty," said one of the squad-car men. "If that's what it might be—" he stood back mutely.

"Oh, *muy lindo*," said Mendoza. "How pretty." In the trunk, packed in neat cardboard cartons, were thousands and thousands of little plastic bags filled with white powder. "I'll have just one guess. H. More, in fact, than I've ever seen in one place at one time before, but then I've never served time up in Narco. Pat Callaghan's going to be interested in this."

"So I guess that's why they put up a fight," said the other squad-car man. "I will be damned. Just over an illegal left turn. How stupid can they get? If they'd just peaceably taken the ticket, no sweat."

The bigger civilian spoke up in bitter tones, telling them explicitly just what they were and all about their antecedents and what they could go and do. "The interfering fuzz," said Mendoza. "We're forever stopping all your fun and games. Spoilsports from way back, that's us."

The squad-car officers efficiently herded the men into the back of the car, called up another to sit on the Ford until it was towed in, and started off for headquarters. And Grace said suddenly, "My God, I've got to run—I'm due in court at that indictment—see you," and made for his car.

"What—oh, that Seymour," said Palliser. Seymour, with a long pedigree, had made the big time some days ago when he shot up a respectable Negro bar out on Washington, killing four people.

"We'd better get back to our part of the job," said Mendoza.

They were trained to be thorough, and follow up where possible, and Landers, taking a couple of hours more to clear up the Holly thing in more detail, had had a stroke of luck. He had thought there'd be no hope of dropping on whoever had sold Holly a bottle; but about a block up from the Wiki-Wiki Grill he'd noticed a small market on that corner, and a sign that said *Liquor.* He parked and went in, unhopefully. A place like this was not very likely to stay open late.

But the owner was there: the place was open until nine on Saturdays, and the owner remembered Holly because he'd just been closing up when Holly rapped on the door. He'd let him in because he needed any sale he got.

And he said nervously, "He didn't act drunk, I wouldn't've sold him anything if he'd been drunk. He—well, I didn't pay much notice, in a hurry to get home—but he wasn't drunk. I sold him a pint of Scotch."

And that was perfectly possible, thought Landers: Holly with three drinks in him, and not used to it, but he'd walked a block in the night air. Why? Why hadn't he gone home with the bottle and tied one on there? Why had he started drinking on the street, enough to get so confused he couldn't get home? The respectable responsible Holly? The near-teetotaller? They'd probably never know that. People, all of a sudden, doing the uncharacteristic thing.

Landers went over to Crosby Place, to the house where Holly's body had been found. It wasn't an area where the streets got cleaned very often. There was refuse in the gutter there, and in the gutter a couple of doors down from that house, a pint bottle, the brand of Scotch the market-owner said he'd sold Holly. Landers eyed it dubiously. A very long chance that it was the same bottle, would have any prints of Holly's on it; but he picked it up carefully and labeled it for the lab.

And headed back to base to deliver it. And then to have lunch. At least it had stopped raining, he thought.

Hackett, heading back for the office at three o'clock to bring Mendoza up to date, was feeling dubious about what he'd got. He could, as Luis said, get the nuances, and the nuances he'd got from these friends of Robert and Kitty Durand he'd talked to didn't send any hunches up his spine.

Even as the Durands looked like ordinary citizens, so did their friends. Janet Nutting was assistant buyer at a middle-class little dress shop on Sunset Boulevard in Hollywood. She was a middling-pretty girl, very obviously and sincerely distressed about Kitty Durand, and she gave him nothing—anxious to help, but no help to give. Yes, Kitty had met Janet's fiancé, Roy Cameron, just once—they'd only just got engaged. Durand hadn't. Roy worked at Lockheed as a master mechanic. There was, of course, a lot of talk from Janet—whom Hackett had talked to at the dress shop—but that was really the extent of what she could tell him, besides how happy Robert and Kitty had been, how much in love, how pleased about the baby.

The Durands apparently hadn't had many close friends. Young, busy, happy people.

Hackett had seen Jeff and Sharon Lyman. They looked very ordinary too. Very shocked about Kitty, vociferous about offering help and sympathy to Robert. Lyman worked at a men's store on Vermont, and he hadn't raised any objection when Hackett verified with the manager that he'd been there all day yesterday. "I know you've got to look at everybody," he said. "But you don't think—somebody she *knew?*"

Hackett had seen Denis Daley, Durand's old school pal, and he also had been on the job at the Chrysler agency. He too was horrified and sympathetic. None of those was X.

And brooding over a drugstore sandwich, it suddenly occurred to Hackett—but, the coffee. The interns had said, provisionally about noon. It could be Kitty had been having a cup of coffee herself about then. Possibly at that hour she'd have offered a cup of coffee, out of courtesy, to some caller she wouldn't have otherwise. Anything in that? Well, wait for the autopsy; see the other few people they'd known; and the men living in the apartment building.

When he came into the office Mendoza was on the phone. "Yes, a strange little thing, I thought you'd be interested, Pat. . . . ¿Qué? ¡Dios! You don't tell me. Well, at least you can put it out of circulation." He put the phone down and told Hackett about that—an estimated fifty grand worth of heroin in the trunk of that car, and if those damned fools had meekly accepted the ticket, nobody any the wiser. "The guilty fleeing where no man—" at which point Lake burst in.

"There's a jumper on the eighth floor at Bullock's—ambulance and firemen on the way—"

They started for that in a hurry. Palliser was in, typing a report; he jumped to follow them. They hadn't had one of those in a while.

When they got to Bullock's Department Store, a solid square block of building between Eighth and Broadway, the crowds were in the streets staring up. The fire engines were there, the men struggling with the awkward net. Seldom time to get the net fixed. The squad-cars were there, the bull horns ready. And, when the men from Homicide had ridden up in the maddeningly slow elevator to the eighth floor, they found men from the squad-cars already there, and the minister and the priest. Ordinary citizens, happening to be within reach in the emergency—shopping or walking down the street, had been pressed into service. Quite a crowd was there, in the accounting office of the credit department.

A blonde woman about forty, dressed smartly and ordinarily a pretty woman, but now weeping hysterically—"But we just came to get the bill adjusted—more time on it—just *business*—he said I shouldn't've bought that stole, but I didn't know he'd lost his job— he never told me—" A pale distraught-looking man mechanically patting her shoulder. "Now, Mrs. Newman—" A cluster of frightened female clerks half-enjoying the excitement. A quartet of firemen.

The man was out on the ledge there, beyond the tall windows along one side of the office. One of the clerks was repeating compulsively, "But he just ran in—not allowed past the counter, nobody but employees—he just ran in—I always said, dangerous to have those windows open this high up—"

There wasn't much for the men from Homicide to do up here that wasn't being done already. The man, Newman, was out there on the ledge between two windows. The Catholic priest was at one window talking to him calmly in a necessarily raised voice, and at the same time hanging for dear life to the belt of the uniformed man who was halfway out the window also talking to Newman.

"If you'll just listen to reason, James—you don't really want to do this foolish thing. Listen to me, James—"

The Protestant minister was at the other window, with another uniformed man. "Mr. Newman, please listen to me—your wife—"

Mendoza reflected irrelevantly that of the two men of God, the priest was using the better psychology. People often responded more readily to their Christian names.

"But he never—it was all so sudden—if he'd *told* me he'd lost his job, I wouldn't have—but he never said a thing—and we'd just come in to get an extension on the—if he'd *told* me—"

"Now, Mrs. Newman—"

"Just take my hand, sir," the uniformed man was calling steadily. His voice drifted back into the room from the open space he was talking to, out there. "You hear me?—here's my hand. James! Take my hand! You can get back easy, just four steps this way—come on —I'll help you. Come on. Come on back—I'll help you." He was hanging out the window, reaching sideways along the ledge to the left of the window, and the priest had a good grip on his belt.

Mendoza and Hackett were at the other window, looking past the minister, the uniformed man there. "*Pares o nones*," said Mendoza softly. "Odds or evens. What sets them off, Arturo?"

"Human nature," said Hackett as softly.

Down there, eight stories down, the mass of faces upturned, blurred into a single unit, waiting. Waiting for the jumper. Human nature. Say it twice. Cops knew all about human nature, but there wasn't much they could do about it.

"James, listen to me!" The priest renewed his grip on the belt. "You don't really want to do this, you know that—take the man's hand now, James—"

"Take my hand. I'm here to help you," the man in uniform was saying; he was more than halfway out the window now. "Come on —four steps over here, easy—"

The man out there on the ledge had been silent, whether hearing all the exhortations or not. Now he suddenly screamed hoarsely, "You bastards! All you bastards shut up! I can't—I can't—I can't—it's no *use* any more—"

And he went. He leaned away, off the ledge, and with awful slowness he went. The crowd below sent up a wordless moan of shock, surprise, ghoulish fascination.

The priest pulled the uniformed man back into the room, shut his eyes, and his lips moved. The uniformed man stayed on his knees, face white, and said, "My God. My God."

"Just like that," said Hackett.

Mendoza turned away from the window and drew a long breath. "So," he said, "just the paperwork, now."

FOUR

By four-thirty it was getting cleared up gradually: the body taken away, the witnesses making statements, names and addresses listed, and Mendoza was bored with all the routine. There was still a lot of that to do. He left Hackett and Palliser, Grace and Piggott, summoned hastily to help out, busy at it, and went back to headquarters.

The blonde was bothering him again. And not one damn thing had they done—*naturalmente,* they'd had every expectation that there'd be a missing report out on her any hour, and it was damned queer there hadn't been. And there'd been other cases on hand, but they should have done *something* about the blonde. This morning he'd asked the lab to make up some copies of the close-up of her face. Now he went and asked if they were finished.

"Just now. Want one?" Scarne went away and came back with a 5 by 7 glossy photograph. "Of course I won't say it's flattering. Dead people so seldom take flattering pictures. But I think anybody who knew her'd recognize her."

So did Mendoza. It was a sharp photograph, taken full-face. Such a very distinctive blonde—the classic fine features, the shoulder-length hair so professionally styled—He thanked Scarne. He went back to the Ferrari and drove out to Beverly Hills.

Gina, Beverly Hills, Calif., was about all they had on the blonde: the label in the green lace formal. Barring, of course, an eventual missing report.

It was a small but very exclusive-looking shop, black marble front, plate-glass doors, on Beverly Drive. Mendoza found a public lot and walked back. Not being intimidated by snob-value surroundings, he was not awed by Gina's plush and haughty furnishing. There was an ankle-deep carpet, a few showcases standing at odd angles, one evening dress negligently displayed over the back of an (authentic) Regency chair; apparently the rest of the clothes actually for sale were hidden behind discreet double doors at the rear of the shop.

In thirty seconds a slender white-haired woman in elegant gray silk came through the doors and asked serenely, "May I help you?" She was queenly, every white hair in place, discreet makeup, dulcet ladylike voice. No flicker of surprise showed in her eyes for dapper Mendoza instead of a female.

He showed her the badge. "Lieutenant Mendoza, L.A.P.D. We're trying to trace this girl Mrs.—"

"Mrs. Peever," she said. At the badge, she looked surprised. And Mendoza nearly repeated the name incredulously: she looked like a dowager duchess.

"Could you tell me if you know her?" He handed her the photograph.

"Why?"

"Why—oh. Well, she was wearing a dress from your shop."

Mrs. Peever, alias Gina, blinked at him. She looked at the photograph. She frowned. "No," she said slowly, "I don't know her. Who she is. I'm sorry. I—wait a moment—I've *seen* her, you know. I'm sure I've seen her—somewhere. She—it's not a very good picture, is it? I mean, clear enough but—"

"Dead people so seldom take flattering pictures," said Mendoza absently. "You have? In here?"

She gasped. "She's *dead?*"

"You've seen her in here? But you don't know her name?"

She looked at the picture again. "I don't know if it was in here —did you say Lieutenant?—but I've seen her somewhere. If only once. But no, I don't know her name."

"Well, thanks," said Mendoza. She had, then, been in here once or twice to buy something. "You'll have a number of regular customers—she wasn't one of them—" A vague idea stirring at the back of his mind. "Do you have any employees—people who wait on customers, besides yourself?"

"Oh, there's Florence. Yes. My niece. We own the shop together. That's all."

"If she's here, may I talk to her?"

"Well, surely," said Mrs. Peever. She opened the doors and called, and a tall thin freckled cheerful-looking young woman appeared with a sequined cardigan over one arm. "It *is* torn, you know," she said in resigned tones. "And that woman knew it too. Decided to exchange it for a different color! Buying a thirty-eight when she needs a forty-two! If—oh, sorry, I didn't know anybody was here." She looked at Mendoza curiously.

"It's police," said Mrs. Peever. "This girl. She's *dead*, and he says she had one of our dresses on, Flo. Imagine."

"Not really?" Florence was thrilled. Mendoza handed her the photograph. "*This* one. Yes, I waited on her."

"That's how I'd seen her then," said Mrs. Peever.

"When, Miss—"

"Oh, Peever," said Florence. "It was—let's see—about two weeks ago. That's the best I can do, sorry."

"You don't know her name?"

"Well, that's one reason I remember her. I mean, I'd have recognized her vaguely anyway, but I remember it was here, because she paid *cash*. Very unusual, you know. Practically everybody writes a check or has an account with us."

He had suspected something like that. "Did she buy anything else besides the dress? It was a dress she bought?"

"She did," said Florence. "She bought a green lace formal, and —another reason I remember her—that black velvet jacket we'd had sitting around for ages. It came to—the whole bill—a little over three hundred dollars. And she paid it in cash."

"I see," said Mendoza. "Thanks very much. You don't remember that she'd ever been in here before?"

"Not that I remember. And something else I remember about her," said Florence, "was that she had a *rock* on her left hand. Engagement finger. I am telling you. The biggest diamond solitaire I ever saw. Maybe four, five carats."

"You don't say," said Mendoza.

"I do say," said Florence.

Mendoza went home talking to himself about the blonde. "I tell you," he said to Alison, "she must have been missed. One like that. Somebody's darling. Now we hear, bejeweled by somebody. Why the hell hasn't she been reported?"

"Everybody thinks she's in Acapulco," said Alison, pouring his coffee.

"Well, I suppose it could be. But—"

"I heard about that suicide on the news. I never can understand how anybody could do it that way," said Alison. "So many easier ways."

"I think," said Mendoza, "he got pushed over the line all of a

45

sudden, right there on the eighth floor, so—*¡acabamiento!* The most available way. Messy, yes. I suppose Bob and Nick are still busy at the paperwork on it. . . . But that blonde—"

"Something will turn up eventually," said Alison. "No postcards from Acapulco, so somebody'll get worried. How do you like the soufflé? It's a new recipe I got from Angel—"

"Yes, very nice," said Mendoza absently.

Hackett went home, turning over the paperwork to Schenke and Galeano, and told Angel he could just conceive of committing suicide under certain circumstances, but never *that* way. "I get butterflies at the top of a ladder."

"I heard about it on the news," said Angel, stirring something on the stove. "Neither could I. But you'll have to get out the ladder, Art. The bulb in the bathroom fixture went phhtt. You can reach it from the lowest rung," she added reassuringly. And as he sniffed at what she was stirring, "That's not for you. Hollandaise sauce. Too many calories."

"Oh, damn," said Hackett. But it was his day off tomorrow. He'd better cut the lawn. If it wasn't raining. He hadn't been able to do it last week because it was raining.

Piggott had dinner at a coffee shop on Hill Street, went home to his apartment and took a shower and put on a clean shirt. At eight o'clock he reported for choir practise at the church, and met that nice girl Prudence Russell just going in.

"Oh, Matt—I wondered if you'd be here. I heard about that terrible suicide on the news—"

"And ten to one the night men still typing reports," said Piggott. "You know, Prudence, I can just see killing yourself, you've got an incurable disease, or maybe you know—not to give the enemy information under torture, something like that—but to do it *that* way —no. I get dizzy thinking about it." But he smiled at her: Prudence was a pretty girl. Only these days, with all that was going on, you wondered if it was sensible to get married, maybe have kids—with Satan traveling around with a vengeance. You really did.

Thursday morning, and Hackett off. Palliser and Grace were the first men in, and there was a call in from the General Hospital asking for cops—a Dr. Goodhart. They went out on that.

It had been a quiet night: for Homicide, only a stabbing over on the Row. Mendoza drifted in before Higgins, Landers, Glasser, Piggott. The lab had sent up a report on Darley, and Mendoza looked at it. They'd picked up some prints in the house and sent them to Records for checking: that was about all it amounted to. The autopsy report was in on Darley, and that said even less. She'd been beaten to death: actual cause of death, fractured skull. She had fought her attacker: there were skin-scrapings and hair under her nails. The hair was light brown. The skin was from a Caucasian.

"Damnation," said Mendoza, thrusting both reports at Piggott. "So go ask her relatives if she'd had trouble with anybody lately. With them. And so on. You probably won't get anything, but we have to look." Piggott, muttering about the routine, went out reading the autopsy report.

The second call of the day came in—a body in a rooming house on Temple. The squad-car men thought, a natural death: an old man. Landers went over to look at it.

"This blonde," said Mendoza to Higgins. "We really should be doing something about her, George. I—George!"

"What?" said Higgins, coming to with a start.

"I swear to God," said Mendoza, "it's worse than just after she married you! I said, this blonde. We ought to be looking. I got something—not much—at that dress shop." He relayed that. "Now I say we get that shot run in every paper around."

"Yes. Obvious thing to do. You want me to see to it?"

"*Por favor.*"

The inquest on Edward Holly was set for this morning. Landers got back just in time to attend it and give evidence for the police. There had been another corpse reported in a cheap hotel on Virgil: Glasser had gone out on that.

At the General Hospital at eight-thirty, Palliser and Grace had asked for Dr. Goodhart and were presently ushered into a cubbyhole of an office. Goodhart was a big lanky man about sixty, with a shock of white hair and tired-looking blue eyes behind horn rims. The men from Homicide introduced themselves. "You've got a suspicious death, Doctor?" asked Palliser.

"Well, not exactly—of course we'll do an autopsy—no, and we'll hope we pull the others through, though it doesn't look hopeful— but it *is* a sudden death, your business, and we've got to find the parents, you know," said Goodhart.

"The parents?" said Grace.

47

"Yes. Five youngsters—age seven on down to six months. We only know the last name, Yocum. It's the baby who's dead. The others very critical. We think some form of botulism, though as I say we'll do an autopsy. It was apparently a neighbor who found them and called an ambulance. I've got the address—" He handed Palliser a slip of paper. "We've been too busy here to go hunting the parents, but we thought you ought to know about it."

"Um," said Grace. "Twentieth and Compton. Colored kids, Doctor?"

"That's right," said Goodhart. "I wouldn't like to swear that any of them'll make it. I should think the neighbors must have told the parents when they came home, but they haven't showed up."

"Some kind of food poisoning?" asked Palliser.

"That's right."

"Well, we'll check it out, Doctor," said Grace.

"Twentieth and Compton," said Palliser as he slid his lean length into the right bucket seat of Grace's little blue racer, the Elva. "Down there, like anywhere, people come all sorts. Good, bad and indifferent. But some of the indifferent ones—"

"Can be mighty indifferent," said Grace. "We'll see what shows."

The address turned out to be a little frame house about fifty years old sitting on bare earth: no sign that anybody had ever tried to grow grass or flowers around it. The house was empty, so they tried the frame duplex on the right, where there was an attempt at grass in the front yard. A plump brown woman opened the door, her pink cotton house-dress neat. They introduced themselves. She looked at Grace curiously, at the badges, at Grace again, fastidiously-dressed Jason Grace with his precise moustache.

"It's about the children, Mrs.—the Yocum children. The baby's died, and we'd like to know—"

She looked distressed. "Oh, that's just terrible. Terrible! I'm sorry hear that. I don't—we don't know the people at all, they just rented the place next door about two weeks back. I couldn't tell you nothing about them. Mr. an' Mis' Yocum, just young folk. They're pickers, is all I know."

"Pickers?" said Grace. "Oh, migrant farm workers, you mean?"

"Yessir. He tol' my husband Sam they don't usual come into town, down here, off season. That's all I could say. Oh, that's awful about the baby. Poisoned food, was it? See, Mis' Yocum she come over yesterday, an' say would I sorta keep an eye on the kids for her, she got some shoppin' to do or such, an' bein' I was home any-

ways it wasn't no never-mind to me, I said sure. The kids was quiet
—stayed inside when it was rainin'." She looked from one to the
other of them, the two men from Homicide, white and black. "She
said as she'd left out lunch for 'em. But comes five, six o'clock, an'
her not back nor him neither, I say to Sam, I better see those kids
get fed again. He was kinda mad about it. We ain't got all that
much, go feedin' kids belong to people we don't know. Sam, he's
janitor at a school. But kids is got to be fed."

"Yes, Mrs.—"

"Mason, I'm Mis' Mason. So I go over there, and—oh, Lordy! It
was awful. They was all lyin' around just terrible sick, like what
my mama call the bloody flux, an' stomach-sick too—just a-lyin'
there a-moanin', poor young ones—an' I see they need a doctor right
quick, I run home an' tell Sam, an' he goes up to the drugstore, call
for an am-*bu*lance. An' that's all I could tell you."

"The Yocums haven't come home yet?"

"Nossir. I been watchin', an' I ask Mis' Carter t'other side watch
too—they did oughta know about their kids—but they ain't come
back. Not since."

"Well, thanks very much," said Grace. "Do they have a car?"

"Yessir, kind of an old one. A Ford or somethin' like that—old
black car."

Grace scribbled the phone number on a card and handed it over.
"When the Yocums come back, would you call this number and
let us know, Mrs. Mason?" But that was probably wasted effort:
when the Yocums came back, hearing about their kids in the General they'd show up there.

This kind of situation was not too unusual or infrequent in areas
like this. Kids were expected to grow up early, take care of themselves. Delayed from getting home for any variety of reasons, the
Yocums—itinerant migrant workers—wouldn't, probably, worry
much about the kids. They'd be back some time.

Palliser and Grace went next door and found the front door unlocked. Past the front door of Mrs. Mason's side of the duplex they
had seen a rather shabby but neat and clean living room, a couple
of upholstered chairs, a thin old rug on the floor, a little portable
TV, an electric-blue couch with a dimestore landscape over it. Past
this front door they met utter squalor.

The only furniture in the tiny living room was a stained mattress
on the floor, a couple of folding chairs, a woman's bright red wool

coat flung over one of them. There was a foul smell in the house, and everything looked very dirty.

They went past a bedroom—also bare save for a mattress—down a narrow hall to a kitchen. There was an ancient gas stove on one wall, encrusted with the grime of years, with a large enamelled pot standing on one burner. There was a table and two chairs in the kitchen; and there was bloody vomit all over the floor and in the tiny back porch beyond. There was a smell from the pot too.

"Doctor didn't say if he'd had samples of what they'd eaten, but I don't suppose he has—the ambulance brought them in," said Grace, sniffing and sighing. "My good God Almighty. I suppose we'd better get a lab truck here, take samples of this. Evidently this was all they had—I don't see anything else around." They looked. The cupboards were mostly bare: there was cornmeal, evaporated milk, sugar, an unopened box of oatmeal cookies, a box of crackers, some canned soup. Grace peered into the pot. "Cornmeal mush, I think. You know, John, this is funny. Maybe."

"Come again?"

"Migrant farm workers," said Grace. "Following the crops. Sometimes coming into town, off season. Great uproar about them being exploited and underpaid, but I was hearing some of the actual figures a while back—talking to one of 'em. That fellow who accidentally killed the drunk—traffic accident. The fact is, John, that those people make damn good money. Up to twenty bucks a day they make. Enough to live pretty well when there aren't any crops to pick."

"They do?" said Palliser.

"A fact. Of course," said Grace, looking around, "they come all sorts too, don't they? Most of 'em—like people anywhere—the ordinary honest citizens. Some of them, no. Spending all the money on liquor, on clothes, gambling— Well. We'd better call the lab. Those poor damn kids."

Bertha, who spent her Tuesday and Thursday afternoons at the Mendoza house on Rayo Grande Avenue, was still feeling annoyed at Mrs. Spencer. Like everybody else, she thought righteously, Mrs. Spencer should know she had payments to keep up, the house and all, and it was over twenty dollars Mrs. Spencer owed her.

She was washing the front windows of Mrs. Mendoza's living room this afternoon, occasionally interrupted by Mrs. Mendoza's cats or that great big dog they'd just got—Bertha herself owned what she referred to as her Germing Shepherd, Fritz, and any day she'd have one like that Cedric, all that hair to be brushed every day—and she kept an eye out, on the Spencer house across the street. At a quarter to four the older Spencer boy, Jim, came up the street and went into the house. Bertha dropped her drying cloth onto a sheet of newspaper, hastily dried her hands, and went right over there and rang the bell. . . .

"You sure your ma didn't leave my money for you to give me?"

"Well, gee, I'm sorry, she didn't, Mrs. Hoffman," said the boy. "I mean, what can I say? I guess, they were in such a hurry and all—Grandma getting sick—she just didn't think of it."

"Well, it seems funny," said Bertha. "She's usually right on time. You heard anything from your ma and pa?"

"Yeah, we had a couple postcards yesterday. I guess Grandma's still pretty sick."

"Well—" Bertha went back across the street. But she was still feeling disgruntled, and when she went out to the kitchen for more hot water she said so to Mrs. MacTaggart. "Not that I don't know how it is, sickness in the family all of a sudden, but she's always been considerate-like."

"A nice woman," said Mrs. MacTaggart, who was alternately keeping an eye on the twins in the back yard and mixing up her special shortbread. "But a sudden sickness calling her away—you'll just have to put up with it. Until they come home."

"And where they've gone I haven't any idea. Or for how long. And that seems funny too—"

When Higgins got back to the office after arranging the cooperation from the newspapers—which promised to run the shot of the blonde in their next editions—he was chased out immediately on the latest call. Police work was like women's: never done. There was always something coming up.

What had come up this time was a new corpse over on Pecan Street this side of the Santa Ana Freeway. The neighbors had called for cops, and Higgins found the squad-car men still there to report to him.

"His name was Harry Tidwell," said one of the uniformed men. "The other one—the one who knocked him down the front-porch steps and cracked his skull—is Terence McKay. Tidwell was on Welfare—so's McKay. They were sitting here drinking and got into an argument, from what we've heard."

"They will do it," said Higgins. The ambulance was waiting, the interns standing around smoking. "O.K., boys, you hang around to ferry him in, hah?" Tidwell's body lay where it had fallen on the sidewalk where, obviously, he'd been knocked backward off the steep front porch. There were little knots of neighbors out in front yards, watching, talking. One woman in the next yard had on a very revealing scarlet chiffon negligee and, at first glance, nothing else. Join the cops and see life, thought Higgins.

Terence McKay was a big hairy man about forty. He was sitting on one of the rickety porch chairs, hands hanging between his knees, with the other squad-car man standing over him. Tidwell had been nearly as tall, Higgins estimated, but not as heavy by thirty pounds. There was a woman standing at McKay's other side, a goodlooking slattern about thirty, with an eye-catching if generous figure plentifully revealed by a tight blue sweater and a tighter blue skirt. She looked belligerent, defiant, scared, angry and sullen.

Higgins produced his badge. "I didn't go to kill him," said McKay sullenly. "I just—I never meant to—"

"Listen, cop," said the woman, "a husband's gotta right pertect his wife, don't he? When somebody insults a decent girl, her husband's gotta right—"

"All right," said Higgins, "what happened here?"

"We was just talkin'," said McKay. "Just sittin' here talkin'—and he insults Doris. So I hit him. I didn't mean to—"

Higgins felt a little tired. "You're on Welfare?"

"Sure. So was Harry. Why?"

"So why weren't you both out hunting jobs?" A silly question. McKay looked at him uncomprehendingly.

"Look, cop, it means anything, I earn maybe like three-fifty per, diggin' ditches for the city. I get four-twenty on the Welfare. We was just sittin' here. I—"

"Over," said Higgins, noticing the bottle on the porch, "a little drink of rye."

"Yeah, like that. And he insults my wife. Calls her a name. I gotta right hit a guy insults my wife."

"What did he say?" asked Higgins.

"That guy—he said right out Doris was—was—" McKay's brow wrinkled—"pulcrit-something—pulcritudiny, somethin' like—an' so I hit him. A man's gotta right, somebody sayin' a thing like that about his wife—"

"You're damn right!" she said shrilly. "Callin' me a prostitute! I

52

was a virgin when we got married inna church—nobody got no call to—"

Higgins looked at Tidwell dead on the sidewalk. Tidwell, even on Welfare, slightly better educated? Poring over the dictionary?

Pulchritudinous, thought Higgins. She was indeed, Doris. He said, "Come on, Mr. McKay. You can make a statement at headquarters." Better warn him, all the rights and so on, then. He nodded to the interns; they could have the body.

He got a statement from McKay down on paper and booked him into the jail on Alameda, and it then being after twelve he dropped into Federico's for lunch. Mendoza came in ten minutes later and heard about McKay. Mendoza was amused.

"*Ridículo*," he said. "They do say, failure of communication these days."

"As far as I'm concerned, it's just depressing, Luis," said Higgins. "Anyway, your blonde's picture will duly appear in the papers. Should by rights turn up somebody who knows her."

"Should is the operative word, George. Did the *Citizen* have time to get it in today?" Of all of them, that paper came out in the afternoon.

"They said so."

"*Bueno.*"

But as it transpired, the newspapers were not to play a part in identifying the blonde.

At two-forty-five Sergeant Lake put through an inside call to Mendoza.

"Mendoza? Carey here. Have you still got that fancy body you mentioned to me? Unidentified? You have? Well, I think maybe I can give you some help. Be with you in five minutes."

And five minutes later Carey came into the Homicide office, accompanied by four people. One of them Mendoza knew: a tall balding impeccably clad man named Claude Serio. He was a Fed —F.B.I. There was also a rather handsome man about fifty, well-groomed, haggard of countenance, with a belligerent look in his eyes, and a nice-looking woman about forty-five, very smartly dressed, with an expensive bleach-job and a drawn face and shocked blue eyes. And a very angry and upset and goodlooking young man about twenty-five, also impeccably clad, who was saying furiously, "I *told* them to call the police! I *said* from the first we should call the police—I've said so right along—"

53

"Serio," said Mendoza, standing up. "What—"

"And *I* told them," said Serio. "For God's sake. Three days delay on it. Should have called the police *and* us right then. But when they finally did—about forty minutes ago—decide to call us, naturally I got onto Missing Persons—it being your stamping ground —and Carey remembered something you'd said. And we'll be sitting in, in case it was a kidnaping—attempted or accomplished. But Carey says you've got a body to show us. Excuse me, this is Mr. and Mrs. Stanyard and Mr. Paul Trulock."

"Kidnaping?" said Mendoza. "What is this?"

"I *told* them," said Trulock in an impassioned voice. "I *told* them —but they were so damn sure it was—wait for a ransom note! My God! When she just *vanished*—it wasn't possible, she just—one minute there, and then just *gone*—my God, if I'd had the sense to call the police *then*—"

FIVE

"So what have you got for us?" asked Mendoza. "This is on the un-identified body found on Monday night?" He reached into his breast pocket and handed over the photograph. Serio glanced at it and gave it to Stanyard, who took one look and uttered a wordless moan.

"Oh, God. Oh, my God. Michele—it's Michele—" He put his face in his hands.

Paul Trulock took it from him. His strong jaw clenched and a vein moved in his temple, but he didn't do any emoting. "If I'd just called the police then! If I'd—oh, my God, but how did it happen? How could it? I don't understand—my God, what did happen to her?"

Mrs. Stanyard was weeping hysterically. Mendoza went out to the anteroom and told Lake to get a policewoman up here. "Who's in?"

"George and John."

"Shove them in," said Mendoza.

Higgins and Palliser came in, and within three minutes a motherly-looking policewoman arrived and shepherded Mrs. Stanyard out. Stanyard made a halfhearted effort to go with her. "She'll be looked after, Mr. Stanyard," said Mendoza. "This is Sergeant Higgins, Sergeant Palliser. Mr. Stanyard—Mr. Trulock. We know you're upset about this, we're sorry, but you'll understand we have to ask questions. To find out the circumstances."

Stanyard nodded dumbly; young Trulock said savagely, "So ask anything you want! If you can make head or tail of it—God, if I'd only called the cops right then—"

Mendoza looked at Serio. "Suppose you start the ball rolling."

"Sure," said the F.B.I. man. "Mr. and Mrs. Stanyard and Mr. Tru-

55

lock came into our office about an hour ago and told the tale to me. Miss Stanyard—er—vanished early last Monday evening, while on a date with Mr. Trulock. They were engaged to be married. Mr. Stanyard was convinced his daughter had been kidnaped, and didn't call the authorities, expecting to receive a ransom note. But no ransom note has been forthcoming, so he finally agreed to notify us." Serio spoke in precise tones, unemotionally, but Mendoza knew he was annoyed at the stupid civilians. Jumping to conclusions: delaying the hunt. Stanyard, thought Mendoza: vaguely he recalled seeing the name—social page?—no, there'd been some big deal in oil, a merger, details escaped him, but that was the connection. Stanyard obviously was Money: old, substantial, discreet Money, by his quiet tailoring. Trulock looked very well endowed too. "I advised them to contact the police at once. Here we are. So now we know the girl's dead. You can get your formal identification later." He shrugged. "I don't think it's anything for us. What've you got on it?"

"Nothing," said Mendoza. "The autopsy report says she was killed between eight and ten P.M. Monday night."

"How—how was she—?" Stanyard looked up, gray.

"She was—someone tried to strangle her, or just to keep her quiet, and her neck was broken, Mr. Stanyard. She died instantly—there wasn't any pain."

"Oh. Thank God for—but she was only twenty-one! Only—and our only child—oh, God—"

"But how, how, how?" demanded Trulock. "It's impossible!" He was pacing, hands clenched in front of him, jaw set.

"Tell us what happened. You were out together? Sit down, Mr. Trulock. Have a cigarette. Just tell us."

Trulock dropped suddenly into a chair. He was a very good-looking young man, tall, wide-shouldered, dark smooth hair, good strong features. He said, "All *right*. Of course you don't—thanks." He took a cigarette, bent to Mendoza's gold lighter, and took a deep drag. "All *right*. Michele and I went out last Monday night. I picked her up at the house about—about six o'clock. We were going to dinner, early, and then on to the theatre. I—"

"On Monday night, sir?" asked Palliser. Most theatres were dark on Mondays.

"What? Oh, it was a Little Theatre play—Michele had some friends in it. We went to Le Renard Bleu for dinner. That's a restaurant—"

"We know it, Mr. Trulock." The Blue Fox was rather a small phenomenon as restaurants went, its history perhaps matched only by La Golondrina on Olvera Street, that tourist attraction maintained as of historic interest. The fashionable restaurants in L.A. County, the places to go, were all suburban—some of them used to be on the Sunset Strip: there was Restaurant Row in the valley, and others in Hollywood, Pasadena, Westwood. The Blue Fox wasn't like any of those, but it had its own deserved reputation. It was in downtown L.A., a dreary and squalid area over on the other side of New Chinatown, right where it had been for forty years when a recent immigrant from Marseilles had opened it on a shoestring. Its reputation was for excellent food and wine and good service. "We know it," said Mendoza.

"Michele—it was one of her favorite places," said Trulock. "We went there quite a lot. Well, we went there Monday. We were early on account of going to the theatre, curtain time was eight-thirty. We got there about, oh, a quarter of seven. We had dinner, and a half-bottle of wine with it. It was about—what?—a quarter of eight when we started to leave. M-Michele said she'd go powder her nose, meet me at the front door. I had to get change for the tip, and then I waited for her. At the front door. And she—" he flung his hands wide—"she never came! She just—didn't come. I waited, and then I didn't know what to—it was nearly eight o'clock, and I —finally I got hold of the waitress, the one who'd waited on us, and asked her to check the ladies' room—and there wasn't anybody there! Nobody. Michele—she'd just vanished! I couldn't understand it—I *don't* understand it. And now—you're saying she might have been dead already—when I—"

"Then what did you do?" asked Mendoza. "Why didn't you call the police right then, Mr. Trulock?"

"I—" said Trulock. "Dear God, if I had! But—oh, hell. It wasn't *like* Michele to do such a thing, but I did just think—I—well, it's silly. I was a damned fool even to think about it. But we'd had a— little fuss—at dinner, nothing really but—I did just wonder if maybe she'd been—annoyed enough—to walk out on me. Just go home. I thought—before *I* raised any fuss, I'd better—call the house and find out. I—" He looked at Stanyard, who took his hands from his face and looked up slowly.

"All right, Paul," he said heavily. "You've every right to call me a fool. Mr. Serio hasn't said it, but I suppose he thinks so too. When Paul called and told me what had happened, I—I suppose every man with any money has always got that at the back of his mind, if he's got children. And there's just been that case back east—the girl about Michele's age, kidnaped and held—I was afraid it was that. And Louise—my wife—was terrified. I wouldn't let Paul call the police or even the F.B.I. If we did, and then there was a ransom note—saying—not to—I said we had better wait, if a ransom note should—and then—"

"Kidnapers are usually prompt on that bit," said Serio. "You waited nearly three days."

"I was *terrified*," said Stanyard. "You've got to understand that! I was sure that's what—I didn't see what else it could be. I thought there'd been—some mix-up—about the note, maybe. I didn't—what else could I have thought? Louise had told us Michele hadn't a dime on her when she left with Paul that night. Not a dime. Just—her cosmetics, things like that, and cigarettes, in her little evening bag. And—just spirited away somehow—she must have been— What else could we think? It was a nightmare—a nightmare—waiting."

"And then finally I persuaded them to go to the F.B.I.," said Trulock, "and—you say she was found—the same night—oh, my God. But how could it happen? Who—"

"The operative question," said Mendoza. "What was the argument about, Mr. Trulock?"

Trulock made an angry gesture. "Nothing—important. Nothing to do with—"

"What was it about?"

"Oh, hell, this friend of Michele's. This Eileen Rodney. I didn't like her. Michele had taken me to a party at this girl's place, last week, and I didn't—well, approve of her as a friend for Michele," said Trulock stiffly. "I'd said so then, and the subject came up again Monday night. And, well, one thing led to another and—I suppose Michele felt—well, some kind of loyalty to old friendship, they'd been at school together, but I—not only this Eileen, some other people there, a wild bunch, and I think there may have been drugs floating around. Michele said I was Victorian about it. But it wasn't anything—well, you see."

"Yes," said Mendoza. "She took her bag with her to the ladies' room, of course."

"Yes, sure. I—what I did, after the waitress said there wasn't anyone there, I asked if she'd seen Michele. She hadn't, since we left the table. I asked the cashier, and she'd seen her start for the ladies' room but hadn't seen her come out. I went out and looked in the parking lot but there wasn't any sign of her, so then— That was when I thought it was just *possible* she'd—"

"Walked out on you. How long had you been engaged, Mr. Trulock?"

"Since—since Christmas," said Trulock. "We were going to be married in June." He hunched his shoulders, bent his head, his hands clasped together.

"Did you have many arguments? About her friends or anything else?"

Trulock shook his head. "Never before," he said numbly. "Never."

"You said she 'took you' to a party at this Eileen Rodney's place. Where was that?" asked Palliser.

"Well—if it matters—that was another reason I didn't— She, this girl, she's moved away from home, I think Michele said her parents live in Bel-Air, but she's got a rathole of an apartment in Boyle Heights. And that out-and-out bum she called her boyfriend—I didn't like the whole setup. Not by a damn sight. But that wouldn't have anything to do with Michele getting—getting—" He shook his head.

"Well, we'll be talking to you again," said Mendoza after a pause. "You know we'll be doing all we can on it. Right now, I'm afraid one of you will have to go down to the morgue and make a formal identification."

Trulock said in a dragging voice, "I'll do that, Mr. Stanyard. You'd better take Mrs. Stanyard home. When—when can we—"

"You can claim the body at any time, the autopsy's been done." Mendoza looked at Palliser, who got up and said he'd take Trulock to do that. "Oh—before you leave—could you describe Miss Stanyard's bag?"

"It was—a little black velvet clutch bag. Not very big."

"Wasn't she wearing a wrap of any kind?"

"Yes—a black velvet jacket—she took it with her to the—"

"And she was," said Mendoza, "wearing her engagement ring? A diamond solitaire? Do you know the size of the stone?"

"Four and a half carats," said Trulock drearily.

"Was she wearing any other jewelry?"

Stanyard said, "Her grandmother's necklace. It had only come to her on her twenty-first birthday last November, and she loved it. She always wore it if she was going out in the evening. It's— diamonds and emeralds, rather old-fashioned—"

"Any idea of its value, sir?"

59

"I don't know. I think it was appraised when my mother died—it's an old piece. Her—her jewelry was taken? Do you think—"

"I don't know," said Mendoza. "We'll be looking. I'd be obliged, Mr. Stanyard, if you could find a copy of that appraisal for us. And—" he looked at Trulock—"an expert description of the diamond solitaire. We'll be talking to both of you again. Mr. Stanyard, I think you'd better take your wife home."

They went out quietly, Palliser behind. Mendoza squashed out his cigarette and lit another. "Well, that is quite a story, isn't it, boys? What do you think of it, Serio?"

Serio said promptly, "If Trulock's leveling, it's a hell of a story, Mendoza. How in God's name was she spirited away out of a busy restaurant?"

"Is Trulock leveling?" said Higgins.

"He sounds damn straightforward," said Serio. "He's with his father's firm, incidentally—Trulock, Morgan and Davidson. Not a member of the firm, of course—he just passed the bar last year. Money. Big money."

"Honest money?"

"So far as we know. Reputable firm. Father has private money too. Young Trulock came into an inheritance of about a million from his grandmother when he turned twenty-one."

"Them that has gets," said Higgins. "Nice for him. What do you think, Luis?"

"I think," said Mendoza, "that I'd like a good look at the inside of Le Renard Bleu, and the terrain around it, at about the same time Trulock says he mislaid Michele, three nights ago. Suppose you and John meet me there about eight o'clock, George."

"Might give us a few ideas," agreed Higgins. "O.K."

"If you'll excuse me," said Serio, "I think I'll bow out. As they say, hold a watching brief. I don't think this is anything for us—if you turn up anything you'll let us know. But do let me know what you do turn up, I'll be interested."

"Yes," said Mendoza. "Damn it, why all of a sudden so many funny ones landing on us? The things *muy extraño*. That blonde worried me all right before we knew who she was—now she worries me all the more."

"It's a rigmarole, what Trulock says," said Higgins, "but the simple explanation's usually the best one, isn't it? It could just be kind of simple. So, the girl was mad enough to walk out on him.

And what he said about the Rodney girl—Michele phoned her to come pick her up, and she winds up with the wild bunch in Boyle Heights. Stripped of her diamonds. Or, she arranges to meet the Rodney girl on a corner down there and while she's waiting the hood comes by and sees the diamonds."

"*Conforme,*" said Mendoza. "Either way possible. Or something else."

"Well, you'll keep me informed," said Serio, getting up.

"And thank you so much for our new problems," said Mendoza.

Piggott had roped Glasser into helping him out on the routine on Darley, and they had wasted the entire afternoon down there, asking futile questions. They had a little new, but nothing that said much. They'd talked to Felker again. He told them Marion Darley was a dirty old woman—and a nuisance. So, people said, lonely, but she was a damn nuisance—coming right into peoples' houses, staying. She'd done that to the Felkers a few times after they'd moved here, until his wife had told her off. Why hadn't he told them that before? Nobody had asked him. But everybody knew how Mrs. Darley was, around here. A nuisance. And some of the time half-tight on beer.

They talked to the Dawsons again. The only Dawsons at home, Mrs. Dawson and the seventeen-year-old Ron, said evasively, well, the poor woman had been lonely. They saw other people up and down the block, the Smiths, the Fishers—middle-aged couples with nearly grown-up families, and got much the same thing. The Powers, five houses up from the Darley house, were more forthright: they were an older couple living alone; Powers was retired from the railroad.

"She was a pest," he said. "Come around, invitin' herself right in, and sit here hours watchin' the TV. I and my wife had enough, told her not come no more. The gall that woman had—not that I ain't sorry for her gettin' killed like that."

They didn't find that there'd been any rumors about Marion Darley having a fortune stashed away in the house.

"There's nothing more to get on it," said Piggott gloomily as they sat over coffee at a drugstore at four-thirty. "I think it was the spur of the minute thing, Henry. Some hood, or a punk needing a fix, hit the first house he came to when the idea occurred to him, and took her off for what was in her purse. Leaving us no leads at all."

"And that could be," said Glasser. "Records make any of the prints they lifted in that house?"

"They did not. I think the quicker we shove it in Pending the better. Anyway, I'll have to put in a follow-up report on it—let's get back to the office."

The autopsy report on Kitty Durand came in just as Mendoza was leaving the office, and he scanned it rapidly. Any big-city police-bureau occasionally gets disorganized with the spate of business: absolutely nothing had been done on Kitty Durand today. And something else might come along at any minute, which was a depressing thought.

Kitty Durand had been forcibly raped. She had fought hard against her attacker: three of her fingernails had been ripped to the quick, and one front tooth broken, possibly in an attempt to bite him. Provisional time of death, between eleven A.M. and one P.M. on Tuesday. She had been about six weeks pregnant. There was dried blood under several of her fingernails: it was Type A, and her blood was Type O. Interesting. And that was about all the autopsy gave them.

Mendoza went home, and if he had brooded over the blonde before, now he was brooding harder. Now she had a name. Michele Louise Stanyard. Pretty ex-debutante. A minor socialite. Girl with money engaged to handsome young man with money. Both looking like clean, upstanding, high-class people.

That tale of her vanishing. Well, look at the restaurant. Look at—

With an effort he put it all out of his mind as he came in the back door. He had a private life and a family to think about too. He kissed Alison, busy at the stove, and went down to the nursery to find the twins being read to by Mrs. MacTaggart preparatory to their baths. Johnny and Terry were very full of *el pájaro* and his doings, and alternately explained to him about *el pájaro's* wife and nest and children. "Pretty soon, *todo el mundo* fly away!" said Johnny. "*El pájaro* bite Bast," said Terry solemnly, "and Bast *corrió rápido!*"

Absently Mendoza thought Alison was quite right, saying the twins ought to get Spanish and English sorted out. They'd be three this year, after all. But how to go about it—

"Good day, *cara?*" he asked over dinner.

"Fine. But there is something we—"

"We've got that blonde identified," said Mendoza. "I'll be going out again on that. And a very funny tale that is, too—" He buttered a roll absently. "What did you say, *amante?*"

"Nothing—it'll keep," said Alison. "Tell me about the blonde."

At eight o'clock he met Higgins and Palliser at Le Renard Bleu. Fashion was such a chancy thing: when the immigrant from Marseilles had opened his little restaurant on a shoestring, forty years back, he was merely hoping to make a modest profit serving local customers; but he had innocently run his restaurant on old-fashioned principles. The word had gone out among the ultra-sophisticated —but, my dear, such atmosphere, really you'd think you were in France—and real gourmet cuisine—you really must try it. And in the end Le Renard Bleu, in this unlikely location, had acquired as customers a far different crowd from the humble local residents. Like La Golondrina over on Olvera Street, like several restaurants in New Chinatown not far away. In the heart of downtown L.A., not a very savory neighborhood.

"No attendant in the parking lot," commented Higgins, locking his car.

"No, there wouldn't be," said Mendoza. "I think, still the family operation. No pretensions." It had never pretended to be a fancy place. The parking lot, grown to be a necessity in these days, had been simply created by buying two lots next door, knocking down the ramshackle houses on them and blacktopping the land. Le Renard Bleu itself was, in fact, an old rambling two-story house converted into a restaurant. There had been a narrow front porch, now enclosed; a little foyer and double doors leading into a tiny anteroom. There a cashier sat, not at a counter but at a little gilt table, with an old-fashioned metal cash-box on it. The cashier was a pretty darkhaired woman about thirty.

"Messieurs—*vous êtes trois?*"

Mendoza showed her his badge; alarm sprang up in her eyes. "Just a few questions," he said. "About a couple of your regular customers. You do have a number of regular customers?"

"*Oui,*" she said faintly. "Is it that I should call Monsieur Robineau? The proprietor?"

"If you'd like. We'd better talk to him too. We just want to look around here a little, if we may—we won't disturb anyone. And ask a few questions." He smiled at her reassuringly.

"I will call Monsieur. Police—they go where they will, who is to say no?"

"Well, we like to be polite about it. Which way is the ladies' room?"

She raised her brows, shrugged and pointed.

The enclosed front porch had created the little anteroom and a narrow hall running down from the foyer. The hall led from directly inside the foyer-door down to the right, where a door was labeled *Gentlemen,* and took a right-angle left turn to a cross-hall which would back up to the partition behind the table in the foyer. Halfway down the ten-foot hall, on the right side, was a door marked *Exit;* Mendoza tried it and it was unlocked. Probably a former door to the side porch, possibly put in in obedience to the Fire Department. At the end of the little hall was a door labeled *Ladies.*

"Well," said Palliser. "So she could have given Trulock the slip if she wanted to. He said he waited by the front door."

"Mmh, yes," said Mendoza. "Let's see." He went back to the foyer, Higgins and Palliser trailing him. Behind the foyer a wide arch admitted them to the dining room, which was T-shaped, the cross-bar of the T to their left. Nearly the whole of the ground floor of the old house had been given over to the dining room, a space partitioned off for kitchens at the back. There were perhaps fifty tables scattered about the dining room. The décor, the atmosphere, was expectable: red-checked tablecloths, mottoes in French stenciled on fake beams, a display of French flags over the stone-manteled hearth where a log fire blazed. At eight-ten, the place was well-filled, a hundred or more diners. The lighting consisted of a candle-lamp on each table, flickering, and a large central chandelier which held many, but small-wattage, bulbs high over the room.

"Hay más," said Mendoza simply.

To the left of the dining room ran the original outside wall of the house; and along there were two sets of double French doors leading out. A sign lettered in Gothic said simply, *Terrace.* Vaguely they could see a few more tables out there. For the alfresco dining in nice weather. "And—" said Mendoza. He turned and led them back to the foyer, and the door. In the five-foot-square anteroom, between the double front doors and the door to the foyer, a narrow lighted showcase had been built into the wall on either side: displayed on narrow shelves was a probably valuable collection of French coinage. Each shelf was labeled as to period, names of coins. Mendoza regarded it interestedly.

"He said he waited by the front door. But, in the foyer, or here?"

"If he was here," said Palliser thoughtfully, "studying the antique coinage while he waited—even part of the time—she could have gone that way too. Sneaking past the cashier, out the other side of the dining room."

"Let's ask some questions," said Mendoza.

When they turned back to the foyer, Monsieur Robineau was there—plump, elderly, bald, anxious to be helpful. They showed him Michele's picture. Did he remember her coming in, with a young man? Yes, he did.

"You understand," he smiled, "nowadays I do not wait on the customers—I have grown old and prosperous. But I stroll about, I keep an eye on my business. Yes, the young lady I know, she and this young man come in often—oh, maybe once in ten days, the last four, six months. . . . Monday night?" He shrugged. "It could be the last Monday night they are here, one night is like another."

They desired to speak with the waitress who had served them? He would ask, find her. It was to be hoped they would not detain her long, they were busy, the house had a reputation for good service. Ten minutes later the waitress was produced, a buxom young woman with a moustache, an air of open frankness, and a heavy French accent.

"Yes, the blonde young lady I remember. A pretty girl, and her young man so handsome. They come frequent, they sit most times at the table which is in my part of room—the room. By the fire. The man, he leaves good tip always. I remember."

She remembered Monday night too. Because it had been something unusual. After they had gone, some time after—who could guess the time, but she had meantime served two tables with the full dinners, and *apéritifs* to a third—the young man had come back, asked her if she had seen the lady. She had not. He had then asked her to look in the *toilette* for the lady. But she was occupied; she could not leave her tables, she had apologized. So he had gone to speak with Mademoiselle Margot. Mademoiselle Margot Guillaume, who takes the money. No, indeed, she had not noticed the young lady and gentleman arguing as she served them.

"Well," said Palliser thoughtfully. "He said he got the waitress to look in the ladies' room."

"He was worried," said Higgins. "If he's leveling. A detail."

Margot Guillaume was not as anxious to be helpful as her employer, who hovered nearby while they questioned her.

"Yes, of course I remember that—it was sufficiently unusual—last Monday night. This young couple, they had been in often, I know

65

them. No, not their names, of course not. I do not know the time exactly, it was early. They came earlier than they usually come. It is later on the man comes to me, asks me to look in the ladies' room." She shrugged; cynical amusement showed in her dark eyes. "She has —what is the phrase?—stood him up, walked out, *hein?* So, I am not busy, to oblige I go and look. No one is in there."

"There isn't an attendant in the ladies' room?" asked Palliser.

"For what? No."

"You didn't see the young lady—mmh, walking out on him—slip past your table out there, maybe to get out through the terrace door in the dining room?" asked Mendoza. "Maybe you thought it was a little joke, didn't tell him?"

She laughed, full-throated. "And maybe I would not tell the *flics* if I had! *Mon ami,* any girl is a fool who does not on occasion show a man she is not the—the easy mark! I think that one, he is—" she wrinkled her admirable nose— "a very correct young man. A rich but what the English call a very stuffy young man! Oh, his beautiful tailoring, his nice manners! I was amused—he was so *distrait!*"

Mendoza said softly, "I think you'd better tell us, Margot. Because the young lady is dead. Somehow, she walked out of here and very shortly got her neck broken. By somebody. We'd like to find out who. That's why we're here, asking questions."

"*Le bon Dieu!*" She stared at him, her olive skin going chalky. "That pretty young one—dead? *Morte?* Mother of God!"

"That's right. Did you see her slip past your table here and go back into the dining room?"

"*Non!* I did not! I do not lie to you—murder is not a game! The poor young lady—no, I did not. They come out, he asks me for change to make the tip. She goes toward the ladies' room, he back to the dining room. He comes back. Then, presently he asks me to—"

"Did the young man wait right here in the foyer, until he asked you to look? Or was he out there where the coinage is displayed?"

She shook her head. "I am not sure. There were people came in, and others coming up to pay. I do not know. But—the young lady, she could have gone out the side door, from the *toilette*. I did not see her again, and I am right here until ten when Monsieur Robineau takes the money while I have coffee."

Robineau was exclaiming, asking questions—the young lady murdered? Near his place? What an atrocity—the wanton violence in these terrible times—

"So what do you think, Luis?" asked Higgins. "You pay your money, you take your choice."

"*Como sí*," said Mendoza. "I want to talk to Trulock again. Oh, yes. This is an odd one, George. Along with a couple of other odd ones. There's Kitty Durand too— This one could be a double bluff, indeed."

"How do you mean?" said Palliser. "Oh—"

"Oh, yes, I saw that too," said Higgins thoughtfully.

SIX

On Friday morning it was raining again—a thin wet mist that couldn't be called real rain but got everything very damp. Mary interrupted a spirited argument between Steve and Laura on the respective charms of baby sisters and brothers, to say disapprovingly, "You need a new raincoat, George. That thing is disgraceful."

"I've heard that wives are always trying to give away our comfortable old clothes," said Higgins, shrugging into his trench coat. "It'll do. Why take a nice new coat out in the rain? And listen, Laurie —you wait for your mother to pick you up with Steve, this afternoon, if it's still raining. And you be careful driving, Mary." It was in that rainstorm last fall the hit-run driver had nearly killed Steve.

"Yes, yes," said Mary. "You do fuss, George." She smiled at him.

"Well, I've got something to fuss over." And suddenly Higgins thought about Robert Durand. His Kitty. They had just been starting out on the fun of a family—and then fate, or something, stepped in.

Durand—well, some work ought to be done on that, of course, and what with the Stanyard thing breaking yesterday, nothing had been. When Higgins got to the office Mendoza was saying the same thing, and the work fell to Higgins. "Art and I will be kicking around several ideas on Michele," said Mendoza. "You go and see if you pick up any more on Kitty Durand. The funeral's tomorrow—I suppose somebody ought to go." Just now and then, and more particularly on a violent killing like this where, ten to one, the victim and killer hadn't been acquainted, a killer did show up at the funeral. Only it had looked as if Kitty Durand had known her killer. Those coffee cups. *Three* coffee cups, which looked a little odd.

Higgins went up to the lab and asked if they'd got anything useful from the Durand apartment. "Some prints," said Scarne. "Strange prints—not hers or Durand's. They weren't in our Records, we sent 'em back to Washington. Wait and see. There was just coffee in that decanter, in the cups. No clear prints on any of those. The lipstick on one cup was Elizabeth Post, coral-rose. There was such a lipstick in the bathroom. Lessee, we gave you the info on the fingernail scrapings and so on. That's about it. Pity it wasn't raining last Tuesday, he might have left some footprints."

Higgins set off for Westmoreland Avenue in slightly harder rain. Salesmen, he thought vaguely; had there been any salesmen going door to door down there that day? And what about the men living in that apartment building? By the photograph in the *Herald* on Wednesday, a strikingly goodlooking girl: any man might have lost his head a little.

Landers was off, but the follow-up on that body he'd covered yesterday had to be done. Piggott abandoned Marion Darley without regret, reading Landers' report. It was just one of those tiresome pieces of routine.

The body had been that of Samuel Revilo. Forty-nine, widower, skilled watchmaker: had his own small watch-repair shop on Alvarado. He had a room in a rooming house on Temple, and he'd been found yesterday morning by his landlady when she went in with clean towels, supposing he had left for work. The interns had said it looked like a deliberate overdose of some barbiturate. There had been a glass, used, beside the bed; the lab had it. No note left. No medication of any kind, pills or whatever, found in the room or the communal bathroom: there were three other roomers.

There was, said the landlady, a son, Alfred Revilo. She didn't know where he lived, just that it was somewhere here and he was married, Mr. Revilo used to go there for Sunday dinner sometimes. Landers had found four Alfred Revilos yesterday, from the phone book; none was the right one. The son should, of course, be notified. Equally of course they ought to find out where he'd got what he had taken.

Piggott pessimistically called the lab to find out if they'd identified that yet: normally the lab liked to be thorough and leisurely, but for once they'd got on it right away, and Duke told him it had been a certain brand of prescriptive sleeping-tablets. "About thirty of 'em, from the sediment in the glass. He must've meant to make certain. The autopsy'll give you something more definite on that. Yes, his prints on the glass."

"Thanks so much," said Piggott.

He drove down to Temple Street and talked to the landlady, Mrs. Pitman. She didn't know a thing. Mr. Revilo such a nice quiet man, lived here four years since losing his wife. He never said much about himself, she wouldn't know if he'd been going to a doctor.

The nearest pharmacy to Revilo's shop on Alvarado was on the next corner. Piggott went there and asked. The pharmacy had no record of filling any prescriptions for Revilo. The nearest pharmacy to the rooming house was on Glendale Avenue; that pharmacy had no such record either.

The other three roomers were all at their jobs, but the landlady had said they didn't have much to do with each other, didn't fraternize much. She had added brightly that poor Mr. Revilo had been keeping company with Mrs. Wooley down the street. He hadn't been an old man, her a widow, and it'd have been nice for him, have a proper home again.

So then Piggott went down the block to find Mrs. Wooley. Mrs. Leda Wooley. She was home, in an old General Grant house neatly kept up. She was a slightly scrawny woman, blonde by request, and grief-stricken over Mr. Revilo. "Such a fine man he was—his own business, and a kind, good man too—it's not every man would have been so kind to Mother, but he was always so thoughtful, he even brought her candy last Mother's Day—"

"He was that," chimed in the old lady. "Poor man. Poor man, and him not fifty yet." She was a little thin white-haired woman, bright as a button, with a perky voice.

They didn't know anything; he hadn't told them anything. They'd only just heard he was dead. Mrs. Wooley did, however, know the son's address: Manhattan Place in Hollywood.

Which was a step further on. Piggott started out for Hollywood in a rain that was, again, more like mist than rain.

"The double bluff," said Mendoza; he was swiveled around in his desk-chair looking out at the gray veil of sky, mist, fog blended to one grayness. "It just could be the double bluff, Arturo. And it would make it so much simpler." And that was at eight-fifteen.

"Oh, I know, I know—I see it," said Hackett. "I saw it when you first told me this little tale. Of course, you've met him—I haven't. Do you think it goes that way, Luis?"

"I don't know. He's putting it over just fine if it is an act—not," said Mendoza, "overplaying his part. If it is a part."

"Simpler, certainly," said Hackett, "than the rigmarole about Michele vanishing away from the ladies' room."

"And he wouldn't be taking too much of a chance. Margot Guillaume tells us that between the time she saw Michele head for the ladies' room and the time Trulock asked her to check it for him, there were people coming in, going out. She wouldn't estimate how long a time that was at all. That foyer's not very big. So it could be that Michele emerged from the ladies' room on schedule, out they went to the car, Margot not noticing. And continued the argument in the car. Mmh, yes—he had to tell us about the argument, otherwise he'd have had no reason for not calling the police then and there. The little argument—over Michele's far-out school-friend— or was it? Was it? And so he can say he thought it possible she'd walked out on him. But all right, they're arguing—in the car, in the unlighted parking lot. And Trulock loses his temper, and grabs her, maybe to shake her. I'd say he has a fairly quick temper, you know. And she was a small, slight girl. He wouldn't have intended to kill her, but he's a big powerful man. So he's left, all of a sudden, with a corpse."

"You're building it," said Hackett. "His fiancée? All right, maybe partly for the money, but he's got it too, it wouldn't have been just the money. She was a pretty girl."

"No. No, he's no cold-blooded egotist—but in a situation like that, Art, a man does tend—however horrified or remorseful or frightened he is—to think about himself. ¿Cómo no? He's no fool, and he's a lawyer. He knows he didn't mean to do it—it was an accident—but it's done. He'd think, what good to ruin his own life and career for an accident? Don't tell me he wouldn't have tried to cover it up."

"I'm not. If he's one like you say." Hackett looked at the open County Guide, to page forty-four: downtown L.A. "Elmyra Street is three short blocks from that restaurant. Strip her of her jewelry, make it look like robbery with the assault secondary. Dump the body the first dark and handy place. Back to the restaurant to play out his little drama. Yes, and he'd been there before—he'd know about that side exit down from *Ladies*. I'll tell you one thing," said Hackett. "If all that's so, it wasn't any of his doing that it all got delayed when the parents jumped to the conclusion that she'd been kidnaped, and held off on calling us. If she'd been found right away, how much more plausible that story would have sounded. Michele walked out on him, after a little spat, and went up Spring to catch a bus home. The hood jumped her, spotting the diamonds, and getting stuck with a corpse, dragged her a little way down that alley to give himself time to get away. All quite natural."

"*Como sí*. So the mother tells us she hadn't a dime on her, couldn't have meant to catch a bus—she couldn't be sure. And the diamonds will be locked up tight in Trulock's safe-deposit box at the bank, and there they will stay."

"Did it happen that way, Luis?"

"I don't know. It could have. It's a thing to keep in mind, is all. Meanwhile, we haven't done any asking around where the body was found. The Hurleys, who found her, were out—but other neighbors mightn't have been. Did any of them see anything around the Hurleys' side of the place that night? And so on. Go and poke around. Later on, I think, you and I will go poke around at Mr. Paul Trulock—ask him some questions. It could be—that's another angle—that he'd never expect us to look at him at all, and the very fact that we do might shake him up. We'll see."

"O.K. And what will you be doing, Sherlock?" Hackett got up.

"Just in the event—which is also possible—that Trulock is telling us gospel truth, I think I'll look up that Eileen Rodney," said Mendoza. "Ask the Stanyards about her. Because—" He swiveled around and looked at Hackett meditatively. "Twenty-one, Michele was. That part of Trulock's story rang true to me. By all the implications, she was a very sheltered young lady. Maybe a little immature. And —young. Private schools, of course. Youth is always so damned idealistic—and inexperienced, *naturalmente*. If all that is so about the Rodney girl—and he'd know we can check it out, of course—I can see one like Michele, with the muddled ideas about loyalty to old friends, defending the girl, and even maybe running to the girl to tell her so, all righteous. Just to teach him a lesson. And—Boyle Heights—the Rodney girl slumming? If she went to the same private school as Michele?" He got up, slim and dapper, and said, "It's a tangle. Let's reach in and pull threads. Meet you for lunch at Federico's."

At the General Hospital at nine o'clock, Palliser and Grace found the Yocums. They had showed up this morning at the old house, been informed of the children's illness by Mrs. Mason, and come to the hospital. Dr. Goodhart had called Homicide an hour before to report the death of the fifth and last child.

They talked to the doctor before they saw the parents. "Any idea what it was yet?" asked Palliser.

"We'll do autopsies, of course," said Goodhart. "Probably some time today, but of course we're busy. Those samples you brought in are in our laboratory now." He shook his head. "Pure carelessness. Neglect. Ignorance. The riffraff." And he glanced sidewise at Grace.

"Doctor," said Grace, "the riffraff come all colors, as we all know. You're probably quite right."

"Parents carried on like mad," said Goodhart. "Which figures— we see it all the time. Neglect the kids, leave 'em alone, and then wail and weep if the kids get into trouble. I gave the mother a tran- quilizer—she was getting hysterical."

In the little waiting room down the hall, they found the Yocums and introduced themselves. The Yocums were both under thirty, on appearance; Yocum very black, bullet-headed, a stocky short man wearing old jeans, a shirt without a tie, a ragged sweater. The woman was lighter brown, hair uncombed, a trifle plump: she had on a rather dirty cotton dress, no stockings, high-heeled pumps; the bright red coat they'd seen at the house lay beside her on the couch.

Yocum was rocking to and fro, his voice high. "Oh, my kids, my poor kids, my dear Lord, why'd You'd take my kids away?" Grace got him quiet enough to look at the badge.

"You understand we have to ask some questions, Mr. Yocum."

"Oh, oh, oh, my poor little kids—oh, I can't stand to think about it—" He pulled out a dirty handkerchief and blew his nose. "You policemen, sir? About our poor kids—I guess you hear how it happen, they get bad food some way—my wife, she didden know, an' us away from home—"

The woman huddled on the couch, looking to be in a half stupor: the tranquilizer. She looked up dully. "Police? About the kids? Oh, dear Lord, my li'l Fanny an' Billy an' Joey an' Annie an'—Oh, I can't hardly believe it—all my childern gone—"

"There has to be an official report," said Grace patiently, and his nose wrinkled slightly at the odor emanating from Yocum: old and new perspiration, unwashed clothes, a whiff of onion, and beer. "We have to ask you questions, Mr. Yocum. You left your kids alone, which is a misdemeanor. Why? Where were you?"

Yocum blew his nose again. "The kids, they stay alone a lotta times before," he said defensively. "They was with Mae—my wife. I—I—been down Long Beach with a friend o' mine, he get me a good deal onna new car—see, I got about a thousand bucks saved up from last season. Oh—oh—I gotta terrible shock, I come back, they tell me my kids—"

"What about you, Mrs. Yocum?" asked Palliser. She looked at him unresponsively. "You went off on Wednesday afternoon and didn't come back. Where were you?"

"I—" she said. "Oh, dear Lord, Eddy sayin' he gotta shock—what about me? *My kids*—all dead! My li'l Fanny, real good at managin' all t'other young 'uns—I never thought but they'd be O.K., jus' overnight! I—I went see this friend o' mine, sir, Millie Fosdick, I ain't seen her inna long time since she get married 'n' moved down here—we ain't been near L.A. a long while, we usual stay up north 'tween pickin' seasons. An' I got terrible sick at her place, that day— the fever like, an'—an' I couldn't get home, but I thought they be O.K. Fanny real good to manage—an' there was stuff there, cornmeal an' such—"

Grace shrugged at Palliser. Given that type, that rang true enough. It was possible that the woman had suffered a milder dose of whatever type of food-poisoning had killed the children.

"I'm sorry, Mr. Yocum," said Grace, "but you'll both have to come into the office and make statements. We can take you in now if you'd—"

"Oh, I guess—get it done with," mumbled Yocum, wiping his eyes. "Whatever we gotta do—I just can't hardly take it in like—just all of a sudden—"

Durand hadn't gone back to work yet. Kitty's parents had flown in from Chicago for the funeral. They were all in the Durand apartment when Higgins, hearing that from Mrs. Otten across the hall, knocked at the door.

Durand let him in resignedly. "I don't know what else I can tell you," he said dully.

"I just thought you might have, thinking it over, Durand." The parents were nice-looking people in the forties, looking grieved and turning slightly indignant eyes on Higgins, as representative of the law which hadn't protected Kitty. "Had your wife ever mentioned any man around here—oh, trying to make up to her? You know—"

Durand shook his head. "You said—I mean the other man said —somebody she knew, because of the coffee cups. Nobody we knew would have— There wasn't ever anything like that, that I remember.

"I—I did think, I said to the other officer, she was so beautiful, some-body might—might have followed her. Like that. But I—"

"But there was!" said Mrs. O'Connell, sudden and sharp. "There was! It never came to my mind until just now when the officer—she wrote me about it!"

"About what, Mrs. O'Connell?" asked Higgins. A lead at last?

"She didn't tell Bob, she didn't tell anybody here, because she knew Bob'd be just wild and the other man was a big fellow and she was scared Bob'd get hurt. But she wrote me all about it. It was around last Christmas, because I remember the letter came the day I mailed her presents. *It could have been him—it could have!*" She sobbed suddenly. "My darling Kitty—such a terrible way to—if it was him, you just *get* him!"

Her husband had his arm around her, comforting. "Now, Nellie. This is the first I've heard about—you women keeping secrets—but you'd better tell the officer all about it, whatever it was."

She blew her nose and sat up straighter, a woman once nearly as pretty as her oldest daughter, the same regular features, and her gray eyes with their long black lashes were like Mary's. "It was then," she said. "The man at the market. The market where she usually shopped for groceries. He was one of the checkers—a big young blond man; she didn't know his name except he wore one of those tags, you know like they do, with his first name, and it was Lance. He—he'd asked her for a date two or three times, and he'd said—you know—suggestive things, and then that day when she was there, he was in the aisle putting things on the shelves when she came past, and nobody else around, and he tried to grab her and kiss her. She slapped him and got away, and that time she went to the man-ager and told him, and I guess the fellow got fired because she said he wasn't there any more, thank God. If it was *him*—"

And this was a lead indeed. Higgins ignored Durand's indignant exclamations and the woman's excited speculation for a moment: this could be a hot lead, or could it? Three months and more later? Well, the fellow could have been out of town and just come back. Or just sparked by the sudden impulse, seeing her in the street for the first time since she'd lost him his job.

"Do you know what market this was, Mrs. O'Connell?"

"She usually went to the Safeway over on Vermont," said Durand. "By God, if I'd heard about that then I'd have—"

"That's just what she was afraid of, Bob. I know I wrote her back that—"

Higgins' mind made a sudden leap. They'd been saying that the coffee cups implied she knew X. They didn't say any such damn thing. The other people in the building said there were occasional salesmen coming by, not often; she'd have opened her door when the bell rang. What the coffee cups might say was that she'd had a couple of visitors earlier, acquaintances if not friends, and served them coffee. Then, after they'd left, before she took the tray out to the kitchen, X arrived and rang the bell. The man from the market or whoever.

If so, why hadn't the friends come forth to say so? That they'd been here? They might not know about Kitty. Not everybody read beyond the headlines. They could have been away somewhere. It was a thing to think about, anyway. And do some work on.

Take the market first. The manager could give him the fellow's last name.

It had stopped raining, or misting, or whatever it had been doing. Higgins, feeling that little glow of satisfaction at the back of his mind that always accompanied a new lead, started for that market. But also at the back of his mind was the sly, wistful, persistent little thought that had been nagging at him ever since they knew for sure about the baby, last week. He hadn't said anything to Mary. They hadn't got round to discussing that yet. Some time he'd get up his nerve and ask.

If, *if* the baby was a girl—maybe she'd at least think about naming the baby for his mother. Margaret Emily.

He'd ask her. Some time.

"Yessir, I swear on a stack of Bibles!" said Mr. Reinfeld emphatically. "I saw what I saw. It never crossed my mind it meant anything till you asked, and I remembered it. When I think back. Acourse we heard about that dead body Mr. and Mrs. Hurley found, but it never came to my mind—I suppose it coulda had something to do with it."

"What, Mr. Reinfeld?" Hackett had spent the morning down here, poking around, hitting no pay dirt. The men first on the scene where Michele was found hadn't got anything for the lab: the alley was blacktopped, so no tire-tracks visible. Nothing said any of the miscellaneous refuse in the alley connected with the body; it was unlikely. She'd just been dumped, whoever dumped her. None of the neighbors had seen or heard anything unusual that night.

The people who lived on the other ground-floor side of the apartment, the Reinfelds, hadn't been home when he landed here. Now they were, and he was hearing something possibly a bit more useful.

"I tell you how it was, see, officer—" Reinfeld was looking excited. "We'd took a parcel for Mr. and Mrs. Hurley—roundabout five-thirty it was, mail truck come by and the man come over and asked would we take the parcel. So the Missus says sure, they're good neighbors. So we was kinda lookin' out for the Hurleys to get home, time we could give 'em the parcel, see. I guess it was from her sister up in Oregon, name on it."

"I thought the Hurleys had just gone out to the movies," said Hackett. "They were gone by five-thirty?"

"That's right," said Mrs. Reinfeld. The Reinfelds were older people than the Hurleys: Reinfeld retired and on the pension. "They'd gone to his brother's for dinner—it was Mr. Hurley's birthday—and then to the movies."

"So we was kinda watching for them to come home," said Reinfeld. "So, I seen these lights turn up their drive, headlights, see, and I say to Martha, they're earlier home than we expected, I get up and go to look out the window."

"Yes?" said Hackett.

"See if it is them. And it wasn't. Because this car, it just turned in their drive, an' it went up past where I couldn't see it no more, up by their side o' the house, see, and then about thirty seconds later it come backin' up again and off it went. People just turnin' around."

"But it stayed up the driveway there about thirty seconds?" Long enough for a strong man to heave a slight body out into the alley, climb back in the car.

"About. I didn't think nothing about it then."

"But you're sure that was Monday night?"

"Sure I'm sure. There was the parcel, see. It was a birthday present for Mr. Hurley."

"I see," said Hackett. Fortunately, that could be checked with the post office. "I don't suppose you could describe the car at all?"

"Oh, now, that I couldn't tell you a thing about," said Reinfeld. "It was dark. It was just a car. I think it was a sedan but that I couldn't swear to. Or how old, or anything like that. But you come askin', anything different that night, and all of a sudden I remember it."

"Yes, thanks very much," said Hackett.

At about the same time Alison was staring absently out into the back yard, absently smoothing her shoulder-length red curls, absently watching the twins and Cedric playing uproarious tag around the rose-beds, and saying indecisively, "Well, it's really none of our business, Máiri. Is it?"

"I will say," said Mrs. MacTaggart vigorously in her most Scottish tone, "I'm not one for meddling in other folks' business, *achara,* and you canna say I am. But by the same token, a body can do wrong not to interfere, times. There was that puir woman stabbed to death back east and not a soul so much as calling the police. And I just say—"

"Well, yes, I know," said Alison. "And you know her better than I do. But—"

"There could have been an accident. It's queer, the whole thing. And those two children—for they're nought else, you can't deny—"

"Well, yes," said Alison. "I'd just like to ask Luis what he thinks."

"I am only saying—"

Out there in the yard the mockingbird broke up the game of tag. He swooped down and pecked Cedric hard on his round tailless bottom, and swooped away. The twins yelled excitedly. Cedric barked indignantly. The mockingbird came to graceful rest in the alder tree and emitted his perennial battle-cry: "Yankee Doodle came to town Yankee Doodle came to town—coroo, coroo—YAWK!"

"Well—" said Alison.

"So it's still up in the air," said Hackett. "If that car means anything at all. What does Trulock drive?"

"I don't know," said Mendoza. "We'll find out. Up in the air you can say." He looked at his shot-glass of rye, dissatisfied.

Higgins came up to their table and pulled out a chair. "I've got a pretty hot lead on Durand," he said, and started to tell them about that. The waiter drifted up. "Scotch and water, Adam, and the steak sandwich." Hackett looked disgruntled; he'd been up to two hundred and twelve again and was back to the lean ground round, cottage cheese and tomatoes. "I've got the guy's name from the manager there. One Lance Ambrogianni. After Kitty Durand complained about him, he got fired all right. I don't know where he is now— I've got the address where he was living then, we'll look. But I ran a make on him, and he's got a pedigree."

"Isn't that nice," said Mendoza. "What?"

"J.D. record of car-hopping. But the rest of it—one count of statutory rape and one of attempted assault—I like. He hasn't served much time—he isn't even on parole." Which figured, the state of the courts these days.

"So we go look for him," said Mendoza. "A nice lead indeed, George. But on Michele—"

"That thing. It could be the double bluff. Trulock," said Higgins.

"Oh, *de veras*. It could also be something else," said Mendoza. "I had one little fleeting thought. There are regular patrons at Le Renard Bleu. Michele and Trulock were fairly regular patrons, but only since a few months back, and evidently nobody there knew them by name. Unless it was Robineau. We can ask him. But very likely, other regulars there, from a longer period back, whose names will be known. To Robineau, to Margot. So, ask them about any of those there Monday night? Go and ask the regular patrons whether they noticed anything? It's just a thought. Not much in it."

"We're supposed to be thorough," said Hackett. He contemplated his diet plate with no enthusiasm. "We can ask. You were going to look at that Eileen Rodney. You get anything?"

"*Ya lo creo*," said Mendoza. "That could very conceivably be some of the story too, Art. If Trulock is leveling."

"The big question. So?"

"I think," said Mendoza, "we'll go lean on him a little. Let him see we haven't taken him at face value. See what emerges."

"O.K. with me."

"And George can—George!"

"Hm?" said Higgins fuzzily, his gaze focussing. "What?"

"I swear *to* God, all these domesticities are demoralizing to the department," said Mendoza. "It was bad enough when he was just pursuing the female." Higgins blushed slightly.

"I was listening. You want me to follow up on Ambrogianni?"

"*Por favor*. I'd better chase back to the office, see what's in from the other boys on the current list. And then we'll tackle Trulock, Art."

"You didn't say what you got on Eileen Rodney."

"This and that," said Mendoza. "That could be interesting. I'll bring you up to date. But Trulock—I could bear to know, yes or no, on Trulock." He finished his sandwich and groped for a cigarette.

SEVEN

Mendoza had landed at the Stanyard house at nine-fifteen. It was one of the older places in Bel-Air, a dignified pile of Norman-provincial, with a vast lawn in front and probably a swimming pool and three-car garage behind. A white-jacketed houseman led Mendoza, after a wait in a large square hall, down the wide hall to a small breakfast room where Stanyard sat alone at the table over coffee. There was breakfast before him, in covered silver dishes, but his plate was clean.

"I'm sorry to disturb you again, Mr. Stanyard, but you understand we have to ask questions and then more questions."

"Any way we can help you, Lieutenant," said Stanyard dully. "My wife isn't up, she—hasn't been sleeping well. But I don't know what— Oh, sit down. Joseph, bring another cup. You'll have some coffee, Lieutenant." He looked drawn and gray, but his instinctive courtesy was still operating.

"Thank you. And you see, Mr. Stanyard, some of the questions we have to ask turn out not to have any bearing on the truth at all, when we find that out. But we have to ask—to be thorough. You might not understand why I'm asking you these things, but I hope you'll be good enough to give me some answers."

"What do you want to know?" asked Stanyard wearily. The servant came back and poured Mendoza a cup of coffee.

"Did you know all your daughter's friends?"

"I don't know," said Stanyard, "I suppose so. Young people, they have their own set, it's hello and goodbye, isn't it? Surely I knew most of her closest friends, I think—Sue Ransome, Wanda Hauck, Sandra Rooney—why?"

"Did you approve of all of them?"

"Approve? Why—like young people anywhere—they're all right, I suppose. All good families. Michele was never—*wild*, like some of the youngsters these days. . . . She went to the Comstock Academy, that goes through high school—she wasn't interested in going to college. She hadn't any particular interest to follow up; it wasn't necessary, of course."

"She had an allowance?"

"Up to her twenty-first birthday," said Stanyard. "Her—her grandmother had left her a hundred thousand, that came to her then. Last November. She—got quite a thrill out of having her own money. Of course it was administered by a brokerage. She—"

"Was she in the habit of carrying much cash around?"

"What? Well, sometimes she did, yes. I told her often enough it wasn't wise—of course she had her checking account—but she did. But what bearing—my wife told you Michele hadn't any money in her purse on Monday night. She wouldn't, going out with Paul. She—"

"Did she have her own car?"

"Yes, we gave her a Porsche on her eighteenth birthday."

Oh, really, thought Mendoza. How nice. "Do you know an Eileen Rodney? One of Michele's school friends?"

"I don't remember—but wait a minute. Yes." Stanyard massaged his neck wearily. "It was Paul. Just—just last week he mentioned the Rodney girl. He said he didn't think she was a good influence on Michele. I think—I gathered—Michele had just met her. For the first time since school, that is. I told him—I thought—since they were engaged, that maybe he could persuade Michele—talk to her about it—better than I could. I don't know any more than that, Paul didn't go into details. Oh—now I remember—he mentioned her in your interview with us. Do you think—"

"I don't know, sir. We're just being thorough. Did these other friends you mentioned go to school with her?"

"Yes, I think all of them—Wanda and Sue and Sandra, at least. But what—"

"Was your daughter out most evenings? Days? She had some—hobbies, interests?"

"What? Well, since she and Paul were engaged, they'd be going out two, three times a week—sometimes more, I suppose. Yes, she was interested in this Little Theatre group—oh, not in the acting part, she was always a little shy, you know, didn't like to—put herself forward—but Wanda was in with them, and some others Michele knew, and I think she'd given them money for costumes and so on.

81

And she liked to ride—we keep some horses at a stable in Malibu—and she was a fine swimmer. But I don't see what bearing—"

"It just gives us a clearer idea of her. What she might have done that night. If—"

"But she hadn't any money with her," said Stanyard. He lit a cigarette; his hands were shaking. "She wouldn't have left Paul—not voluntarily! If you're thinking that—it's impossible. It's no good going on that premise." For the first time he showed some emotion. "She wouldn't have—how could she, with no money? Listen, Lieutenant. Listen. Paul said they had this little argument. He said—I just remember—it was about that Eileen Rodney. But Michele—she hadn't that kind of hot temper, to—to—oh, she might argue, sulk, but she was really rather timid, if that's the word I—ten minutes later she'd be all over it. She had a—happy nature. I can't see—"

Which told Mendoza a little something more about Michele. He was aware that Stanyard thought the police were wasting time. You didn't always know the right questions to ask. But the picture was building for him, of Michele: not a silly girl, but possibly what used to be called flighty: inexperienced, sheltered, surrounded with that nice padded cushion of money. And very probably thinking of herself as a sophisticated, knowledgeable adult, when she was anything but.

He thanked Stanyard; was shown out by the solemn-faced houseman. He found a public phone booth along Sunset and looked in the book. The Comstock Academy was in West Los Angeles. Very unlikely he'd get anything over the phone; he drove back there. He had to use all his authority and charm, beyond the forbidding stone wall and wrought-iron gates, in the foyer of the tall stone administration building, but eventually he was admitted into the presence of Miss Fenwick, the headmistress. Miss Fenwick was a characterful-looking middle-aged woman with pepper-and-salt hair, an abrupt voice, and a sense of humor.

"Oh, you're the officer investigating that awful thing," she said. Her office was businesslike, plain. "Sit down, won't you? Michele Stanyard. I'd have said, the last one to have such a thing happen to her." She took his offered cigarette, bent her head to his lighter.

"Oh? You were here when she attended the Academy?"

"Been here twenty years. Probably be here till I go senile."

"And why would you have said that about Michele? What did you think of her, Miss Fenwick? Just off the record?"

She cocked her neat head at him. "What the Victorians called a flibbertigibbet. But a nice one, Lieutenant. A good kind girl, sentimental and a little shy, but basically a good girl. Why? Oh, well, she was—unadventurous. Conventional."

"Yes," he said. "I begin to gather that."

"But what would that have to do with—I'd gathered she was killed more or less at random, in the course of robbery?"

"And it could be. There are always ramifications in murder," said Mendoza. "What I really want from you is some different information. A girl named Eileen Rodney. Was she here when Michele was?"

"Oh, dear me, yes," said Miss Fenwick. "For my sins, she was, Lieutenant." Once she'd seen the badge, she wasn't holding back. "A difficult girl. Very headstrong. Undisciplined. A good mind, if she'd cared to use it. She didn't. A very pretty girl—and that, she used. She was expelled six months before graduation, for getting out at night to meet a boyfriend. She'd had a duplicate key made for the main gate—charmed our grounds-keeper into letting her borrow the key, you know. I might add that he was fired at the same time! We really can't have that sort of thing going on. Her mother was in a state about it, and we gave it out that it was illness —covered it up—but of course every girl in the school knew about it."

"That would be about three years ago?"

"That's right. . . . The address? Well, it was Westwood, I think. I can look it up in the files."

"If you would, please."

The address was Tavistock Drive in Westwood. It was a newer house than the Stanyards'; very groomed and fashionable. A Japenese gardener was cutting the grass with a purring motor-mower as Mendoza went up the walk to the one step of the porch-entrance. For once, he reflected sardonically, they were moving in somewhat higher circles than their usual beat down at Central. All this money floating around. . . . But behind the elegant façade of the house he met a very unhappy woman.

He wasn't sure that Thelma Rodney understood who he was at all, or why he'd come. She was, he thought, a dreep. Once a pretty girl in the chocolate-box sense, but never very much in the way of brains. She dithered at him when he mentioned Eileen. "Is she in trouble? You said police? I don't understand—oh, I just don't understand any of it." He had never seen anyone actually wringing her hands before. "That was a very fine school we sent her to,

83

Frederick said—goodness knows it cost enough—downright wicked it seemed to me, but then of course I wasn't brought up with money—not that Frederick was either, just the farm, but then there was all that oil—I never rightly understood it—"

"If you could just tell me where your daughter is living now, Mrs. Rodney?"

She stared at him. A little thin gray-haired dreep of a woman, probably looking much older than her actual years. Her dress was an expensive one, and she made it look dowdy; her hair had been professionally waved, and the precise blued curls looked out of place above her lined thin face with no makeup. You could guess, for all the money, no close friends, no interests, nobody to talk to, nothing to do. A futile woman. "Oh, dear," she said. "I really don't know what to *do*. She was always such a difficult girl. And exactly like Frederick—like her father. Well, who *else* would she be like, of course it was only natural, but they used to shout at each other so—it was nerve-wracking, what did you say your name is?—so bad for Frederick—he had high blood pressure and the doctor warned him not to get excited and lose his temper—might as well have said it to the man in the moon, of course—and Eileen yelling at him, and him yelling back—and of course the doctor was right, he had that stroke. He passed away two years ago, only fifty-three he was. And Eileen—"

"Mrs. Rodney, all I want is the address—"

"It wasn't right, her going off by herself. Some of the boys—*and* girls—she used to bring home, why, just horrible, looking like dirty tramps. But you can't talk to her any more than you could Frederick. He'd set up this fund, they call it, for her—trustees and all—I think it's about fifteen thousand a year—neither to hold nor bind, like they say, and she—"

"The *address*," said Mendoza, and she stopped in mid-flight, mouth open.

"Oh, yes. I didn't know it—she never comes home—but Mr. Turner, he's one of the trustees, he said I ought to have it in case. Of anything. I'll look it up for you—I wrote it on the telephone pad, I think—"

It was Chicago Street in Boyle Heights.

She faced him there in the doorway of the old apartment in the run-down, dilapidated old building, and she was quite indifferent. Uncaring. About anything: the whiff of wildness coming from her

84

almost tangible. She could have been a very goodlooking girl, thought Mendoza. Good figure, curly dark hair, dark eyes. She had on stained blue jeans, and a man's dirty white shirt too large for her, and no makeup, and no shoes. Her bare feet were grimy.

"Fuzz," she said incuriously to the badge. "Be my guest. Walk in, walk in. Tommy's still asleep. You want him?"

"No, I want to talk to you, Miss Rodney."

"What about?"

"Michele Stanyard." Mendoza came in.

"Oh, that one. I think maybe I'll have some breakfast today," said Eileen dreamily. "For kicks. I wonder what's here." She wandered past another door into a kitchen. Mendoza followed her.

"Miss Rodney, you were at school with Michele—"

She turned to look at him lazily. "School. That was hell for you. All those old bats. But I got away from the whole bit, and I stay away. Yeah, man. Just the way I want it. Eileen's out of the rat race for good. Do what I want when I want where I want. Don't want to do anything, don't. Stay in bed all day—listen to rock all day—sit in the park all day—the good life." She yawned. "Right now I guess Eileen'd like a li'l drinkie, decide what to do today. Or not do." She opened a cupboard and took down a bottle of vodka.

Mendoza looked around in fastidious incomprehension. His grandmother used to say that Luis Rodolfo Vicente Mendoza would get up off his deathbed to straighten a picture crooked on the wall; and here, the sheer magnitude of disorder and dirt and clutter distracted him like the spine-tingle of a fingernail drawn across blackboard. It was, he thought, obviously months of monumental indifference. Clothes dropped where they were taken off. Glasses left where they were emptied. Ashtrays overflowing to the floor. Nothing picked up, put away, washed. The whole place stank of dirt. Expensive stereo in one corner, covered with dust. Cushions on the dirty floor. An empty vodka bottle under the stereo. From an open door across the bare living room, presumably a bedroom, came the sound of snoring.

She gulped vodka, standing at the dirty sink piled with dishes. She grinned at him fuzzily. "What a party!" she said. "Like last night, or was it the night before? Fun, man, fun. That's all there is any more. What you want, anyway? I don't know any fuzz."

"Michele Stanyard," said Mendoza again. Irritation and contempt sharpened his voice. Fun for Eileen—because of the nice fifteen thousand per, Eileen didn't have to work like the peasants. Eileen,

85

on the way down fast. Eileen, probably drawn here by her low-class pals—the natural taste for low company? Tommy? Nice for Tommy too, probably, and the rest of them—the free drinks, free meals, and—"She's dead, you know," he said sharply.

"Who's dead?"

"Michele Stanyard."

"Oh, zat so? Accident or something?"

"Or something. She was murdered."

"You don't say so," said Eileen. "Well, people get killed every day. What a drag that one was. At school, tagging me around—little snotface innocent Michele. God. No guts, stand up to anybody."

"But you'd met her again just lately, hadn't you?"

"What? Yeah, yeah, of all places I run into li'l Michele at Robinson's. Tagging after me again like at school. *Oh, Eileen, I think you're so brave, just leave to live your own life.*" She threw back her head and shouted with laughter, sounding loud and coarse. "Life's to live, no? You're a hell of a long time dead." She poured another drink. "Oh, I let her come—party night every night here —everybody comes to Eileen's parties. But, man, you should've seen the guy she brought here one night—that was a real scream! Tommy had fits. A real—"

"Did you see her last Monday night?"

"Who notices days? I don't know. I don't think so. Nope, she wasn't here then." Eileen swallowed vodka, and suddenly threw her head back and began to sing in a nasal voice—

> "Railroad Bill mighty bad man,
> Shoot dem lights outta de brakeman's hand—
> Was lookin' for Railroad Bill!

> "The ole sheriff had a special train,
> When he got there, was a shower of rain,
> Was lookin' for Railroad Bill!"

"But what the hell," said Hackett, "was any attraction for one like Michele, Luis? That I don't see at—"

"Maybe just contrast," said Mendoza dryly. "A funny sort of attraction, Art, a negative one, but I can just see it. Given one like Michele, the staid conventional background. Eileen said Michele tagged her around in school. The wistful admiration of the docile, shy little girl for the one with the guts to defy authority. And a kind

86

of holdover there, this while later—could you say, an unwilling fascination for anything different?"

"If you want to sound like a head-doctor, say it," said Hackett. "Call themselves nonconformists—the biggest bunch of sheep there ever was, all doing their thing the same way. We used to call them bums. And you can see why Trulock—"

"Mmh, yes. That's a very squalid little place, daytimes, Art. You can see all the dirt. But at night, with just a few lamps on for the romantic atmosphere, and the beat music, and a few drinks—maybe looked pretty glamorous to Michele. And I'll tell you something else. There's malice in Eileen. So far as she might have any purpose—do any planning ahead—she'd have taken a little pleasure in—mmh—corrupting Michele. No, I don't buy the idea that these people unconsciously realize how far down they are, and want to pull everybody else down too—they've just opted out, doing what comes naturally. And I also think," said Mendoza, braking for a light, "that I'll pass that address on to Pat Callaghan. Very conceivably there could be dope floating around there, of this kind and that."

"So now we try to scare Trulock. In case he isn't leveling."

"And that could be too," said Mendoza.

Higgins had found Lance Ambrogianni right at the address the market had had for him. He was just leaving the apartment where he lived with his parents when Higgins arrived. Higgins brought him back to headquarters and with Palliser and Grace started the questioning.

Ambrogianni was surprised and indignant. "What the hell do you think you've got on me? I've done noth—"

"Kitty Durand, Lance," said Higgins.

"Who's she?"

"The girl who lost you your job at the market, round about last Christmas."

"Oh, that one," he said. He shrugged. "I haven't seen her since." He was a presentable fellow, if not handsome not ugly either, and he spoke well; he'd graduated from high school, they knew, the parents honest people. He was neat and clean in a navy suit and white shirt, and he was evidently capable of holding a good job— one like that he'd lost, demanding some intelligence. But by his record, his trouble was women: he couldn't leave them alone. They'd gone into his background a little now and they knew he'd lost a couple of other good jobs because of complaints similar to Kitty's.

He hadn't looked for a job since losing that one. He'd had the unemployment insurance, and some savings, he said; and he'd had some luck at poker down in Gardena. But he also had, at the moment, a couple of deep scratches on his face and another on his neck. "I cut myself shaving," he said. "That's all."

"Those don't look like razor cuts to me," said Palliser. "You got fresh with a girl maybe? What girl? Was it Kitty Durand, last Tuesday, Lance?"

"I told you, I haven't seen that one since. I didn't even know her name then. No, no, I—it's an old razor and I—"

"Can you tell us where you were last Tuesday, between eleven A.M. and one P.M.?"

"What's with this? I haven't done anything—last Tuesday? I was —oh, yeah—I was at Benny's pool hall downtown. Just hanging around. I had a pizza at the place down the street for lunch—it's Third Street—No, I wasn't with anybody exactly, that is anybody I know very well—I shot a couple of games with this guy came in alone too. I don't know his name, maybe Benny does."

"You're sure you weren't over on Westmoreland, raping and choking Kitty Durand, Lance?"

"R—*me*? I never did such a thing in my life," said Ambrogianni passionately. "Listen, that old count—that was a bum rap, that girl looked a good twenty years old and she made the deal for a quarter-century herself—it was her old bat of a mother brought the fuzz in!" And that was very possible, too, considering that the charge had been statutory.

"What about these scratches, Lance? Where'd you really get them?" asked Grace.

"Oh, hell," said Ambrogianni. "Oh, hell. I never raped a girl— I wouldn't do a thing like that. But a guy makes a pass, O.K. It was Tuesday night—I was out with Marge. So I throw a pass, she lets me know I'm out of line. Marge is kind of hair-trigger, you get me. So that's that. That's all. . . . Well, Marge Luzon, she works in that pizza place down from Benny's."

Grace went out to try to check that, while Higgins and Palliser went on at him some more. And, of course, any confirmation that might be forthcoming from customers at Benny's would not constitute the perfect alibi; but as that turned out, even Benny couldn't say Ambrogianni had been there; one day was like another, he might have been or might not. Grace did, however, get instant confirmation from Marge Luzon that she had been responsible for Ambrogianni's facial decorations, on Tuesday night.

"What do you think, George?" asked Palliser. "He doesn't really look so good for it. A little pedigree, but he's not really over the line. He holds jobs pretty steadily, and he doesn't smell right for one like this."

"He's still possible," said Higgins, massaging his jaw. "We'll keep him in mind. And he looked so hot for it, too. But there's nothing on him. Let him go, bear him in mind."

And just then a new call came in—a stabbing over on Leeward Avenue—so they let him go, and Higgins and Palliser went out to look at that while Grace finished typing the latest report on the Yocum children.

Mendoza and Hackett got nowhere at all with Paul Trulock. They found him in his modest office within the offices of that austere and important legal firm, which had its own very modern and handsome office building on Wilshire Boulevard—the right end of Wilshire Boulevard. There were glamorous-looking secretaries, the correct impressionist reproductions on the walls, the deep carpets, the broad polished desks. Even Trulock's small office, relegated to the most junior member of the firm, had the carpet, the painting (possibly bought by the yard and cut up for framing, thought Mendoza in passing). And Trulock, that good upright citizen, started answering their questions openly, willingly, cooperatively.

No, he hadn't had any arguments with Michele before. She was just a little fool about some things, couldn't see any harm in that Rodney girl. What the hell, a wild bunch like that, beatniks, whatever—he'd just tried to make her see it. And it wasn't a big fight, just a disagreement. No, of course she hadn't threatened to break off the engagement. Well, yes, he had—for just a while there—thought it was just possible Michele had ditched him on that account. Well, no, then he admitted it was a little more than just a disagreement, but *now* he didn't think it was possible she would have done that. It wouldn't be like Michele. Of course he'd wanted to call the police right away, but Mr. and Mrs. Stanyard—

Well, he had a temper, he supposed, as much as the next man. Yes, he had gone out for athletics at college—football and boxing.

He was about as strong as any man his size, he supposed. But what—

"Just this, Mr. Trulock," said Mendoza gently. "We do have to look at all the angles, you know. You could just be playing a double bluff here. It could be that Michele met you at the front door that night and you went out to your car, continuing the argument—that you lost your temper and—"

"*I* killed her?" said Trulock. "You think that?" His voice held naked astonishment. "*Me*? You think—"

"We just have to look at all the possibilities," said Mendoza. "Did you?"

Trulock got up from his desk, unexpectedly saying nothing, and walked over to the window. After a moment he said, "I'm not a fool, Lieutenant. But—that you'd think that, it never occurred to me. Now I can see where you'd think it might be a possibility. That I—was covering up. All I can say is, it's not so." He swung around to face them. "I was in love with her," he said simply. "I don't have that hot a temper. Everything I told you—was just how it happened." He spread his hands.

"All right, Mr. Trulock," said Mendoza equably, "we'll take it from there."

And Hackett said in the car, "Not only didn't we scare him, Luis, he sounded pretty straight. That sounded like the natural man."

"So maybe he's a good actor," grunted Mendoza. "I want to see Robineau again. If that's a forlorn hope—but you never know where a lead will show up."

Piggott finally located Alfred Revilo at three o'clock, and took him down to the morgue for the formal identification.

The new one, the stabbing on Leeward Avenue, looked like another anonymous little thing, but it had to be worked. Higgins and Palliser spent the rest of the afternoon asking questions, and hoped the lab might give them something on it eventually, but it didn't look hopeful.

"We seem to get the queer ones lately," said Palliser. "What the hell was a burglar—a daylight burglar—doing here? Practically nothing to steal."

"Anything is something to some of the types you run into," said Higgins. It was getting on for five then, and he yawned. "Damn, that Ambrogianni. . . . He could be, he couldn't be. And no way to say yes or no. . . . I'll type the report on this one, and be home late. I'd better call Mary."

And at five o'clock Mendoza and Hackett were at Le Renard Bleu, talking to Robineau.

But of course, said Robineau, the regular patrons. Like the poor Miss Stanyard and Mr. Trulock. "Of course the young man's name I know, not hers—he would call in for the reservation. Of course, other names—people who come regularly, called in the reservations. Last Monday night?" His broad brow wrinkled, he said seriously, "But it is a thought. Most definitely it is a thought. You are thinking, perhaps others here—some whose names I could give you—that night, perhaps one of them has seen something of significance. About Miss Stanyard. We will consult the reservation book, gentlemen, and you are welcome to all I can tell. It is well thought of, but then one is aware that our police here are known for their brains, *hein?*"

"We'd be obliged, Mr. Robineau. It's just an outside chance, but possible."

"So we look." Robineau turned briskly from his stance in the open arch leading to the dining room. "It is—*tiens!* Pardon—" as he staggered against Mendoza. "Manuel, you *petit drôle!* You are early. Only one party is here as yet. See, messieurs, an entrepreneur of the free enterprise! Manuel Chavez."

The boy grinned up at him. "I'm sorry I trip you, *señor.* Is it O.K. I go in?"

"You will not sell more than one newspaper, but go," said Robineau, smiling. The boy was eleven or twelve, a slight frail-looking boy, narrow-shouldered, liquid-eyed, his made-over trousers and white shirt clean, a bundle of late *Heralds* under one arm. His sharp-featured face was alert and intelligent. Robineau patted his shoulder. "Here is one with ambition, gentlemen. That's right, Manuel, you work hard—however small the beginning—and perhaps you end as lucky and rich as Papa Robineau!" The boy went into the dining room. "Always I have respect for ambition. The reason I let the boy come in with his papers. Now, gentlemen, we see."

Margot Guillaume was at her table. Beside the cash-box on it was a small ledger. Robineau picked it up, leafing back through its pages. "Last Monday night, yes. There are several names here I know. There are the Gallards—Monsieur and Madame Gallard. Parisians, long citizens here but they like to come to my place for the cuisine. The reservation was for seven-thirty. Mr. and Mrs. Easterfield, they come off and on. Mr. and Mrs. Wright. He is something to do with films, I think with Disney. Mr. Plunkett. Him—" Robineau grimaced. "An old lecher, always he comes with a pretty girl, he will have money I think, by his clothes and how he tips the girls. The other names I don't know, and the other reservations were for later, it is not likely the people were here when Miss Stanyard—you think this may help you?"

"We don't know," said Mendoza. "But thanks very much, Mr. Robineau. Never know where something will turn up."

Hackett had been inspecting the terrain: that side exit down from *Ladies,* the terrace doors from the dining room. "I'll just say, Luis," he said as Mendoza finished copying the names into his notebook, "Trulock sounds on the level to me. And she could have, couldn't she? Ditched him. If she wanted to."

"¿A son de qué?" said Mendoza. "If we take Trulock's word for gospel, Art, she wouldn't have wanted to."

Jason Grace had just signed the report in triplicate and stood up and stretched and said to Glasser, "Well, that's that—three minutes to six, another day, another dollar—" when Sergeant Lake looked in and said tersely, "Doctor over at the General, asking for Palliser or Grace."

"Oh?" said Grace, and picked up the phone. "Detective Grace here. . . . Dr. Goodhart, yes. We'd appreciate copies of the autopsy reports, if you—"

"You'll get them," said Goodhart in a peculiar tone. "Oh, yes. It was arsenic. They were loaded with arsenic, all five of them. The Yocum children."

Grace held the phone away and stared at it. He said, "What?"

EIGHT

"Oh, I don't believe it," said Palliser. He'd come in as Grace was relaying that to Lake. "I don't—*arsenic*? It was—"

"Common rat-poison," said Grace. "As sold in rural areas. This is one for the books, John. Five kids—I will be damned. There's really only one answer, isn't there?"

"Accident," began Palliser weakly.

"Accident be damned," said Grace. He looked grim. "And overtime or no, I think I'm going out to find Mr. Yocum right now. Jimmy, will you call my wife or have the night man do it?"

"I think maybe I'm with you," said Palliser. "My God—five children! But, Jase—Jimmy, call Roberta—"

"But me no buts," said Grace. "I want to ask some questions of Brother Yocum—and his wife."

"If they're home," said Palliser, "and not out gallivanting."

The Yocums were not only at home, in the shabby old house on Twentieth Street, but they had company. When Grace pushed the bell and the door opened cautiously, they saw that there was now furniture in the living room. Not much—a couch, two chairs, a portable TV, a couple of straight chairs, a coffee table. Sitting in one of the upholstered chairs with some papers spread on his knees and a briefcase beside him was a very respectable-looking young Negro in a neat gray suit, white shirt and dark tie. He looked up as Grace and Palliser stepped in.

"Uh—what you want?" asked Yocum nervously. His wife was sitting on the couch sipping beer from a can.

"The answers to a few questions," said Grace. "In."

"I—we tell you ennathing we can, sir—" Yocum backed nervously into the room away from him—"but I thought as you asked all you needed to. About our poor li'l kids. I still can't hardly believe it—Mae, you remember the nice police gennelmen—"

"And who might you be?" asked Grace of the neat young man.

That one looked a little bewildered, standing up politely, clutching his papers. "David Dickens, sir. You're police officers? I'm with Acme Mutual, sir—insurance all types. Mr. Yocum has policies on all the children—what a terrible tragedy—when he called me to—"

"Oh, you don't say so!" said Grace, sounding savage. "Well, that about ties it up, doesn't it, Brother Yocum? Policies on all five kids, even the baby!"

"I—I dunno what you mean, sir—it was Mae's notion. Travelin' around like we do, might be an accident or—"

"Accident!" said Grace. "Or the sizable dose of rat-poison dumped into the cornmeal mush? And you both casually walked away and left them to die—you are really a prize specimen, Brother Yocum! Did your wife know about it, or did you happen to have a policy on her too? What about it, Dickens?"

Dickens' pleasant smile faded and he began to look horrified. "What? Poison—why, no, there's no policy on Mrs. Yocum—what did you—"

"So maybe you knew about it too, Mrs. Yocum?" Palliser hadn't immediately leaped to the same conclusion as Grace had, but any doubt in his mind had been dispelled by the expression in Yocum's eyes as he recognized them there on the step. He'd thought he was finished with the cop part of it. Now Palliser turned to look at the woman.

She was sitting as if frozen there, beer can half raised, staring at them, her eyes frightened. Palliser felt incredulous, disgusted; he wasn't sure what he felt. It just wasn't possible, this kind of thing —except sometimes when it happened.

"Do you mean he— Poison?" said Dickens. He was only twenty-two or three, but suddenly he lost about ten years and looked like a scared kid. "He *killed*—his own— Oh, my God. My God. For the —and I sold him the policies—oh, my God, let me get out of here—"

"Sorry, sir." Palliser caught his arm.

"Nobody's going anywhere but down to headquarters," said Grace. "We want to hear chapter and verse on those policies. And both of you are coming too, Brother and Sister Yocum—get your coats."

"I ain't done nothin', you can't arrest us—"

"If you want to make a statement, we'll advise you of all your rights at the office. You'll have a lawyer. You like to explain how the rat-poison got in the kids' lunch, Yocum?"

"I—I ain't sayin' nothin'. You got no call—" Yocum tried to back away from him.

"*In the kids'*—" Dickens looked ready to faint. "Oh, my God."

They called up a squad-car to ferry them in. At the office, with Schenke and Galeano sitting in, they got nothing from Yocum but sullen swearing and nothing from the woman but frightened sobs. But when Dickens told them that the insurance policies on the children were less than four months old, that and the Yocums' reactions drew the picture clear. They booked the Yocums into the Alameda facility; start the machinery on the warrants tomorrow.

It was, of course, sheer ignorance on the Yocums' part that made them think they could get away with it. That the coroners' office would pass off the arsenic as food-poisoning. All the same—

"But for sheer gall," said Grace at home, as Virginia got his belated dinner, "that really takes the cake. My God. For once I kind of regretted that cops are all nice polite fellows these days and don't go in for the rubber hoses. Those poor damned kids—his own kids. *Their* own—"

"Horrifying all right," said Virginia. "But—people, Jase. People always coming all sorts. The woman is harder to understand—in a *way*—but then, of course, your Mr. Kipling was quite right. The female of the species—"

"What a thing. I hope we can get 'em to talk. Though if we don't tie it up tight, the damned court decisions throwing out a confession. I tell you," said Grace suddenly, "I guess what upset me, Ginny, is—well, here you are trotting to a specialist and all, trying to start a family, and the Yocums—my God."

"And I'll pass another thought on to you," said Virginia. "When and if we do, Jase, I like to think we'd produce something of a little higher quality than any of the Yocum children might have been."

Grace laughed unwillingly. "The Jukes and the Kallikaks. And how right you are."

Palliser went home and told his Robin all about that. "Some pretty raw things I've seen since I've been at Homicide, but that—my God. And I wonder too, by God, if they'll weasel out of it in court, get the charge reduced to negligence or something."

Roberta said all the expectable things, setting out his dinner kept warm in the oven. And presently said, "Mr. Griffin called this afternoon. The house'll be through escrow in about a month, and you know something, John? Those monthly payments are starting to look awfully big to me right now. I had on rose-colored glasses maybe. I just thought—" They had signed all the papers on the forty-thousand-dollar house on Hillside Avenue in Hollywood last week.

"We can make it. I'm due for a raise in six months."

"No, but, John, I thought if I went back as a substitute the rest of the school year, and then on full time in September—"

"I don't approve of wives working," said Palliser.

"Well, it's not as if I'd be neglecting a family. Be reasonable. Until we do start a family—and it'd help out a lot on the payments. I really haven't enough to do all day anyway, and I'd like to—"

"Well, I don't know."

"We'll think about it. Because there's furniture too, and all the appliances we haven't got—"

"Well," said Palliser. He sat back and lit a cigarette. "I wonder if Jase called the Lieutenant? I think I will. A hell of a thing—"

"*¡Parece mentira!*" said Mendoza on the phone. "*¡Vaya historia!* You don't mean—*¡Dios! Five*— Yes, and it's all too possible they will slide out from under—accidental death due to negligence. Though with those insurance policies—yes. What a thing indeed. People, people. . . ."

When he hung up, Alison asked, "What was that?"

"More evidence," said Mendoza, "that the hopeful souls who think mankind is ready for Utopia, has made progress since the days Neanderthal walked, are wrong again. But I interrupted you —or John did. What were you telling me?"

"Well, we just think it's a little queer, Luis. You see—"

Mendoza listened. "Well, after all," he said, "a seventeen-year-old's not a baby, *cara*. The little I've seen of him, he seems a responsible kid. And the other one's not a baby either—what, fourteen, fifteen?"

"But Máiri says it's odd, and she knows her better than I do— they're both gardeners, you know, exchanging slips and so on. Shouldn't we do something?"

"What? It's good policy to stay out of neighbors' business, *amante*. I suppose they know what they're doing."

"Well, but—well, I *suppose* so," said Alison.

In the middle of the living room, Cedric lay sprawled with Sheba between his large shaggy paws; he was washing her head lovingly. Nefertite was cuddled against one furry flank, Bast on the other. "I think," said Mendoza, regarding this tableau of the Mendoza livestock meditatively, "I'll have a small drink to take the flavor of Brother Yocum out of my mind. You want anything?"

"No, thanks. Who's—"

"Tell you when I come back." At the magic word *drink* El Señor woke suddenly on top of the credenza, followed Mendoza out to the kitchen, and loudly demanded his share of rye. Mendoza shook his head at him, pouring it, and swallowed a quarter of his own. He thought, the muck at the bottom got so very murky at times—those Yocums. . . .

"Peter," said Laura.

"Gwendolyn," said Steve. "I like fancy names on girls."

"Or maybe Ludovic," said Laura. "I sort of like that."

"Guinevere," said Steve.

"Now for heaven's sake, you two, whose baby is this?" said Mary. She exchanged a private grin with Higgins.

"*Ours!*" said Steve and Laura together.

"Oh, for—look, you'd better get your coats and books. It's twenty to eight. You'll be late, George. . . . I suppose we had better think about names, at that," she added as the children went out still arguing. "I do rather tend toward David if it's a boy—unless you'd like a junior?"

"I would not," said Higgins. "I guess whatever you like is O.K. with me, Mary. We'll think about it—"

"Oh, don't be so diffident. It's yours too. Give me some ideas."

"O.K., O.K.—I *will* be late," said Higgins.

Saturday morning, with Sergeant Farrell sitting in Lake's chair at the switchboard, brought them a really hot lead on the X who had killed Kitty Durand. It came in as Hackett entered the office, and he read it with mounting interest and took it in to Mendoza.

"Something tangible on Durand all right, Luis, only how do we hunt him? You remember the lab lifted some good latents in the bedroom—not in our records so they passed them on to the Feds. Here's the make. He sounds a little offbeat for it, but the prints definitely put him there."

"Who is he?"

Hackett read from the teletype. "Richard Arquette, thirty-six now, six-one, a hundred and eighty, hair brown, eyes brown, no scars or marks. He did a hitch in the Army, fifty-two to fifty-five, honorable discharge. He hails from Philly originally, and the last time the law had occasion to look at him that's where he was. He's got a pedigree of little stuff—car-hopping as a J.D., and then petty theft—that was after the Army, of course—D. and D., a hit-run he got off on, one count of statutory rape, two paternity suits. His wife divorced him four years back and he's behind on alimony. He's evidently, so say the Feds, attractive to women—and vice versa. He's worked as a laborer, waiter, service-station attendant, roofer's assistant, truck-driver—jobs like that. Then back in 1962 he pulled a real rape—positively identified, and lab evidence on him too— and he ran. There's been a 'want' out on him since. How does he sound for Kitty Durand?"

"I like him, I like him," said Mendoza. "Do we read it that he spotted her on the street, followed her? But it doesn't matter, with his prints in that bedroom. I also like George's little brainwave about the coffee cups. That she'd served the coffee to a couple of previous visitors, who haven't come and told us because they're out of town, or shy, and that X arrived later. And considering, Arturo—"

"Yes?"

"Considering everything, the rape charge included, he may just have enough sense not to be going around carrying the flag of Richard Arquette. Am I second-guessing or having a hunch? He could still be known to Kitty Durand by another name. Known to Durand. I think we'd better ask him if he knows anybody fitting that description."

"Well, naturally," said Hackett. "I—my God, that funeral—there's a requiem High Mass at nine o'clock—I'd better run if I'm going to make it."

Palliser looked in to say he'd written a preliminary report on that stabbing over on Leeward Avenue yesterday, and he and Higgins were going out to look around some more on it—there were formal statements to get and so on. "I'll see the report some time," said Mendoza inattentively. "I think I'll be doing some legwork myself today. Just for fun."

But before he left, another lab report came in. It was on that bottle Landers had picked up as possibly having been Edward Holly's bottle, dropped there as he fell. The lab had found several of Holly's prints on it. *"Muy extraño verdaderamente,"* said Mendoza to himself. People did the damndest things. But that one was dead: cleared away. This was just the finishing bow on the package.

"I dunno what else to tell you," said John Weiss stupidly. "I told you all I know yesterday. We was workin' in the garden, and Gertrude she went in to make some coffee, was about three o'clock, and I hear her yell, I come runnin', and I find her on the floor and see this guy runnin' out. I see she's been cut, I run out, and the Wembergs next door seen him too—we told you—"

"Yes, sir," said Palliser. "You'll have to come down to headquarters and make a formal statement, Mr. Weiss. And Mrs. Wemberg and her sister too." Weiss grunted. Palliser exchanged a glance with Higgins: they were both thinking the same thing. At least on this one the spouse was out of the running: there were witnesses.

Leeward Avenue wasn't a slum, but it was in an old part of town and the houses were old. John Weiss's house was an old five-room frame, and it was painted and trimmed and its surrounding lot inhumanly neat. Weiss was a gardener: but not of flowers. The front yard, divided into plots by rows of boards, was planted (by all the signs on stakes) with potatoes, beans, and tomatoes. The back yard boasted a good stand of corn already, and beyond the corn—these were deep lots—were rows of brussels sprouts and carrots. Weiss had told them he and Gertrude grew all their own vegctables. "Rotatin' crops," he had said yesterday.

He and his wife had been out in the back yard, as he'd said, yesterday afternoon, weeding. On coming in, Gertrude had apparently surprised the daylight burglar. Who had stabbed her and run. She was D.O.A. at the General. And next door, Mrs. Augusta Wemberg had been out on her front porch saying goodbye to her sister who had dropped in for a visit, and they had both heard Mrs. Weiss scream and seen the man run out.

Even the ordinarily intelligent citizens were difficult to pry descriptions out of, and John Weiss, retired laborer for the city, was slow-minded, taciturn, inarticulate, and unimaginative. They tried again to get something more useful from him.

"Could you have a guess at the man's size?"

"Dunno. Maybe about as big as me. I only saw him a second, then he—"

"How was he dressed?"

"Uh—only thing I could say, his coat and pants didn't match. I dunno."

"Did he move like a young man?"

"I dunno. Maybe."

"Well, the car—you saw him get into a car?"

"Yeah. Out in the street. I couldn't say any make. It was a dark color." Mrs. Wemberg had said it was a Buick or Olds or Chrysler, something like one of those: and she said it was light blue and her sister said it was a light green Ford. Both said it was a sedan.

"Now, Mr. Weiss, you told us nothing is missing from the house? We asked you to check and be sure. He didn't, maybe, have time to take anything before Mrs. Weiss came in and surprised him?"

"I reckon so. Nothin' gone, anyways. He didn't find nothing," said Weiss in satisfaction. "But he hadn't no call to go killin' Gertrude."

"Have you any valuables in the house, Mr. Weiss? Anything anyone might have known about?"

Weiss shut his tight mouth harder. "Does it look like it, mister? We ain't rich folk down here. Gertrude an' me, we worked hard all our lives, save up for our old age—no kids help take care o' us. Savings we got, sure. No fancy antiques or silver spoons, a thief'd be after. But killin' Gertrude—there wasn't no call—she couldn't've stopped him, likely, he was bigger than her."

"Well, we'll take you downtown to make a statement," said Higgins. "John, suppose you see if Mrs. Wemberg's available to come along." Unless the daylight burglar had left some prints—and was known to their records or the F.B.I.—it didn't look very hopeful that they'd ever lay hands on him.

And possibly, as Hackett admitted to Mendoza later, it had been the wrong time to tackle Robert Durand. Just after his Kitty was buried, after the solemn requiem High Mass at St. Joseph's, and the long slow procession out to the Holy Cross Cemetery in Culver City. But this was such a hot lead they had, Hackett was anxious to get Durand's reaction to the description of Richard Arquette.

He caught Durand as he and Kitty's parents left the cemetery. He apologized, explained. "You see, this man is definitely placed in your apartment—in the bedroom, Mr. Durand. He's a very hot suspect for your wife's murder. And it's not very likely he's using his own name, so you may know him as someone else. I'd just like you to listen to his description, and—"

Durand listened, but not as if he was concentrating on it. "I'm sorry," he said wearily. "I don't know anyone who looks like that—I don't know him. I want to help the police, but right now—right now I don't think I—"

And Mrs. O'Connell said, "Think you'd have better sense than to bother us now! Of course we want to help you, but when we've just—my poor Kitty—" She took Durand's arm, her husband at his other side; they went off toward the waiting limousine.

Bad timing maybe, thought Hackett. Tackle Durand again tomorrow. Meanwhile, just how to go about looking for Arquette? Well, the usual routine. . . .

Mendoza covered a good deal of ground that day, and up to six o'clock he didn't get much for all the legwork.

He managed to locate, and talk to, Wanda Hauck, Sue Ransome, and Sandra Rooney—said to be Michele's closest friends. He heard this and that from them—the nice upper-class girls busy at their upper-class lives, parents with money, the girls playing at the Little Theatre bit (Wanda), the Junior League charities (Sue and Sandra). They all remembered Eileen Rodney from school—"She was *awful!*" said Wanda. "You never knew what she'd do next." They'd been interested, but not very much, that Michele had run across Eileen again recently. What Michele had told them about Eileen, the apartment in Boyle Heights, hadn't surprised them; they'd thought Michele was a little idiot to take up with Eileen even casually. After they'd all said so to her, Wanda adding a warning about drugs—"And Eileen just the kind to think it was funny to spike a drink with LSD or something—" Michele hadn't mentioned Eileen again.

"It was funny," said Sandra thoughtfully, "now I think about it." She was the sober type, feet on the ground. "We took it for granted she'd stopped going to see Eileen, but she never said so. To me, anyway. And at school—well, that was years back, but she seemed sort of fascinated by that awful girl—like a bird with a snake. Because she—Eileen—was different. I never understood it, but—well, Michele was always a follower, if you know what I mean. Given to crushes on people."

Which was interesting, in a way. Mendoza went back to Chicago Street in Boyle Heights, but the apartment was apparently empty: no answer to his knocks. Eileen off doing her thing somewhere else. As he turned for the stairs, a man reached the top landing and came in his direction: a young man in a blue shirt and jeans, leather jacket. He had a key in his hand. As he spotted Mendoza, he stopped short.

"And who the hell are you? I just bet, that Latin lover fuzz Eileen was tellin' me about. She's not home. I don't know when she will be."

"Tommy," said Mendoza. "I would take a bet. Have you got another name?"

"Smith," said Tommy reluctantly. "If it's anything to you." Mendoza had not moved from the door. "Look, I wanta get in. It's cold out here." It had begun to rain again.

Mendoza took Michele's photograph from his breast pocket. "Have you ever seen this girl here—at Eileen's?"

Tommy looked. "A couple times, that's all. I don't know her name —I mean, I don't remember it. Sorry." He was being sarcastic.

"Did you see her here or anywhere last Monday night?"

"No," said Tommy hurriedly. "No."

"You're sure?"

"I'm sure, I'm sure. She was just some creep come hangin' around Eileen. We didn't *know* her—she wasn't one of the crowd. Now, come on, let me go inside, will ya?"

Mendoza stepped aside and he bolted in hastily. Wondering about several things, Mendoza went down and out into the gentle rain again, putting on his hat. He had left the Ferrari in the headquarters lot, taken a cab down here. As he set out for the drugstore on the corner to call another one, his gaze passed over a man sheltering under the canopy of the newsstand next to the apartment, reading his paper, and just then glancing out at the bus-stop as if checking on his bus. He looked back to his newspaper, and Mendoza slid into the little stand beside him and said, "Boo!"

"For God's sake, scare me out of—" They went out into the rain, to the canopy over the drugstore, out of earshot of the newsstand clerk. "This one of your things, Luis?"

"I don't know, Steve. Pat put you on the apartment?"

"On this Tommy Smith. Another tail on the girl," said Steve Benedettino.

"Well, let's hope something turns up for you at least," said Mendoza. "A Narco charge is better than nothing."

He came back to the office at four o'clock to find Hackett and Higgins kicking the Durand thing around. Higgins had got out all the photographs the lab had taken—long shot of living room showing the coffee table, bedroom door—close-ups, shots of the bedroom; and as Mendoza came in and sat down he said suddenly, "There's one thing we hadn't spotted before, Art. Look here. The living room's neat as all get-out. No signs of any struggle. That's all in the bedroom—things knocked over where she fought him."

"That's so," said Hackett, taking the photograph. "But what does it say? For God's sake—that it *was* somebody she knew, she let him in and turned her back and started for the bedroom, and that's where he jumped her? I hope to God I can get Durand to think seriously about Arquette's description."

Grace and Palliser were down at the jail still prodding at the Yocums. Always the new calls coming in—most of them entailing only the paperwork—and Piggott and Glasser were out too.

Those regular patrons of Le Renard Bleu—Robineau had given him the Gallards' address, but Farrell hadn't reached them yet. Mr. Wright, Disney Productions said, was on vacation. Plunkett—Farrell was going through the phone book.

Mendoza read the current reports, did some brooding over Michele and Kitty Durand, and was still sitting there of inertia at a quarter to six when Farrell put through an outside call to him.

It was Robineau. "*Mon ami,* I have got some information for you. You will laugh at me—but I am concerned, such a thing even beginning to happen in my house. And just now, Monsieur and Madame Gallard arrive, and the madame tells me this which I think the police should know—"

"They're there now? *Bueno,* I'll be with you in ten minutes." Mendoza reached for his hat.

The Gallards were very cosmopolitan, well-bred people in their sixties. Madame with frankly dyed black hair, still smooth skin, artful makeup, and the good bones of former beauty: he a big hearty man, a little too gallant of manner, now grave as befit the situation. They were sitting over *apéritifs* at one of the tables near the fire: Robineau introduced Mendoza, sat down with them.

"I don't suppose it is of great value, what I have to tell you," said Madame Gallard in nearly perfect English. "But Mr. Robineau seemed to think—" She shrugged, a very Parisian shrug even forty years from the Right Bank.

"What is it, madame?"

"You will take a glass of wine—" The amenities must be observed before business. To avoid argument he took it, a drink he detested.

"This poor young one murdered—" Mendoza handed her the photograph, and she nodded at it. "This is she. Poor girl. It was last Monday night? Yes. We were here. We arrived at—" she considered—"seven-thirty, perhaps. We had been visiting friends at Malibu, and it was a tiresome drive back, the traffic—the rain. I said to Jacques, I will go to tidy my hair, powder my nose, before dinner. Which I do, in the *Ladies* out there. I am there perhaps, oh, three, four minutes. And as I come out, I see this girl"—she tapped the photograph —"coming up the hall. She passes me, she goes into *Ladies*. That is all."

"Oh," said Mendoza. "This would be about, say, twenty-five to eight, a little later?" The times fit: Michele and Trulock had had an early dinner, on account of the theatre.

"About that, I would say." She sipped wine.

"Was—"

"You wanna buy a *Herald*, sir?" It was the young Mexican boy, coming up to the table. Gallard smiled at him and fished for change in his pocket.

"Our small entrepreneur," said Robineau.

"That is well, boy," said Gallard paternally, taking his paper. "Hard work never hurt anyone."

"Was there anyone else in the ladies' room when you entered or left it?" asked Mendoza as the boy went on to the next table.

"But no. It was empty when I entered it, it was empty when I left. But I saw this Michele enter it immediately afterward. That is all I saw. Mr. Robineau seemed to think you should hear this."

"Yes," said Mendoza. "Thank you very much, madame; you may have given us an important piece of evidence." He got up and wandered out to the foyer, with Robineau after him.

"You think it *is* important, *hein?* I thought so too."

"But what the hell it might say—" Mendoza went down the hall to pause just outside *Gentlemen*, looking down the cross-hall toward *Ladies*. "So we know she went in, at least." He noticed suddenly that just opposite to the side door there was a public phone on the wall. "What does that—? I'm woolgathering, damn it. First rule of detective work—haven't I said it before?—the idiot boy and the lost horse. If I was a horse—" So, Michele with no money, Michele probably not walking out on Trulock (maybe unsold on Eileen, knuckling under to Trulock's much stronger character?), but— "She couldn't have been waylaid here," he said, thinking aloud, "or could she? People all around, she'd have managed to make some noise—

waylaid in *Ladies,* for God's sake?—but of course she was a small, slight girl. . . . But, *imposible también,* even if she'd wanted to ditch Trulock, she couldn't have. She didn't have even a dime for a phone call. I'll tell you what it comes down to—" and he was talking to himself, dimly conscious of the big restaurateur beside him—"what it says to me, whatever happened to her must have started to happen here. Right here. Because she hadn't any money on her—for a phone call, a cab, the bus."

"*My* place," said Robineau. "It seems impossible."

"If she'd had even a dime on her, to have left voluntarily—"

"*¿Señores?*" They turned. It was the newspaper boy, Manuel Chavez. He looked at Mendoza rather timidly. "*Perdón,* but I cannot help but hear—you're talkin' about that blonde young lady got murdered? I seen it in the papers. Right here she was, last Monday night. You said about money—you a policeman?"

"Yes. What about it?" asked Mendoza. "Did you see her here? You were in then?" He should have thought about the boy—evidently coming in at different times with his papers.

The boy hesitated. "Sure, I was in here then. And I seen her. But you're wrong about that, sir—she did have some money. I saw." He looked at Robineau. "Señor Robineau, he don't mind I come in with my papers—"

"When did you see her? You're sure it was—"

"*Sí.* That picture you was just showin' Missus Gallard, it was her. I was—I was just comin' out from the rest room here"—he gestured at *Gentlemen*—"when I saw her. I guess it was about ten minutes to eight. And—*honestamente, señor,* she had some money. Some bills and some change, she dropped a dime and a quarter and I picked 'em up for her and she thanked me. *Honestamente,* I saw."

And that, of course, opened up some wider possibilities.

NINE

Hackett went home and told Angel about the Yocums; today was the first the day-shift men had heard about it, of course. Angel stared at him with a handful of silverware poised; she was setting the table in the dinette. "Their own—well, honestly, you can hardly believe there *are* people like that, can you, Art?"

"Jase was kind of upset," said Hackett. "You know, his wife's been trying to start a family ever since they were married, I gather. Doesn't seem fair in a way." He reached for an olive from the relish dish and Angel automatically told him how many calories were in it. "Oh, hell," said Hackett.

"The *things* you Homicide cops run into!" said Angel.

Higgins went home and told Mary about the Yocums. Her gray eyes were horrified on him. "But their *own*—well, it's hard to believe. The things you see on this job—"

"Grace was upset about it. They're trying to have a family," said Higgins. "Yes, and not the least of it is, it gets into the papers, with photographs, and everybody says—"

"Yes," said Mary. "They're all like that . . . talk about riffraff."

"Nearer Neanderthal," said Higgins. "Or maybe I'm maligning Neanderthal man. He didn't know anything about insurance policies. What's all the argument in there?" Steve and Laura could be heard busily at odds, but merrily, in the living room.

"They're still naming baby. Steve's latest contribution is Camilla and Laura's is Gareth. It sounds so romantic." Mary's eyes twinkled. "We really had better decide about it, George, and put the collective foot down."

"Well, anything you like," said Higgins.

Piggott went to choir practise—they were rehearsing for the Easter program—and told Prudence Russell about the Yocums. "But, Matt!" she said. "Their own—how perfectly awful. You can hardly believe it. And maybe, so many terrible things happening these days, the reason some people think there isn't any God, it's all—at random."

"Just the devil getting into men's hearts," said Piggott. "You know something, Prudence, the smartest thing the devil ever did was convince a lot of people he doesn't exist."

When Mendoza came into the office on Sunday morning he found Hackett leaning on Lake's desk. "There are some freak ones, of course. All the tomatoes you want and nothing else. Or nothing but cottage cheese and lettuce. But—"

"I am not a rabbit," said Lake. "A man's got to eat, and I tell you, Art, I just don't count lettuce, and cottage cheese, and lamb chops with about four bites on them, as eating. I damn well don't. It isn't that I have a sweet tooth, I couldn't care less about dessert—"

"Oh, neither do I," said Hackett. "It's just, a meal isn't a meal without—"

"Bread and butter, and potatoes, no, it isn't—all the starch, I know, but, damn it, what the hell is lean ground beef if it isn't on a bun with mayonnaise and pickle relish and—"

"Cheese and all the trimmings," said Hackett. "I know. And—"

"Break it up, break it up," said Mendoza. "You can reminisce together some other time. George in? *Bueno.* Anybody here had better hear what I've turned up on Michele. In my office."

Landers and Glasser were in; Piggott had taken a call almost as soon as he'd come in, and was still out. Mendoza told them what he'd heard from Manuel Chavez last night. "So she had the wherewithal to duck Trulock if she wanted. This is all up in the air—have I been misreading Michele? Had she—mmh—depths we haven't plumbed? It seems a little funny, in a way, that she'd be fascinated with Eileen, that crowd. Oh, you can say glibly, attraction of opposites—attraction to something different from anything she'd ever known. And of course, the holdover from school-days—evidently Eileen the adventuress had fascinated Michele then. And maybe Michele hadn't grown up very far in three years. And another thing—a girl like Michele—not to sound like the head-doctor—a very much weaker character than Paul Trulock, maybe exactly the kind to run out on him on impulse, teach him a little lesson, knowing all the while she'll come meekly back and knuckle under to him."

"Yes," said Hackett. "If she did, that was the way it went."

"Just a lovers' spat. With a penitent reconciliation scene in the offing," said Landers. "So, did she run to Eileen?"

"Put down your bets," said Mendoza. "Eileen and her crowd as slippery as eels. Hard to put a finger on. But this I'll say. I'd take a bet at least some of Eileen's crowd is playing around with the dope—pot or speed or H or whatever. And Eileen's modest, if nice, fifteen G's per year isn't going to be enough to support a communal habit. Particularly if there's H floating around. So if innocent bird-with-snake Michele ran in a pet to old-school-friend Eileen on Monday night, very likely nobody there—if the crowd was there, and whoever the crowd consists of—would have had the slightest compunction about—mmh—subduing Michele to get those diamonds off her. If none of the crowd knows a fence, the dope-seller will. And, finding that Michele had been subdued a little too hard, what easier than to stash her in that alley and forget her?"

"I think you just said something, Luis," said Higgins. "That could be just the way it went."

"Well, we wait to see if Callaghan gets anything on any of them. Maybe, if nothing else shows up, find out who the crowd consists of and bring some of them in to lean on," said Mendoza. "If Pat gets any of them on a definite Narco charge, and they know they're in for trouble anyway, maybe one of them would be all the quicker to sing a pretty song."

"That's so," said Hackett. "I want to tackle Durand on that description again today."

"And I want to see Trulock again," said Mendoza.

"I've still got to get out a report on that corpse in the hotel," said Landers. "Routine. Natural death."

"Well, let's get on the horse," said Higgins. "Likely something new coming along any time."

The early call to Homicide had been from a Dr. Egon Gerner. He said he had some information on Samuel Revilo, so Piggott went to see him. His home address was on Arden Boulevard above Wilshire. It was a modest, pleasant apartment; Dr. Gerner was a widower. He was a man about sixty, with a mild manner and a crest of white hair, and he was very distressed at what he had to tell Piggott. He had only just learned about Revilo's suicide yesterday, from another patient.

"You see, I've always felt that a patient should be told the truth.

Oh, with some hysterical females it'd be madness, of course—but Mr. Revilo seemed to be a rational man, self-contolled and sensible. I felt too—a man in business—he'd appreciate knowing the facts, to put his affairs in order. But he must have—I feel very bad about this," and he shook his head sorrowfully. "But that must have been it, of course. . . . What? Oh, terminal cancer. Of the bowels and pancreas. He hadn't six months to go, at a rough guess." They hadn't seen the autopsy report yet; that would confirm it.

"I see," said Piggott. "And you told him that?"

"I did. With poor judgment, I see now. But he seemed—"

"Well, we'd like a formal statement on that, Doctor, and you'll be testifying at the inquest. It's scheduled for Tuesday at ten."

"I'll be glad to do anything necessary," said Gerner mournfully.

It was at headquarters, when he was making the statement, that Piggott asked him if he'd prescribed sleeping tablets for Revilo. No, he hadn't. "I wanted to think over the medication, and he wasn't having much pain yet that aspirin wouldn't alleviate. Later, of course —and now I recall, he told me his wife had died of cancer of the stomach, so he'd know too well what was in store—poor devil."

"How did he happen to come to you, Doctor? Just at random?"

Dr. Egon Gerner looked at him over his bifocals and said mildly, "Why, no—another patient of mine recommended me, he said. Mrs. Duggan. In fact both she and her daughter, Mrs. Wooley, are patients of mine."

By that time, summoning a squad-car to take Dr. Gerner home, Piggott looked at his watch and found he'd have to hurry to get to church. But after church he thought he'd pay a visit to Mrs. Wooley and her mother.

Palliser and Grace had again brought the Yocums up from the Alameda jail for a session in depth, trying to get the bare admission from one or both of them. There was a policewoman there, and a silent lawyer from the public defenders' office sitting in—interested for once. As before, Yocum twisted and turned, now sly, now playing dumb, and his wife sat with head bent refusing to say anything.

They had just found out that Yocum had bought a five-year-old Cadillac from a lot in Long Beach, paying cash for it.

"You bought the rat-poison," said Palliser, patient and grim. "You admit that."

"A lot o' varmints up where we was last—yeah, yeah. It's not—"

"All right. Did your wife know you'd brought it into the house, here, from the car where it was with the rest of your luggage?"

"I dunno."

"When you took out the insurance policies on the children," said Grace, "did you plan to collect on them then, Yocum? You didn't wait long, did you—four months!"

"I never heard nothin' about that *in*-surance before, it was a lady Mae got talkin' to, last job we was on up north. Mae just said, maybe—" he smiled ingratiatingly at Grace.

They had been at this all morning, around and around, and it was getting on for noon now. All that time, the woman hadn't said a word, even to the policewoman. Now, she raised her head and looked at her husband. "You gonna put it on me?" she asked huskily.

"I don't mean nothin', Mae—"

"You try put it on me, you bastard—sure, so I hear how they's that *in*-surance thing, you get money, people dyin'—Mis' Peters she got two thousand dollars, her man drops dead, two th—but who says, about the kids. The damn kids alla time yellin', gettin' in the way, I couldn't work nearly all last season accounta the damn baby —who had the idea, you bastard? You did, that's who! You the one said, come down here where ain't nobody knows us—you the one finds out how to do about the *in*-surance—you try say it was me—"

"Goddamn you, woman, you didn't put up no fight on it, did you?" Yocum half-rose, ugly and snarling at her. "You jump at the notion, all right! Get rid o' the Goddamn kids an' get that money besides—easy it'd be—an' I dunno how the damn fuzz drop on it—.

There was some more of that, and they ended up signing statements—prodded by the lawyer—and at one-thirty Palliser and Grace took them back to jail and started out after a belated lunch.

Grace was still grim. "One for the books," said Palliser. "Where d'you want to go, Jase? Coffee shop O.K.?"

"Any place with a liquor license," said Grace. "A drink I could stand."

Piggott and Landers went to see Mrs. Wooley and her mother after lunch. Piggott had had a sudden brainwave, and at the last minute asked Dr. Gerner whether he'd prescribed that brand of sleeping tablets for either of the women. "We still don't know how he got hold of them, you see." And Dr. Gerner had said, Why, yes, Mrs. Duggan took them regularly.

Possibly Revilo, calling on Mrs. Wooley, had managed to steal some. It was just more of the boring routine, tying it up for the coroner.

Both women were there in the old house, and Mrs. Wooley said, Whatever we can do to help, just a terrible thing, poor Mr. Revilo's son all broken up. Yes, Mr. Revilo used to drop by, evenings, and they'd play three-handed rummy or just talk. Such a gentleman he'd been, and—sleeping tablets? Why, yes, Mother took some the doctor had—

"We don't know where he got those he took," said Piggott, "and they were the same brand you take, Mrs. Duggan. Is it possible he could have stolen some of yours when he was here one night?"

"Oh, I shouldn't think so," said Mrs. Wooley vaguely. "Mother would have missed—he'd have to take a lot, wouldn't he?"

"*Have* you missed any tablets, ma'am?" asked Landers of the older woman.

She regarded him perkily from where she sat primly on the couch, a thin, upright, white-haired old lady with bony hands and still-sharp blue eyes. "I haven't *missed* any, young man, because I knew where they were. Knew why. Since you know so much, down to brands and all, and I guess this is the only place he could have got hold of any such, I'll tell you. The poor man come by just after the doctor told him about his trouble." In Mrs. Duggan's youth, the dread word was not bandied about. "You weren't here, Leda. He said he wanted a drink of water, went to fetch it. *I* knew what he was up to. Didn't let on. He knew about my tablets. It was his trouble and his choice. Not to make any trouble for people, takin' care of him. I never said a word, but when he'd gone, I looked, and he'd took all the rest of the tablets in the bottle. So"—she sniffed—"I just hollered out the window at that Harrison girl—the oldest one—and give her the money and ask her to run up to the drugstore and get the bottle filled up again. Nobody the wiser, and"—she looked at them defiantly—"it's not on my conscience, neither. His own choice, the poor man, and a peaceful end, and God rest him."

"*Mother!*" gasped Leda Wooley.

And Landers said, "I'd have to look up the statute. I don't know there is one covering that. I'll be damned."

"What statute *would* it be, Tom?" asked Piggott as they got into Landers' car.

"Be damned if I know, Matt. And anyway, a poor white-haired eighty-year-old, what jury'd convict her? I will be damned. People," said Landers, and started the engine.

The pleasant-faced gray-haired matron at the house on Wallace Avenue in Beverly Hills had told Mendoza that Paul had gone to see the Stanyards, and that was where Mendoza found him. Michele's funeral was scheduled for tomorrow, up in Forest Lawn. When the houseman showed Mendoza in to the large formal living room, and he apologized for disturbing them again, Stanyard looked up and said heavily, "No trouble, Lieutenant. I had meant to call you—you asked about the appraisal of Michele's necklace. I looked it up. It was valued at approximately five thousand dollars."

"And a four-and-a-half-carat diamond at around the same figure," said Mendoza. "Yes. Mr. Trulock—"

"Won't you sit down?" said Louise Stanyard with an effort. She was gray-faced, empty-eyed, but mechanically courteous. Mendoza thanked her. Even in their absorption with grief, the Stanyards and Trulock were obviously feeling some surprise at Lieutenant Mendoza of Homicide, his elegantly-tailored gray Italian silk, gold cufflinks, and Sulka tie.

"Mr. Trulock, at any time that night did you happen to see inside Michele's evening bag?"

Trulock looked astonished. "Why, no—of course not. She was sitting across from—well, let's see, she opened it to get out a cigarette —she didn't smoke very much, one after dinner, like that—but of course I—"

"Mrs. Stanyard. You told us you were sure Michele hadn't any money with her that night. How were you so certain?"

"Well, I—she joked about it. I—I'd come into her room just as she was getting out her evening jacket, and putting a lipstick, her compact, into her bag. She said something like—like,"—Mrs. Stanyard swallowed—"oh, I haven't even a dime of mad money with me, hope I don't need it. You know, an expression that—"

"Yes," said Mendoza. "And after that? Try to think back, please."

"Well, I—we started downstairs—Paul had come about ten minutes before—and then Michele said she hadn't a handkerchief and she went back to get one—but she wasn't more than half a minute, hardly that—"

"But in that time, back in her room, she could have put some money in her bag?"

"Well, I suppose, but it never crossed my mind—she didn't say— and with Paul she wouldn't—"

"But evidently she did," said Mendoza. "That we know now."

"For certain?" asked Trulock abruptly. "I'll be damned. So she could have—the little idiot—mad at me, but she'd have been over it in half an hour, for God's sake—my God, did she run to that—that beatnik bitch?"

"*Paul!*"

"Oh, sorry, Mrs. Stanyard, but you don't know—did she?" he asked Mendoza.

"We don't know. Do you think she might have?"

Trulock looked miserable and mutinous. "God, I don't know either. It sounds crazy—Michele and one like that—and I see now, maybe if I hadn't said anything at all about Eileen, the—glamor'd have worn off. Glamor, by God. But the minute I did say anything—just to be contrary, she had to defend her." He shrugged. "I guess she might have. I don't know."

"Who—who do you mean?" asked Louise Stanyard tremulously. "Who's Eileen?"

Trulock said to Stanyard, "I *told* you! I tried to tell you about that Rodney girl. Didn't you understand what I said about her? Didn't—"

"Well, I thought you must be exaggerating—a girl at school with Michele—"

But these days, thought Mendoza, or maybe any time, any type at all getting pulled down into the muck at the bottom. And some of them deliberately wallowing in it.

"Wait a minute," said Trulock suddenly. "Wait a minute. One thing I remember her saying"—his face twisted. "Monday night. Just—just before we left the table. I'd been saying this and that, and Michele said—said, she'd just like to hear what Eileen'd say about such horrible accusations, I was just jealous and didn't want her to have any friends at all— My God, does that say she did maybe run to that bitch? You say now she had some money—"

"It's possible," said Mendoza. "Oh, yes."

When Hackett got to the Durand apartment he found it in a state of confusion. Mrs. O'Connell was busily and helpfully sorting out her dead daughter's clothes and personal effects, a labor of love and saving Durand the agony. Durand was sitting drinking coffee at the kitchen table, and he welcomed Hackett lackadaisically.

"I know you weren't feeling like concentrating on this yesterday, Mr. Durand," said Hackett, sitting down opposite him. "But this man is a very hot suspect, his fingerprints picked up in the bedroom here. We have a description of him, and I'd just like you to think it over and tell me if he sounds like anyone you know."

"You keep harping on that—somebody we knew," said Durand. "I never did think that was possible. Just somebody following her in the street, it could have been. And ringing the doorbell."

"Well, if you'll just—" Hackett read him the description of Richard Arquette. This time Durand listened.

"No," he said, shaking his head. "I can't think of anybody—but it's a sort of general description, isn't it? A lot of men might be six-one, weigh a hundred and eighty, brown hair, brown eyes. It says no scars or anything. It might be anybody."

"But it doesn't ring any bells?"

"No. I'm sorry. I still think it was just—one of the wild ones roaming the streets these days."

Mrs. O'Connell bustled in. "I'm sorry I was rude to you yesterday, Sergeant. I know you're trying your best. Bob, you should have offered the sergeant some coffee." Deaf to Hackett's polite Don't bother, she got down a cup, poured coffee for him. Coffee, of course, was another thing, thought Hackett gloomily; he simply didn't care about coffee without cream and sugar. "Bob, I sorted out a bag of things for the Goodwill—clothes not good enough to keep. But I know you won't mind—Kitty and Bridget wear the same size—that's my second daughter," she added for Hackett's benefit, "and it's not sensible to waste good clothes. I'll take the better things home for Bridget. Is that all right?"

"Yes, sure," said Durand dully. "Only—sensible."

"That's right." She bustled out.

Hackett couldn't think of anything else to ask him. And, of course, the official description of Arquette might fit a lot of men. The same statistics—but the individuals poles apart. Unfortunately, Arquette had never been mugged anywhere. Hackett drank black coffee absently. He said, "Those coffee cups—" Because it seemed funny, if she had just served coffee to some acquaintances that morning, they hadn't come forth to say so.

Mrs. O'Connell came in again. "Bob, do you want any of her jewelry? You're welcome to it—not much, of course, but her birthstone ring and the cultured pearls we gave her for her eighteenth birthday and her high-school ring—"

"I—I'd like her engagement ring," said Durand. "Please."

"Surely." She patted his shoulder and went out.

"I always said," said Durand, "it wasn't—what you thought. Just somebody—seeing her, wanting her—she was such a beautiful girl

—and these days, all the criminals getting let out, roaming the streets—"

"All right, it could have gone like that," said Hackett, "but these prints definitely place Arquette here, and he's got the right record for it. A hundred to one and no takers, it was Arquette who killed your wife, Durand."

"And you can't find him?" said Durand.

"If you'd—" Hackett bit back the retort. Excluding the coffee cups, it wasn't likely the Durands had known Richard Arquette. And it was just a general description.

Mrs. O'Connell came in looking rather pink, with a big manila envelope in one hand. She laid it on the table in front of Durand. "I suppose you'll want these," she said rather abruptly, and went away.

Durand opened the clasp of the envelope with listless fingers, and a sheaf of glossy black-and-white photographs slid out on the table. Hackett caught a glimpse of just the top one, an 8 by 10: a very sharp photograph—the art study, in the jargon—provocative nude, a magnificent female figure, the thrusting upright breasts, the artful lights and shadows—

"Oh," said Durand. "Oh." He shuffled the photographs—more 8 by 10's, smaller ones, down to wallet-size, back into the envelope. His dark eyes held inexpressible pain. "She used to—pose for me. For practise . . . never took any of those to class, of course. I—I suppose I shouldn't even—carried some of them—in my wallet. But—" He bent his head over the envelope. Hackett thought, the young people so happily in love, Kitty the beautiful. Laughing over the sexy photographs—taken for practise. Out there in the cold ground in Holy Cross Cemetery, because Richard Arquette had seen her, wanted her?

He got up. "Well, thanks anyway, Mr. Durand. You know we'll be hunting him."

Durand didn't look up as he left.

Landers had wanted to see Mendoza, ask him about that queer one on Mrs. Duggan—was there a statute that covered it?—but Mendoza was out somewhere. Eventually, thought Landers, and began to type the report on that. He heard about Palliser and Grace breaking the Yocum thing—and what a thing that was—and congratulated them in passing.

He'd finished the report and was talking over the Yocums with

Piggott, who was being rather eloquent about the devil, when Sergeant Lake looked in and asked if anybody knew where the boss was, Lieutenant Callaghan wanted him.

"No idea, Jimmy," said Landers.

"Hell," said Lake, and went out. Fifty seconds later he was back. "Shooting at a bar out on Figueroa," he reported. "Go and look at it."

"The devil very busy these days, Tom," said Piggott.

"I believe you," said Landers. "Take my car?"

At the bar on Figueroa, they found two squad-cars, a lot of excited civilians, and the ambulance just arriving importantly, the interns hopping out.

"We've got him for you," said the uniformed man holding back the crowd out here. "Inside."

Landers and Piggott went into the bar. It was the ordinary darkish place with booths on one side, high stools at the bar itself. The squad-car men had herded the half-dozen Sunday-afternoon customers to one side; one of them said to the Homicide men, "Plenty of witnesses for you anyway."

There was a dead man stretched out on the floor: a young man, probably goodlooking when he was alive, blond, in tailored sports clothes, gray trousers and matching shirt, a braided leather bolo tie. He'd been shot several times in the body, by the blood. The civilians were gabbling excitedly. There was a young brunette sitting in a booth sobbing loudly and exclaiming tearfully between sobs, "But he had to *work* on Tuesdays—he had to—"

There was a chunky, dark man about thirty-five gripped securely between two of the uniformed men, looking sullen and belligerent. The fourth uniformed man stepped forward and said to Landers, "We've got his gun, sir. I tried to be careful about prints, but of course a lot of witnesses saw it. It's a Colt .38, sir. He just came in and started shooting, by what we've heard."

"You're damn right," said the bartender: Landers identified him by his apron. "Never said a word. Just up with the gun and shot Wayne there. Wayne Billings. Jesus Christ, I never saw such a thing —he just—"

"His name's Bernard Schwartz," said the uniformed man. "We got that from the I.D. in his billfold, sir."

"So, Mr. Schwartz," said Landers, confronting him. "Why the shooting, Mr. Schwartz?"

Schwartz said, "That's my wife. My wife Myra. Sittin' there." He

116

jerked his head at the sobbing brunette. Schwartz had a pugnacious bulldog face and protuberant brown eyes.

"So, she is?" said Landers. "Why the—"

"We got an *agreement*," said Schwartz aggrievedly. "An agreement we got—Myra and me. See?"

The brunette sobbed, "But he had to *work* Tuesdays! You didn't have no call to—"

"An *agreement*," said Schwartz stubbornly. "She can go see her boyfriend Tuesdays an' Thursdays, you unnerstand? Only Tuesdays an' Thursdays. An' this is *Sunday*."

"You can't deny that," said one of the uniformed men *sotto voce*. Another one laughed involuntarily.

Almost, Landers laughed. He looked at Schwartz incredulously. "You mean you—just because—"

"This is *Sunday*," said Schwartz doggedly. "She's got no business meetin' her boy friend on Sunday. Only Tuesdays an' Thursdays. That's the agreement. But I suspected, an' I followed her an' she's meetin' him. On Sunday."

Somebody said, "For God's sake—"

Landers nearly said it himself. "All right, you'll have to come with us, Mr. Schwartz," was what he did say. He caught Piggott's eye. The devil going up and down. . . .

They took him in, and the brunette, and got statements from them. Get the warrant on him tomorrow. They were just about to book him in when Higgins and Palliser came in to hear about it.

"My God," said Higgins. "How the other half lives."

"I'll take him in," said Piggott resignedly, and marched him out. They'd sent Myra home in a squad-car.

Higgins lit a cigarette. "That Gertrude Weiss—the daylight burglar —it is dead, we'll never nail that one. No leads at all. But we have to go through the motions. We haven't got a statement from that Mrs. Wemberg yet."

"I know, I know," said Palliser. "And we'd better shove the Darley thing in Pending too—another dead one. Where's the boss?"

"Who knows?" said Landers. "Narco wants him on something. I wonder if they've pinned something on that Rodney girl—the Michele Stanyard thing. That's a funny one all right. The beautiful young socialite."

Sergeant Lake thrust his sandy head in the door of the sergeants' office. "Good, at least a handful of you Sherlocks here to pick from."

"What's up, Jimmy?" Always something new, thought Landers resignedly.

"Don't know," said Lake. "A call in from Traffic. They had a routine call—a 415 down on Cortez Street—" that was the code for a disturbance—"about half an hour ago. It was a real brawl, by what they said, and they've brought in four guys on the disturbance charge, only one of 'em is yelling for Homicide cops. Loud and clear. Traffic wants to know the score."

"Cortez Street," said Landers. "Don't tell me—"

They all went out on it.

TEN

They got down to the jail on Alameda just in time to run into Piggott at the main desk; he'd just seen Schwartz booked in. "What's up?"

Landers explained, and the desk-sergeant said, "Oh, you from Homicide? Sergeant Wentworth wants you in the interrogation room down the hall." He added directions.

In the interrogation room they found four civilians somewhat the worse for wear as to bruises, four men in uniform, and Sergeant Wentworth who was staff personnel at this facility. Before anyone could say anything one of the civilians sprang up and, eluding the men reaching for him, ran up to Palliser.

"You—it was you I talked to you before, after he murdered Ma! I got to tell you—it was him did it! It was him—that was why—"

"Take it easy. You know these men?" asked Wentworth.

They did, three of them. The man clutching at Palliser was Charley Darley, and sitting glowering under the watchful gaze of the other squad-car men were Fred Dawson and his gangling teen-age son Ron. "Listen," said Darley excitedly, "that's my brother Bill, you didn't meet him before, listen, as soon as Rose showed me that letter I knew it was *him* killed Ma—and I and Bill went down there—" The fourth man bore a strong family resemblance to Charley; he was scowling under beetle brows at the Dawsons.

"What letter, Mr. Darley? O.K., Sergeant, this seems to be Homicide business, you're welcome to sit in, but—all right, Mr. Darley, we'll listen to you, but take it easy and tell us one thing at a time."

"Well, look, Rose, she's been sortin' out the place, see, Ma's place, the funeral yest'day, and she's goin' through things an' this letter it fell outta one o' them old magazines, an' as soon as Rose showed it to me I knew it was *him*, and I and Bill—well, I didn't exactly mean to start no fight, but I was mad, naturally, and when they—"

"What letter? Where's the letter?" asked Landers.

"These damn cops come up, haul us down here—I guess Rose's still got it—"

"There were some females on the sidelines," said one of the squad-car men. "I don't know whether Feeney and Gomez brought 'em in."

"So let's find out," said Palliser resignedly. The Dawsons just glared sullenly.

The women hadn't been brought in, just cautioned; so they sent a car back to Cortez Street for Rose Darley, and Bill's wife who'd been helping her in the house, and Mrs. Dawson. With instructions to bring the letter.

The letter, when Rose handed it to Palliser—"The minute I read it I guessed it was him, that no-good bum—and I showed it to Charley and he—"

"Yes, yes," said Palliser. The letter was interesting, all right. It was written in a vile childish scrawl on a dirty piece of dime-store paper: the envelope was there too, and it had been through the mail. The postmark was clear, the date February tenth. Without salutation, it called Marion Darley a lot of names and warned her to "stay awey from our plase you ole bat we dont want no dirty old bich like yur sort yu are a pein in the nek stay awey or som day I kill yu like you desarve too be." And it was signed "Yur freind R. Dawson."

"Well, I will be damned," said Palliser where they passed it around out in the hall. "Of all the queer ones. Let's talk to Charley and Rose first."

The Darleys, talked to in another room alone, had calmed down somewhat. "You see what I *mean*," said Charley. "It musta—"

"We see what you mean. Where exactly was the letter, Mrs. Darley?"

"It was in one of those dirty old magazines, it just fell out. I'd been carryin' 'em out to put with the trash, see, and—"

"But Mr. Darley," said Landers, "this letter was mailed nearly six weeks ago. Why do you suppose your mother never mentioned it? We asked you if she'd had trouble with anyone—you'd think she'd have said something about this—"

"Oh, gee," said Charley, hesitant and uneasy. "I—well—I s'pose that does look funny, don't it—"

"*Had* she mentioned it to you?"

"No, no. I—well—the fack is, you see, Ma, she didn't—she didn't read too good. In fack, I don't s'pose she made head or tail of it, see. I got to say that. I s'pose it come—she never got but junk-mail—an' she opened it like you see, but I don't s'pose she figured out what it said."

They looked at each other. "I see," said Palliser.

"But the minute *I* spelled it out, I—"

"But, Mr. Darley," said Piggott, "your mother kept all those magazines around—she had a fight with Mr. Felker about it, even. If she couldn't read well enough to make out a letter, why'd she keep all the magazines?"

"Oh, gee," said Charley. He looked at Rose. They both looked ashamed; neither of them the great brains, but the illiterate relative they were reluctant to admit.

"She liked to look at the pictures," said Rose. "That's all. She'd just go looking at the pictures."

So then they talked to the Dawsons. Ron wasn't eighteen yet so necessarily they handled him with care. They got a lawyer from the public defenders' office and a policewoman took notes. They didn't get anything from Fred Dawson but growls about that old bitch coming round and no loss. It wasn't much trouble to get a lot more out of Ron.

"Criminy," he said sullenly, "she was an ole bitch—always comin' in, sit watchin' our TV, an' she liked those crazy westerns an' talk-shows, an' any time you switch channels there's a big argument, her an' Dad an' Ma yellin' at each other, an' before they stop any show you wanna look at's over! I got fed up—real fed up with the ole bitch, an' so was Dad an' Ma. Sure, I wrote her that letter, but she don't pay no mind to it—I just figure I beat up on her a little, scare her some, maybe she get the idea I mean it. I didn't go to kill her, my gosh, I just—"

Just like that. The slightly backward boy? It could be, and in any case probably not much would happen to him. He was only seventeen. Remanded to the juvenile authorities until he was eighteen, and then probation, or some light sentence.

At least now they wouldn't have to throw the Darley case in Pending.

"My God," said Palliser as they emerged from the session. "Just for that. And we were thinking about the impulsive burglar."

"It's a kind of illustration," said Higgins seriously, "of why I can't read detective-novels. In most of 'em, every killer has got a great big fat important motive—blackmail, or a million dollars, or the plans for the newest submarine. It's not plausible, after you've put in a stint at Homicide."

Piggott was silent, probably ruminating on the devil. And it was after six o'clock; they all went home.

A good deal earlier, Mendoza and Hackett had been up in Narcotics, in Pat Callaghan's office.

"I just thought you'd like to hear, and sit in on the questioning," said Callaghan, who was, incredibly, even bigger than Hackett, with a shock of fire-red hair. "In fact I'm letting 'em stew, while I located you. We've had tails on Rodney and the Smith guy—if that's his name—and a while ago they made a buy from a pusher. Him we've known about for some time, he's loose on a leash—eventually lead us to the supplier, we hope."

"What did they buy?" asked Mendoza.

"Oh, Mary Jane. Twenty reefers," said Callaghan. "We figure the rest of the party was sitting back at Eileen's waiting for 'em to fetch it, have a party. We dropped on the rest of 'em there. You said she might tie up to one of your bodies."

"It's up in the air," said Hackett. "She could be."

Callaghan heaved up his enormous bulk. "So let's go ask some questions, boys."

Mendoza looked at the little collection of fallible humanity in the interrogation room with cold wonder and concealed contempt. There were eight of them. Eileen and Tommy Smith, and six others: Callaghan would know their names. Four of the six had records as users, he'd said, and been picked up before for possession. Four boys, two girls: you had to look twice to tell them apart. They all looked dirty and unkempt, the girls with long greasy hair, the boys ditto, two with sideburns. The sloppy, dirty clothes, the bare feet, the sullen under-brow stares. Eileen had several drinks inside and was feeling no pain. And she was the oldest of them at twenty-one.

Callaghan opened the ball by asking Tommy if he'd bought from that pusher before. "You go to hell," said Tommy. "I'm not sayin' nothin'. I don't have to. You know I don't have to."

"What the hell," said Eileen genially, beaming muzzily at Callaghan. "Why all the sweat? My God, s'only Mary Jane—pretty soon they get it all legal, it doesn't do anything to anybody, God's sake—"

"That's interesting," said Callaghan. "About the time these pretty specimens were getting picked up, Luis, I was reading the latest info on that. Researcher who's spent twelve years at it. He's just found out that even marijuana creates those chromosome changes. Mongoloids in the next generation and so on. . . . You were planning a little party?"

"'At's right," said Eileen. "No harm, little party. What the hell? But I wasn't buyin'—just for me and Tommy. I'm not an idiot." She articulated that carefully. "Rest o' these bums—don't take me. I said, they put up their own bread, didn't I, Tommy? I'm not—"

"Yah, rich bitch don't even put out for a little pot," said one of the six, jeering and angry. "Li'l rich bitch—"

Callaghan stood with his fists on his hips and was silent, waiting. Beside Mendoza, Sergeant Steve Benedittino was equally silent.

"Li'l rich bitch lookin' down her nose—got all the bread there is an' she won't put out for anybody but Tommy no more—"

"You shut up, you bastards!" screamed Eileen, turning on them. "You took me for plenty till I got wise—I'm not carryin' everybody on my back, drinks an' pot an' horse an' acid, for God's sake—I said you find your own bread an' I—"

"Shut up!" said Tommy viciously.

"Well, well," said Callaghan. "Even more interesting. So some of you are on H and LSD, hah? Just now and then? Where'd you get that?" Silence. He looked at Mendoza.

Mendoza singled out the sideburned lout in stained jeans who had first turned on Eileen. He showed him the close-up shot of Michele. "You've seen this girl at Eileen's apartment?"

"Oh—this one. Yeah, yeah, a couple times. Man, a real dog. But those di'monds—like for real, I guess—buy a hell of a lot o' horse, I said t' Benny—"

"Was she there last Monday night?"

"What? I dunno."

"I told you she wasn't!" screamed Eileen. "She wasn't she wasn't she wasn't—"

"Hey, maybe she was," said Sideburns, and snickered. "Yeah, yeah, I guess I remember she was." Eileen began to scream wordlessly.

"For the love of God," said Hackett an hour later in Callaghan's office, "how can we even guess, yes or no? My God, Luis—that bunch—it could even be Michele *was* there and nobody knew it but Eileen and Tommy—or some other pair—if the rest of 'em were high on something. And by all we can gather, that bunch—and probably some more of the same types around—had been taking Eileen for an easy mark, getting her to buy the stuff for them, and now she's not playing any more and they'd just as soon get her in trouble. More than she is."

"*Es duro de pelar*," said Mendoza. "But they knew Michele. And her diamonds. If she'd only been at Eileen's parties a few times. Didn't Stanyard say she always wore that necklace, going anywhere in the evening? And the engagement ring. The diamonds would indeed buy a lot of H. About ten grand worth of diamonds, Pat."

"Holy God!" said Callaghan. "You don't say. She might have been there? With that bunch?"

"I don't know. And you don't need to tell me that if she was, and the notion occurred to any of them—as apparently it had vaguely entered the minds of Sideburns and Benny—"

"Gonzales and Middleton. Jesus Tomás and Ray. Picked up for possession, respectively, four and five times."

"Neither of them would have hesitated to throttle her for the diamonds. But, Pat, would they have known a reliable fence? The diamonds haven't showed, and it's a week ago tomorrow night." If it had been like that, they'd have wanted hard cash for the diamonds *pronto*.

Callaghan rubbed his red-bristled jaw. "They might, Luis. They just might. Down there, a lot of honest people, but also—the fringes. People not remotely connected to the pro burglars might still know about a fence. On the other hand—"

"*¡Demonios!*" said Mendoza. "Yes, that type wouldn't have the brains to cover it up much. They'd have got about a third of the real value from a fence—call it thirty-five hundred—and only a week later, they wouldn't be cussing Eileen for being a tightwad. What was on them?"

"Not much."

"Up in the air you can say. And it doesn't say anything even if your men pick up Michele's prints in that place—we know she'd been there, if only a few times. I take it you've turned the lab loose there."

"What else?"

"Yes, well, we haven't found Michele's evening bag or jacket yet. Both black velvet. If you come across those, we'd have something concrete to go on."

"I'll let you know," said Callaghan.

"You taking any bets, Art?" asked Mendoza in the elevator.

"No bets," said Hackett. "It could be a lot simpler, Luis. She decided to go home, teach Trulock a little lesson about criticizing her. She called a cab and went up to the corner to wait for it. The hood came along and grabbed for her bag, and—"

"I don't think I buy it quite that simple," said Mendoza. "The hood would have left her where she lay."

"Which is a point," admitted Hackett.

"And I sent a query to the cab companies. We should know eventually whether she did call a cab. I think I'll go home," said Mendoza. "I'm supposed to have Sundays off, after all."

"Just the dedicated cop, you."

Mendoza went home, and found Alison in the back yard sketching in charcoal a portrait of their shaggy dog lying contentedly in the shade of the back porch with two cats between his forepaws. "What, spending some time with your family for a change?" exclaimed Alison in mock astonishment.

"*Sarcasmo.*" Mendoza kissed her. "I get fed up with this job occasionally." The twins discovered he was home and flung themselves at him. "One at a time! *¡Dios!* Where do you get the energy, *niños?*"

"It's time they were in anyway," said Alison, putting away her sketching materials. It hadn't rained today but a cold wind was getting up and the sky looked ominously dark. "You can read to them until Máiri comes back, while I put that soufflé together."

"And where," asked Mendoza, "is—*¡bastante!* quiet down, you two monsters—is Máiri?" Mrs. MacTaggart theoretically had Sunday off but in practise was usually home by three o'clock.

"Máiri," said Alison amusedly, "didn't think much of your advice about not interfering, Luis. I'll tell you about it later."

Mendoza took the offspring down to the nursery and read them *Just-So Stories,* which were guaranteed to keep them quiet.

Alison was shredding lettuce when Mrs. MacTaggart came in, her silver curls firm above her round jolly face, and said, "I'm not caring, *achara.* There is something queer and it needs looking into. By what the boy says. If you can get the man to listen—"

"Mmh," said Alison. "I think so too. I won't say a word at dinner—get him in a receptive mood, all relaxed—and then tell him. It is queer, he can't deny that."

But the plans of policemen's wives are frequently frustrated. Mendoza had just finished a satisfactory dinner of pot roast, browned potatoes, a cheese soufflé, and chocolate cake, and had a second cup of coffee and lit a cigarette, with Alison just opening her mouth to broach the subject, when the telephone rang.

"Luis? You said a black velvet evening bag? There was one in Eileen's pad. In a drawer. Empty. Likewise a diamond solitaire. You interested?"

"I am emphatically interested. You at the office? I'll be down—hold everything." Mendoza ran for his hat and jacket. "Expect me when you see me," he told Alison, and was gone.

"Damnation," said Alison.

The diamond ring was not Michele's big headlight of an engagement ring. It was a modest solitaire, perhaps three-quarter-carat, in a plain mounting, not new. Mendoza dismissed it at one glance. But the black velvet evening bag was something else. It was empty, as Callaghan had said, a few loose grains of powder clinging to its satin lining, a faint perfume. A plain little pouch bag, with a gold chain.

"Let's see if we can get a positive ident on this," said Mendoza. "Whether or not, I'll drop it back at your office, O.K.?"

He drove out to Beverly Hills and showed it to the Stanyards. "Why, it's Michele's," said Louise Stanyard, taking it from him eagerly.

"Are you sure, Mrs. Stanyard?"

She handled it, opened it, hesitated. "I—no, I can't be sure," she said slowly. "I can't. It—it looks like the one Michele—but now I look back at it, I—I think Michele's was newer. This has been carried a lot, see where the velvet's worn, and the chain all tarnished. But it's just like the one Michele—I'm sorry." She handed it back. "But it's an ordinary kind of evening bag, there must be a lot like it. I don't think it's Michele's. It's not her perfume in it, she never wore anything but White Shoulders or Maja."

Conventional even there, thought Mendoza. He thanked her and drove back downtown, to leave the bag at Callaghan's office. He went up to his own office to see what was turning up on the night shift. Nothing had: it was being a quiet night. He talked awhile with Schenke and Galeano, and drove home to Rayo Grande Avenue in Hollywood.

"And the next thing will be," he said, coming into the bedroom, "that I find the shaggy dog in bed with me." Cedric, his large hairy self stretched comfortably across the foot of the king-size bed with

Bast and Nefertite cuddled against his side and Sheba between his forepaws, woke up and uttered a small genial *whoof* in greeting. "I do not approve of dogs on the bed. And damn it, this thing is still all up in the air and I simply do not see where to work on it constructively. We haven't found those Easterfields yet, but when we found the right Plunkett, he'd taken off for Europe. They probably don't know anything to tell us anyway." El Señor, who had been sound asleep on the window seat, swore at him for making a disturbance.

"How annoying," said Alison, who was sitting up in bed with a book.

"Say it twice," said Mendoza irritably.

Alison, eyeing him, decided it was not a propitious moment for the queer story.

Monday morning, and Piggott off. The inquest on that jumper, James Newman, was scheduled for ten o'clock; Higgins would cover it, to present the police evidence. The inquest on Michele was scheduled for one o'clock, and the inquest on Harry Tidwell for three. It was quite possible both would be delayed. Monday, in fact, was going to be one of those tiresome days, Mendoza had the hunch.

Palliser and Landers came in together just after Mendoza. "—wants to go back to teaching for a year, help out on the house payments, but I don't much like the idea. Working wives—"

"Well, if it's only for a year—" said Landers. "I wonder if there's anything new in."

There had been a knifing over on the Row. They had yet to get a formal identification on the body of that Wayne Billings. Myra Schwartz had said he had a brother, who hadn't been reached yet; try to find him today, get him to make the identification. Palliser went out on that, and Landers on the knifing.

There was a report on Mendoza's desk from the cab companies, consolidated by Sergeant Lake. Nobody in the vicinity of Le Renard Bleu had called for a cab between six-thirty and eight-thirty last Monday night.

"*Pues bien,*" said Mendoza to Hackett. "So Michele didn't call a cab. Did she call anybody?"

"Eileen?" said Hackett.

Mendoza sighed. "Not that I think for a minute, Arturo, that it'll do us any good, but we do have to try—let's you and me go talk to

Eileen and her pals some more. At least by now she'll be dried out and possibly make more sense."

"And maybe not, too. Did you see John's report on the Darley thing? We were upstairs with Pat or somewhere when it broke."

"I did. Human nature will be so very human, won't it?" Mendoza got up.

As they came past the desk, Sergeant Lake looked up. "If you're wondering where Jase is, there was a hit-run over on Carondelet. A kid."

"It does seem a shame," said Hackett seriously, "that Jase is handling all these kids getting killed. When they're trying so hard to start a family. Those Yocums—"

"Oh, that just got called in," said Lake. "The Yocum inquest. Tomorrow at ten."

And somebody would have to cover that, and it would be a full inquest with the evidence and statements presented, which would take up some time.

Alison was on the service porch combing Cedric—one draw-back about the shaggy dog was, of course, that long coat that so easily tangled and needed frequent combing—when the doorbell rang. It was about ten-thirty. Mrs. MacTaggart was in the back yard with the twins. Alison went down the hall and opened the front door, armed to repel a salesman.

"Er—I beg your pardon," said the man on the porch. "I wonder if you could tell me anything about Mr. and Mrs. Spencer at 304 across the street? They seem to be away—we've been trying to get in touch—" He brought out his billfold, extracted a card and offered it to her. It said, R. J. Titus, Ass't Manager, Bank of America, and an address on Hollywood Boulevard: the nearest branch of the bank.

All Alison's detective-fever flared up. "We've been thinking there's something queer," she said eagerly. "Nobody knows where they are, not even the children. Well, that is, the note said at Mrs. Spencer's mother's—or his, I don't know which. But the children—"

"Children?" echoed Mr. Titus.

"Oh, well, the older boy's seventeen. They're both in school now, of course. Is there something wrong, Mr. Titus?"

He looked vaguely alarmed. "Oh, well, now, we don't want to leap to any conclusions, Mrs.—"

"Mendoza," said Alison. "But it does seem—my—our nurse, she

knows Mrs. Spencer better than I do, and she says she'd never just go away leaving the children—"

He backed off. "Now, there's probably some simple explanation, Mrs. Mendoza. We're just—ah—making a few inquiries— Do you happen to know where Mr. Spencer works?"

"Don't *you* know?" Alison was surprised. Banks—

He looked at her severely. "Mr. Spencer has no outstanding loans with us, has never applied—the checking account merely—" He stopped. Bankers notoriously close-mouthed.

"Well, I believe he's with a brokerage firm in Hollywood. Fox, Holt and something. What's happened, Mr. Titus? As far as we can find out—" She was all primed to tell him the queer story, but he raised his hat and thanked her and turned down the walk quickly.

Alison hurried out to the back yard. "Máiri, there *is* something funny," she said. "This man from the bank just came—he wouldn't say what it was about, but asking about the Spencers. And where Mr. Spencer works. Do you suppose—"

"They'll have been abducted!" said Mrs. MacTaggart. "Those two poor boys—I've felt in my bones there was something aye wrong—"

"But who would kidnap them? Why? And how?" asked Alison practically. "We've simply got to tell Luis about it tonight, see what he thinks. There must be something wrong if the bank—"

"Guidness knows where those poor folk are," said Mrs. MacTaggart. "I just felt *in my bones* there's something terrible wrong. We had best be telling the man indeed, he'll know what to do—"

When Mendoza and Hackett foregathered with Higgins and Palliser at Federico's, they hadn't got anything out of Eileen and her motley crowd they hadn't heard before. Palliser had found Wayne Billings' brother and got the identification made. The warrant on Schwartz had come through. The autopsy report on Tidwell had come up from Dr. Bainbridge's office. Higgins reported that the inquest verdict had, of course, been suicide while of unsound mind.

Landers came in just as they were ordering and said disgustedly, "Just more paperwork. The bums. Both drunk, getting into a brawl. I'll have a Scotch and soda, Adam."

Grace came in and pulled up a chair from the next table; they made room for him. "To paraphrase Lincoln," he said, "God must love fools, He made so many of them. I've sorted out that hit-run. A dozen witnesses, and for a change they all say the same thing.

The driver wouldn't have been held if he'd stopped—the kid ran out from between parked cars, the best driver in the world couldn't have stopped in time—and everybody says the car wasn't traveling fast, about twenty per. He was scared, so he ran."

"Any make on the car?" asked Higgins, looking grim. Higgins didn't like hit-run drivers, even the ones unculpable.

"Gray sedan, middle-sized, not new. Do we ever get it that easy? I'll have a bourbon and water, Adam."

They sat talking desultorily over lunch, until Hackett glanced at his watch and said, "Damn—that Stanyard inquest scheduled for one—I've got to run."

"And I take no bets," said Higgins, "that the Tidwell inquest won't get delayed. Hang around in court—I suppose you'll be going to Michele's funeral, Luis."

"To waste the afternoon," said Mendoza. The inquest a pure formality, no evidence offered, the request for the open verdict, person or persons unknown. . . . It was largely a superstition that a murderer would show up at a victim's funeral. At the moment, Mendoza was more than halfway inclined to think that Michele, innocent Michele running in a fit of sulks from Trulock, had fallen among thieves—Eileen and that crowd: and there didn't seem to be any way to prove it, and as they were all in jail they wouldn't be at the funeral. The very solemn and elaborate funeral, at the Church of the Recessional at Forest Lawn. He remembered absently that the Church of the Recessional was an exact replica of the church Rudyard Kipling had attended. Kipling always had the word for it—how he knew people. . . . *Too much Ego in his cosmos*—the inevitable mark of the killer. But—

He came home at six-twenty to be pounced on by Alison and Mrs. MacTaggart. "You've simply got to listen, Luis! Because there was a man from the bank asking about them this morning, they must think there's something queer too—and besides, Máiri knows her and she says she'd never—"

"Now, *achara*, we'd best tell it all in order, how it happened—"

"*¿Qué es esto?* What are you talking about?" Cedric sidled up to greet him and the twins came yelling down the hall.

"*El pájaro,* he got *los niños* in the nest—Máiri saw—Daddy, *el pájaro*—"

"Bast she go climb after *el pájaro,* an' Máiri—"

"*¡Bastante!*" said Mendoza.

"For heaven's sake, quiet, you two!" said Alison. "All right, Máiri —you start telling him, while I—" She led the twins away. Mrs. Mac-Taggart looked at Mendoza solemnly.

"'Tis the Spencers—across the street. They—"

"Yes, Alison told me that. They've gone to nurse a sick grandmother or something. Why all the concern?" Mendoza shrugged out of his jacket.

"They've *not*. They've been abducted maybe," said Mrs. MacTaggart. "A mystery it is. I thought it was queer from the first, when Bertha told us what Jimmy said. A nice woman Mrs. Spencer is, and a good mother—Jim only seventeen and Dougie fourteen. It's not natural she'd just go off like that. Sudden illness or whatever. I do not care, she wouldna. It is a week ago Saturday, and she wouldna stay away that long, leave the boys alone. I thought it was—"

"We both thought it was funny," said Alison, coming back up the hall, having shooed Cedric and the twins into the nursery. "And so—"

"And so I went and asked questions. There's a time to interfere," said Mrs. MacTaggart sturdily. "And by what Jimmy says—a good lad, looking out for Dougie as best he can, but just boys they are—there's something terrible wrong."

"He told Máiri when he came home from swimming class last Saturday—a week ago Saturday, that is," burst in Alison, "he found a note from his father saying they had to go take care of his grandmother—Jimmy's grandmother I mean—and they didn't know when they'd be back. And there was a check for a hundred dollars, for the boys to get along on until the Spencers did come back. And they left the car, the note said they'd take a cab to the airport—did you find out where the grandmother lives, Máiri?"

"Jimmy said, back east in Pennsylvania, a little town and he didn't remember the name. I wouldna wonder if he was worried about it himself. The strangeness of it. Mrs. Spencer would not be having a holiday in the spring, and he would not just leave his work like that, all on a sudden—"

"The man from the bank asked where he worked. I wonder why the bank's interested," said Alison. "Oh! If that check was *forged*— But you see it's queer, Luis."

"She thinks the world of the two boys," said Máiri. "Fussing over their meals and all. She would never in this world just go off and leave them so long—"

"Luis, don't you think there's something queer?"

Mendoza said, "Queer is not the word. This is what you've been agitating about the last few days? I think it's so funny we'd better get some professionals on it. Abduction? That sounds—" He went down the hall and picked up the phone, dialed. "Captain Eden in? Well, Sergeant Barth?—Barth, Mendoza here. I may have an extraordinary little thing in your territory—"

ELEVEN

By the time Sergeant Barth of the Wilcox Street precinct got there, Alison and Mrs. MacTaggart were arguing hotly over who should stay with the twins and who should go with the men to act as moral support for what Mrs. MacTaggart termed those two poor bereaved children. "You'll both stay here," said Mendoza, and of course was overruled.

Barth, stocky and balding, pulled at his earlobe in habitual gesture and said it sounded very funny to him too. "I mean, down in Boyle Heights or somewhere like that you wouldn't think twice about parents going off, but in a neighborhood like—well, of course you can't generalize. But I think I'd like to ask some questions, all right." Mendoza was tacitly welcome to trail along, but Barth looked a little doubtfully at Alison, who had prevailed over Mrs. MacTaggart.

The Spencer house across the street was early American colonial, partly frame and partly used brick, sitting in the middle of two lots. There were flower beds, a silver birch artistically placed in front; Mrs. Spencer was a gardener. The paved walk up to the porch curved prettily. There was a car sitting at the curb in front, and lights were on in the house. A little pause after the door chimes sounded, and the door opened slowly. The porch light was on, and the boy looked out at them there, behind the screendoor.

Mendoza introduced himself. "You're Jim Spencer, aren't you? Well, Jim, this seems to be a peculiar thing, your mother and father going off so suddenly, and Sergeant Barth here'd like to ask a few questions about it. You mind if we come in?"

"No, sir." The boy opened the screen door. They went into a little entrance hall giving on a large living room furnished expertly and attractively with the early American décor. Another man stood before the used-brick hearth, and Alison hissed at Mendoza, "Mr. Titus."

There were confused introductions. When Titus grasped that Barth was a police officer, he said fussily, "I'm bound to say there should be an official investigation—well, of course there has to be— that check—I must say, for a man of Mr. Spencer's position—and reputation—simply to vanish this way, it's unprecedented. Quite unprecedented. I have checked with his office—Fox, Holt and Thorsen—and they have been trying to contact him too. He has not been in the office for more than a week, and—"

In the doorway to the large square dining room stood the younger boy. He looked a little frightened: a small-for-his-age darkhaired boy with a forgotten ham sandwich in one hand. And both the boys, and the house, bore the marks of neglect. The furniture was dusty. Roses in a bowl on the coffee table had long since withered and died. The carpet needed vacuuming. The boys looked unkempt and dirty, Jim in gray slacks and once-white shirt, Douglas in jeans and a very dirty T-shirt.

"Jim," said Mendoza, "maybe you've been thinking it over, and thinking it's all a little peculiar too." The older boy jerked his head once. He was a nice-looking boy, had his growth early: at least six feet, still gangling and a little awkward, but he had good features, a strong jaw, curling dark hair. "You just tell Sergeant Barth what happened."

"Well," said Jim after a couple of false starts, "well, gee, it was a week ago Saturday." His voice was still uncertain whether it was boy's or man's. "I came home from swimming class about four, and there was this—this note, that's all. On the kitchen table. From Dad. It said they'd got a telegram, Grandma was sick and they were going back east to take care of her. And they'd leave the car, take a cab to the airport. I could use the car—I got a license, I mean a temporary one. And the check for a hundred bucks, for us to buy groceries and stuff with—till they came back. That's all I know." He sounded miserable and worried.

"That check was forged," said Titus. "Not at all a good forgery— it was spotted several days ago—dated the twentieth—"

"That was a week ago Saturday," said Barth. "Yes. Was the note in your father's writing?"

"Well, gee," said Jim, "I *guess*. I mean, when do I get letters from him? I suppose."

"Something was said about postcards. You had one?"

"I—well, yeah, there were a couple of cards—Thursday I think. I told Dougie about that—"

"What was the postmark?" asked Barth. "Did you notice?"

"No, I didn't. Uh—one was from Mom and one from Dad. They just said Grandma was still sick and they didn't know when they'd be back."

"In their handwriting? Could you be sure?"

"I suppose they were," said Jim unhappily. "I—I don't see any of their writing much."

"Well, we'd like to see the note and postcards," said Barth.

"I—I threw them away. I'm sorry. I didn't think—"

"Are any of your parents' clothes missing?" asked Mendoza. "Suitcases?"

"I—I didn't look to see. I suppose, if they took off in a hurry—"

"Where does your grandmother live, Jim?" asked Barth.

Mendoza didn't wait to hear the whole answer. "It's some little town in Pennsylvania, I don't remember the—" He drifted out of the living room and past the younger boy, through the dining room to the kitchen. A big, ordinarily pleasant kitchen across the back of the house, a separate laundry room beyond, the kitchen door giving on a broad paved patio visible because the floodlights were on in the back yard. Mendoza surveyed the kitchen: dirty dishes piled high, evidence of the scratch-meals—in the wastebasket, cartons from frozen pizzas, TV dinners. The linoleum dull and stained. He wandered back to a cross-hall and three large bedrooms. The front bedroom was obviously the Spencers': king-size bed made up neatly with a plain tan spread, everything neat, the little row of cosmetic jars, cologne, on the dressing table. In the double wardrobe, what looked like a complete collection of clothes: suits, slacks, clean shirts on hangers, dresses, rows of shoes. The other two bedrooms cluttered and disordered, the beds unmade. Mendoza went back to the kitchen and had another look at the linoleum, and drifted back to the living room.

"—when they'd never done such a thing before, Jim? Doesn't it strike you as odd?"

"Well, I—I guess I didn't think—I mean—well, I guess it is. Sure."

Mendoza squatted down in front of the other boy. "Douglas— they call you Dougie, do they?"

"M-Mom does. I like Doug better."

"O.K., Doug. Did you see the note, did Jim show it to you? Saying your mother and father had to go away?"

The boy shook his head. "It's *funny*," he burst out suddenly. "Mom never goes away! I—" He was fighting tears. "And—and all we had all week was sandwiches and—"

"Well, I tried my best, Dougie!" said Jim desperately.

"Doug. Did Jim show you the postcards from your mother and father?"

The boy shook his head. "He said—there were some. I thought—"

"Well, for gosh sakes, they were just postcards—"

Mendoza stood up and turned to look at him. The boy was trembling, frightened, nervous, uncertain, immature, agonized. He faced Mendoza rigidly. And Barth stepped up beside Mendoza.

"What did you do with them, Jimmy?" asked Mendoza very gently.

Alison put both hands to her mouth. Titus just gaped.

And after a long dragging moment the boy said dully, "I—I put them—I buried them behind—the garage—in Mom's compost heap. I—"

"Oh, my God," whispered Alison. The younger boy began to cry and automatically she went to him.

"Why, Jim?" asked Barth.

He let his shoulders sag, and sank down on the gay chintz-covered couch. "I—Mom said I couldn't have the car—that night. And about using the phone all the time. I—just got mad and I—hit her—and she fell on the stove and her head—and when Dad came in I didn't know what—and he yelled and hit me and I picked up the—the hammer, Mom'd been hanging a picture and it was right—" He began to sob suddenly, his shoulders shaking.

"*Oh, my God!*" said Titus. "Do you mean he—"

"I—I—Dougie was at Boy Scouts—and I—I put them put them in the front closet till after dark and Dougie was in bed—way late—and I—"

Barth went to find a phone.

Mendoza lit a cigarette, watching Jimmy. And he thought remotely, *Too much Ego in his cosmos. . . .*

It was quite a thing, of course. The lab truck and the cars of men came swarming up, and a crew started digging in the compost bed behind the garage. A squad-car took Jim and Dougie down to Juvenile Hall. Alison, looking pale and shaken, went home to tell Máiri about it. And it wasn't any of Mendoza's business: he saw enough bodies down in Central Division. He could imagine what the police surgeon at Wilcox Street would say about these bodies.

"I won't say thank you," said Barth. "What a hell of a thing. What a—seemed like a nice family, your wife said. The kids brought up O.K.—he looks like a nice boy. What triggers them off, Mendoza? Oh, we say adolescence—my God, we were all adolescents once—and our great-grandfathers—you never got this kind of thing—"

"Don't say never. Once in a while." Mendoza flung his cigarette end off the front porch, and it made a miniature falling star in the darkness. "De veras. You know part of the answer as well as I do—the deliberate wedge driven between the generations—hasn't J. Edgar said it? The rest—I don't know, Barth. I don't know. And he's not eighteen. Stash him away, try him when he turns into an adult. Very likely, all the head-doctors saying this and that. You want to take a bet he's not loose within five years?"

"No bets," said Barth heavily. "No. What a hell of a—"

Mendoza went back across the street and started to answer questions from Alison and a very much shocked and horrified Máiri.

"But what a *hell* of a thing—right across the street, that nice respectable neighborhood," said Hackett. "My God."

Tuesday morning, and Mendoza was telling Hackett and Higgins about his overnight excitement; Piggott and Landers came in halfway through the story and demanded details.

"It's almost enough," said Piggott, "to put a man off getting married at all, isn't it? What a thing."

"Fortunately none of our business," said Mendoza. "We've got enough to do down here, and we'd better get on with it. Have we had anything from anybody on that Arquette, Art?"

"*Nada.* We've spread it to the pigeons we want him. Damn shame there's no mug-shot available." The "want" on Richard Arquette had, of course, been sent to all precincts and all nearby police forces in L.A. and Orange Counties.

"I had just a stray thought about that," said Higgins. "On the Durand thing. She'd been working somewhere up to just the week before. Could it be Arquette had spotted her there? Been attracted?"

"That might be," said Hackett, "though it was a dress shop, I think—"

"Says nothing," said Higgins laconically. "He could have made deliveries there—his pedigree says he's a womanizer, he could have been there with another woman."

"True," said Hackett. "Having nothing else to do on it, I can always go and ask."

"And we haven't thrown that Gertrude Weiss thing into Pending yet," said Higgins. "I have a hunch we will. We never did get the formal statement from that Wemberg woman."

"The daylight burglar, yes," said Mendoza absently. "Sit down, George, and listen to some deducing." Higgins yawned, sat down and lit a cigarette. . . .

There'd been a suicide reported just after the shift changed last night. Landers went out to get the statements, clear up the paperwork on that. Grace hadn't got all the follow-up statements on that hit-run yesterday; he and Palliser were off today, so Piggott started out on that. Glasser went down to the communal detective office to wait for the expectable new call.

Mendoza swiveled round in his desk-chair to look out at the gray sky: it wasn't raining today, but overcast and gray. "It's too late now," he said, "and I don't think it'd have given us anything anyway—to ask questions for a block around that restaurant, did anybody see Michele that night. Because there's nothing around there —a couple of warehouses, public parking lot, row of shops across the street all closed at night. But it's useless for another reason, George, and I've had a second guess about it. Now, Michele might have been a little idiot some ways—as witness her fascination for Eileen, and as far as that goes probably a good part of it was a hold-over from school days and eventually Michele would have got some sense into her head about Eileen. At least we do know that, fascination or no, Eileen hadn't—mmh—corrupted her yet. No evidence of drug-use from the body."

"You're deducing fine," said Higgins.

"So. She was not altogether a fool. And, George, Stanyard being a responsible man of substantial property, Michele would be conscious of property. It is a very safe bet that she wouldn't have been fool enough to start out on foot anywhere, in that area, at night. Wearing all the diamonds. ¿Cómo no? We know she didn't call a cab. But we also know now that she had some money on her. There is a public phone just down from that ladies' room. Who might she have phoned, George? Temporarily mad at Trulock, for trying to order her around? Obviously whatever happened to her, whoever waylaid her, it wasn't in the restaurant. And—she was a pretty girl, George."

Higgins sat up abruptly. "So she was."

"Twenty-one," said Mendoza, and swiveled back to face him. "She must have had other boyfriends before Trulock. They'd only been engaged since Christmas. Feeling annoyed at Trulock, wanting to teach him a little lesson—isn't it at least possible she—"

"Phoned a former boyfriend," said Higgins. "All right, that's nice deducing, Luis. What does it go on to?"

"I couldn't guess. I just saw that far," said Mendoza. "It's possible. I don't know what it might say. Former boyfriend still mad at her for ditching him? Former boyfriend needing some money quick and spotting the diamonds? *No sé*. But I think it's an angle we ought to look at."

"How?"

"Girlfriends," said Mendoza succinctly. "They'll know. Go and ask who she went around with pre-Trulock. Go and look at them. We might just turn up something interesting, you never know."

"I'm with you," said Higgins. "Another place to look, all right."

"So, you go find this Sue Ransome—here's the address. I'll see Wanda and the Rooney girl. Her closest friends—they'll give us some names. So go and look at the boys. I'll meet you at Federico's for lunch."

"O.K.," said Higgins.

"It was about six-thirty when you came home, Mr. Hanson?" asked Landers, taking notes.

"Yes, yes, as usual." Jan Hanson was a fairly handsome fellow in his fifties, with a full head of blond hair and Viking features: at the moment his face was working with emotion. "I have—my pharmacy, it is around on Virgil Avenue, I told the other policeman last night, I opened my pharmacy when Gerda and I came to America, it is nearly thirty years ago, before the war. Now, I have employees, I do not have to be there myself all the time, and I come home every day at six, six-thirty. Oh, my poor Gerda—"

"That's how it was all right," put in the other man. He was a little thin man, older than Hanson, John Elderby. "Mr. Hanson come in regular time, about six-twenty it was. I'm sittin' there in my living room, door open like I usual leave it, I'm home. Those ground-floor rooms get stuffy, I like fresh air. I see Mr. Hanson go past, he sees me and like usual says hello, and not half a minute later he comes rushin' back down the stairs, sayin' his wife's locked in the bathroom and he can't make her answer. So I go back up with him and we break in the door, and there the poor woman is"—he shook his head. "Hung herself from the shower-rod. Terrible. Never thought as Mrs. Hanson'd do a thing like that."

"My poor Gerda!" said Hanson in agony. "I had not realized—how much it had troubled her, how she had brooded—if I had not been so busy at the pharmacy—"

"Now you can't go blamin' yourself, Mr. Hanson."

"Had she been ill, sir?" asked Landers.

"She was losing her hearing," said Hanson. He had very little accent. "She was going deaf, very rapidly it had come on, and the doctor had said, nothing he could do to help her. My poor Gerda, so fond of music, it had grieved her—but I had not realized—"

"Yes, well, you'll both have to make statements, as I said," said Landers politely. "We'll get these notes typed up and you can look them over and sign them." Routine. Another suicide: they would do it. Galeano had typed the first report on it last night; a straightforward suicide.

There was that Weiss thing no work was being done on at all. He supposed after this maybe he should get the Wemberg woman's statement at least. He supposed Mendoza had sent a query down to Lieutenant Goldberg's office asking about any known daylight burglars given to the violence. But whether they'd ever get any kind of lead on that one—it'd probably wind up in Pending.

"My poor darling," said Hanson, "if I had only realized how she was brooding—"

Hackett had correctly assumed that Durand would be back at work. He landed at the Ambassador Hotel at a quarter to nine and asked questions: a bellhop guided him down through a labyrinth of corridors to the vast kitchen premises and turned him over to a white-aproned assistant chef.

"Oh, but yes—Durand—we have all been so shocked to hear of his wife. A terrible tragedy. Durand a good man, reliable. The waiters will be coming in here, sir—you may talk to him here—" The assistant chef led Hackett to the rear of this underground area, past several separate kitchens, a row of dumbwaiters, a row of elevators and lines of serving-trolleys, to a long narrow room lined with steel lockers, a communal shower-room beyond. There were a few men already there, a few of the lockers standing open, as the men exchanged suit jackets for starched white ones. "There is Durand just coming in, sir."

Durand looked tired. He trudged across the room from the rear entrance nearly to his locker before he saw Hackett. "Oh—you," he said. "More questions?"

"Just one, Mr. Durand. You said your wife had been working, at a dress shop—"

"Yes. Until the doctor said—" Durand unlocked the steel door with a key from his ring, and began to take off his jacket. All the men were wearing black trousers, white shirts, dark ties. Idly Hackett speculated, the jackets laundered by the hotel: hotel property. A man came up and unlocked the locker to the right of Durand's. He smiled at him a little awkwardly: an older man than Durand.

"Glad to see you back to work. You feeling O.K.?"

"I'm O.K.," said Durand shortly. "Thanks." He hung up his suit jacket on a hanger and put it in the locker, started to put on the white one. Another man came up to the locker where Hackett was standing, and Hackett moved, apologizing.

"Which dress shop was it, Mr. Durand?"

"Which—oh, it was Peggy Lee's on Vermont," said Durand.

"Thanks. That's all I wanted."

Durand looked at him curiously and might have asked why, but an agitated voice from the double doors leading into the kitchens was demanding haste—"All these Room Service orders—quick, quick!—Etienne, this is the third time you are late"—as a harried-looking youngster dived in and ran for a locker across the room. Durand turned away with the others.

Hackett started for the door, hoping he could find his way out of this place, and bumped into the man hastily donning his jacket at the next locker. "Sorry."

The man muttered something, and in turning from the locker faced Hackett at close quarters for a second. He brushed by. Hackett looked after him.

And it was, of course, a very general description—a good many men might conform to those statistics—but that fellow did, in a general way. About six-one, the right breadth to weigh about a hundred and eighty, brown hair, brown eyes, and a goodlooking fellow by that one glance, regular unmemorable features. Hackett called to him on pure impulse. "You—mind my asking you something?"

The man stopped halfway through the door and turned. "You mean me?"

"Yes." Hackett went up to him. "What's your name?"

"And what business is that of yours?" Hackett produced the badge. "I still don't see what business of yours it is."

"Look, just take it easy," said Hackett. "I can ask somebody else, you know. I was just trying to break the ice. We start over again?"

"Joe Buckley," said the man resignedly.

Hackett looked at him, uncertain and halfway regretting that he'd initiated this. There was nothing at all to say that Buckley was anything but what he looked like. Thousands of men would match that description. Probably if he'd taken any notice, at least a couple of the other waiters here, in that crowd of men just gone out, would match it.

"Look, we're busy," said Buckley. "All the breakfasts. I'm on Room Service and—"

Hackett had on him, as did all the Homicide men this last week, a copy of that glossy 5 by 7 photograph of Michele Stanyard. It was in his breast pocket. He reached there and unobtrusively slid the photograph hard up and down against the pocket lining before he brought it out. He offered it to Buckley. "Have you ever seen this girl in the hotel?" he asked casually.

Buckley took the photograph in thumb and forefinger, in his left hand. Hackett took careful note of the spot where his thumb rested. "No, I never did," said Buckley. "I never saw her anywhere." Buckley didn't read the papers? She'd been plastered over them all during the middle of last week.

"Well, thanks," said Hackett. "That's all I wanted to know." He took the photograph back, casually, between his first two fingers, let it dangle as Buckley turned and went out. Alone in the locker room, he took out a pen and ringed a circle round where he hoped Buckley had left a print.

By asking four different people for directions, he found his way out to the parking lot. He laid the photograph carefully on the front seat and drove back to headquarters. Handling the photograph gingerly, he took it up to the lab and demanded instant service.

"What on?" asked Scarne.

"Inside this area," said Hackett, "is a thumbprint. I hope. It's about ten million to one that it belongs to that Richard Arquette— if you remember, you turned up his prints in the Durand bedroom —but I wish you'd look and see. I feel silly just asking you." He did.

"You want me to look now? Compare them? Look, we're busy—"

"So are we. That one we'd like to drop on before he gets a yen for some other female. How long will it take you?"

"Half an hour," said Scarne, shrugging.

"I'll be down in the office. Let me know as soon as you do."

"Sure."

Hackett went downstairs to the Homicide office. Nobody was there but Sergeant Lake. "What are you doing here?" he asked. Hackett told him, feeling foolish. Wasting time like this. "Well, for my money that's goofing off with a vengeance, Art. Just because this guy vaguely matches that description—say, how come Arquette never got mugged, anyway? I gather he was picked up and charged—"

"Only once in the big town," said Hackett. "A couple of times in the little towns, outside Philly, where the force was a chief and two deputies, and no facilities for the mug-shots. The rape charge, they knew they wanted him—the Philly boys—but they never laid hands on him. All they had were his prints, from the small-town boys."

"Oh," said Lake. He sat back and sighed. "I was a pound and a half down this morning."

"Congratulations."

"I've been on the damn diet a week," said Lake, "and I've only lost three pounds, damn it. The insurance scale says—I'm five-ten, what they call a medium frame—says, between a hundred and fifty and a hundred and sixty. It's not *much* over—a hundred and eighty-six—but Caroline said—and the doctor said—damn it, I've got a job to do, keep up my strength."

"The lean ground beef," said Hackett. "Cottage cheese. I know, Jimmy. The scale says I could go to two hundred and fifteen—which is damn ridiculous. I'm six-three-and-a-half, after all—"

"I never did much like cottage cheese," said Lake mournfully. "What kind of meal is it without the bread and butter? Did you know something I just found out?—not that I like margarine, for God's sake, but it's got just as many calories as butter! I thought—"

"I've been on this kick longer than you," said Hackett. "I did know that." The phone buzzed and Lake picked it up: an inside call.

"Homicide, Sergeant Lake. . . . Yeah, he's right here." He handed the phone to Hackett.

"I don't know whether you've borrowed our Luis' crystal ball or what, Sherlock," said Scarne, "but you hit the jackpot all right. That thumbprint belongs to Richard Arquette."

"It *does?*" Hackett was thunderstruck. "It *does?* Arquette? That's *him?* I will be eternally Goddamned!"

"Oh, I hope not," said Scarne; but Hackett had slammed the phone down. He looked at Lake blankly.

"It's him. Arquette."

"Oh, I don't believe it," said Lake.

"Well, neither do I," said Hackett. Piggott came in and asked what was up. They told him.

"I can only say, Art," he said seriously to Hackett, "the Lord is certainly with you."

"Like to come help make the collar?"

"Sure."

"Jimmy, you can get the machinery started on the warrant," said Hackett. And he still didn't believe it.

At the Ambassador, back in the spreading kitchen premises, they found Arquette alias Buckley just manhandling a serving-trolley into one of the elevators. Nearby other waiters were loading trolleys, coming and going with trays.

"Just hold it," said Hackett to Arquette. "You're under arrest, Arquette."

The man calling himself Buckley straightened and turned and looked at them blankly. He said, "That's not my name."

Hackett had not spoken loudly, nor had Arquette, but quite suddenly there was an instant hush of the noise all around: the clatter of dishes and trays and trolleys stopped dead.

"We're taking you in, Arquette," said Hackett, "and you know what for. For the murder of Kitty Durand."

And in the little pause before Arquette started to say automatically, "It's a lie—I didn't—" there was a harsh loud voice behind Hackett and Piggott.

"*Is he the one? He killed my Kitty—he killed—*" And Robert Durand hurled himself past them straight for Arquette's throat.

The serving-trolley with its load of four breakfasts carefully arranged in the covered dishes went flying in a crash of crockery. Hackett leaped to pull Durand off. For a fraction of a second his mind flashed back to that awful night when they'd caught up with the rape-killer who'd got hold of Alison, and pulling Luis off him after he'd half-killed him—

"I'll kill him, I'll kill him, let me at him," Durand was sobbing.

Other hands took him from Hackett, held him. Hackett yanked Arquette up to his feet.

And Arquette cried in a high bleating frightened voice, "I never meant to! I never meant to! I never—"

By the time they got him back to the office Landers had come in, so he sat in on the questioning. There wasn't any sign of Mendoza or Higgins, and Glasser had gone out on a new call.

"All right, Arquette," said Hackett, "would you like to tell us about it? You know we've nailed you for it, with your prints found there. In the Durands' bedroom. What about it, Arquette? How'd you come to pick on Kitty Durand? You like to tell us?"

"For God's sake, Art," said Landers, "you haven't warned him. The courts'll throw out any confession if he wasn't told all his—"

"Oh, hell," said Hackett, and repeated the little ritual—whatever he said could be used in evidence, he could have a lawyer, he didn't have to say anything. The handcuffs on the cops, all the weight in the scale of citizens' rights on the side of the bad boys.

Arquette looked at them in sullen anger. "It was all *his* fault!" he said. He looked like an enraged bull, head down, trapped and not knowing how he'd been, so unexpectedly, trapped. "*His* fault! Goddamn it, I wouldn't never have—but those pictures—those God-damned pictures—"

"Pictures?" said Landers. "What pictures?"

"The damn pictures in his damn wallet." Arquette hunched his shoulders. "He was—he was—once, a while back, showin' some of us —pictures. Of his wife. That girl. Braggin' on her, how pretty and all. And he flipped past some, didn't show those, but I got a kind of look, pictures of her nekkid they were. And I—while he was in the shower once after that, I get his key and—you know—get a press of of his locker key, a guy showed me how to do that once. I get a key made—so I could see the pictures, that's all. The pictures of her nekkid. She was a real something, you know that? One—beautiful— dame." He looked at them resentfully. "If he hadn't showed the pictures—"

"Not your fault," said Hackett sardonically. "I see. How'd you find where the Durands lived, Arquette?"

"I—followed him home once. That's all. I never meant to do it! I never meant to—I wouldn't't've—only, I just got to thinking about her all the time—those pictures—I—took that day off, I didn't feel like—and I went there, I thought maybe she wouldn't be home but

145

she was. I said I worked with her husband, I come to tell her he had a little accident on the job, that was just to get let in, see, I said he wasn't hurt bad, but—and she went to the bedroom, get dressed—she had on a kind of robe, and God, what a figure, you could see—I wouldn't've—I never meant to—but she fought like crazy, and I was kind of stirred up—God's my witness, I never meant to *kill* her! But I—I seen she was dead, and I thought—make it look like—maybe somebody she knew'd been there—"

The Homicide men looked at each other. All the speculating they'd done about that.

"The coffee cups, Arquette?" asked Hackett.

"I just thought—I was scared then, I never meant—I—there was a coffeepot on the stove, coffee still in it—and I remembered—remembered to pick up the cups with a handkerchief, so's my—"

"But you remembered that too late, Arquette."

"I never meant to do it," shouted Arquette.

TWELVE

"Don't tell me you're starting to have hunches too," said Higgins. "I'll be damned. He was right there all the time—all you had to do was look." Hackett and Landers had come into Federico's to find Mendoza and Higgins already there; Piggott had taken Arquette down to book him in.

"And that poor devil Durand," said Mendoza, "when he hears that bit about the pictures—probably put him off photography for life. *Donde menos se piensa salta la liebre.* But at least we can mark that one off the list. I trust you've applied for a warrant."

"Jimmy," said Hackett. "I think I've earned a drink."

"Calories," said Higgins.

Hackett said calories be damned and ordered a Scotch and water. "And what the hell are you doing here?" he added as John Palliser came up to the table.

"I had to cover the Yocum inquest," said Palliser. "Had all of you forgotten about it?"

"My God, I had," said Hackett. "What happened?"

"The attorney tried for a reduced charge, but no dice. First degree homicide. Lord knows when the trial will come up, of course."

"But just wait till you hear, John," said Hackett. "Luis had a humdinger of a murder right across the street—what a thing—" He started to tell Palliser about that. As Palliser was exclaiming incredulously Piggott came in and said Arquette was tucked away safe.

"*Bueno,*" said Mendoza briskly. "Stop gossiping about Wilcox Street's problems, Art, and hear what we've got on Michele. I had a little brainwave—former boyfriends. I—"

"What?" said Hackett. "Well, that could be an angle."

"So what did you turn up from Sue, George?"

Higgins swallowed bourbon and water. "One Jack Stover, one Christopher Wood, one Adam Fletcher. She said Michele had gone out just a little with Wood and Fletcher, for a while pretty steady with Stover. He's the only one I've seen."

"What did he look like?"

Higgins considered. "Ordinary. Clean. He's a law student at U.C.L.A. Where I talked to him between classes. He lives with his parents in Beverly Hills. Michele had nothing but high-class boyfriends. I asked him about a week ago last night and he said he was at home. Unfortunately he was home alone—parents were out at a party. He said of course Michele didn't phone him, hadn't heard from her, talked with her, in over a year. He's got his own car."

"So," said Mendoza. "I came up with two more former steadies. Wanda and Sandra gave me several names but by what they say Michele only went steady, to any degree, with those three—Stover, and that was a long time back, and Bill Vickers and Duane Patterson. Patterson was apparently the latest before Trulock. He lives with an aunt—Beverly Hills, what else? I haven't seen either of them. I did, however, hear something else from Wanda. A Lester Gerard. Way back when Michele first began to date, apparently the Stanyards pushed her at him—his mother a friend of the family, and one deduces, Lester so safe for Michele. I haven't seen him. I did see Vickers. He works in his father's office—advertising and promoting, Hollywood. He said he hadn't seen Michele in a long time. She didn't phone him a week ago last night. He was home, he says, and he too was home alone. His mother's dead and his father had a business meeting."

"Which leaves it still up in the air," said Hackett.

"Stover," said Higgins, "acted surprised. And I think he really was—to be connected. He's engaged to be married, he says. Said it had all been very casual with Michele and he hadn't thought of her in years. Seen her occasionally, in a crowd, was all. I think he's clean."

"But it doesn't say the brainwave's a washout," said Landers. "I kind of like it. There must be others she went out with. If Patterson was the most recent since she got engaged to Trulock—"

"Yes, I want to have a look at him," said Mendoza. He glanced at his watch as the waiter came up bearing plates. "Art's hit one jackpot today and they do say, never two without three. We'll see what turns up."

"There is, damn it, that Weiss thing," said Landers. "I suppose we ought to—we never did get Mrs. Wemberg's statement down and signed. When I went back next day she wasn't home—"

"Routine," said Hackett. "We'll never drop on that one. Too anonymous."

"Yes, well, you can come help out George and me on the boy-friends," said Mendoza, "and maybe hit another jackpot."

Mendoza, Hackett and Higgins took off from the restaurant; Palliser went home and told Roberta all about the murder across the street from Mendoza, that exclusive neighborhood in Holly-wood. Roberta looked horrified.

"But his own—! Honestly, John, the things that happen these days." She'd just washed her dark hair and had a towel round her head, was wearing a rather shabby terry robe, but she looked beautiful to Palliser. "It's almost enough to make you afraid to acquire the family."

"Well, after all, you bring them up right, with the discipline and all—"

"Even *so*," said Roberta. "The little monsters—" She sighed. "I put my name on the substitute list. And in September—"

"If you really want to—"

"We can postpone the first little monster a year or so. Those house-payments," said Roberta.

Landers and Piggott, dutifully clearing up the routine, went back to Leeward Avenue to see if Mrs. Wemberg was home. At the Weiss house next door, with its growing stand of corn in the back yard, its plots of vegetables in the front, Weiss was on his knees at some gardening job, weeding or fertilizing. He glanced up as they got out of Landers' Corvair, and watched them up the walk to Mrs. Wemberg's porch. She was home.

"Oh, dear," she said, flustered, when they explained. "Come down to the police station? I already told you all I saw—that awful burglar —poor Mrs. Weiss—"

"It's just to have you sign the formal statement, ma'am," said Landers. "The inquest is scheduled for tomorrow, you know. It won't take you more than an hour."

"Well, I can't come now," she said. "I'm sorry. I've just put a cake in the oven, and I'm not dressed to go out. I could come in about an hour and a half, is that all right?"

"Yes, that's fine, Mrs. Wemberg," said Piggott. "We'll send a car for you then."

"Mercy, the neighbors'll think I'm being arrested."

As they came down the walk to the curb, Weiss hoisted himself up from his knees and came over to intercept them. "You fellers find out anything about the guy who killed Gertrude?" he asked abruptly.

"Not yet, Mr. Weiss." And probably never would.

He cleared his throat, spat aside, and said, "Well, I—well, I'm bound to tell you—what I'm gettin' at is, the more I think it over, I —well, I seen that guy before. I know who he is."

They stared at him in astonishment. "You—Mr. Weiss," said Landers, "we've talked with you several times, questioned you, and you never—you couldn't even give us a good description—"

"Now maybe I ain't so handy with talk." Weiss looked aggrieved, not at all abashed. "But I been turnin' it over in my mind, and it come to me who that feller is. I got the picture clear in my mind. Clear as can be. He was that feller sold me the new atenny."

"The—what was that, sir?" asked Landers.

"The atenny for the TV," said Weiss. "Gertrude was sayin' the repair feller said we needed a new atenny. Foolish waste o' money but Gertrude, she liked the TV and she's a hard worker, I had the money. She says they'd send a man up. This feller came and arranged about it. I dunno his name, o' course. And it was him I paid— I went right upstairs and got the money, he give me a receipt and next day they come and put up the new atenny."

Landers and Piggott looked at each other. "Excuse me, Mr. Weiss," said Landers, "how much was it?"

"'Twas a hundred and ten dollars and seventy-six cents. Foolish, but Gertrude—"

"Er—you say you went upstairs for the money. You paid him in cash?"

"Why, sure. I always deal in cash. I don't trust no banks. Never know when they're goin' shut up."

"When was this, sir?"

"About two weeks back."

"Mr. Weiss—the receipt he gave you, could we see it?"

"Sure. I get it."

"Oh, this is wild," said Piggott while they waited for him to come back. "He's imagining—"

150

"Do you really think," said Landers, "he's got any imagination, Matt?"

"Well—"

Weiss came back and showed them the receipt. It was signed in an illegible scrawl, but the heading showed the firm to be the Ace TV Sales and Repair Service on Virgil. Landers took down the address.

"It's silly," said Piggott in the car. "I know the citizens are always doing silly things—and not doing sensible ones—but I ask you, Tom. I ask you. Some one of us has been here two or three times—we brought him down to the office to make a statement—and not a word about this antenna salesman up to now. He hemmed and hawed about what color pants the man had on! And now telling us—"

"The citizens you can't predict, Matt," said Landers philosophically. "He's got a slow mind and he's not good at expressing himself. Though you'd have thought, if mulling over the mental image was going to tell him anything, it would have before now. But just in case, we check it out."

"And it'll be a waste of time," said Piggott gloomily. But Piggott tended to be a pessimist.

Mendoza had found Duane Patterson at home. Nothing but the high-class boyfriends for Michele, all right. It was an old and very stately house in an older section of Brentwood Heights, and Patterson was slightly older than the other boys Michele had dated, about Trulock's age. He didn't turn a hair at the badge, but asked Mendoza in, answered questions openly. He hadn't, he said, seen Michele in over a year—oh, in crowds here and there, was all. No, she hadn't called him a week ago last night. "What the hell?" he said interestedly. "The night she was—*that* was a shock, to see it plastered across the front page. Little Michele. Last one in the world you'd think could be—everybody protected Michele," said Patterson. "Between us, a very nice girl but nothing spectacular in the way of brains." He looked at Mendoza curiously. "You canvassing every male she ever dated, Lieutenant? Think it was—something personal?"

"Something like that," said Mendoza vaguely. "We don't know. Where were you a week ago last night, Mr. Patterson? Can you show she didn't phone you?"

Patterson's dark eyes narrowed. "You're not asking me for an *alibi?* Well, I'll be damned. As a matter of fact I can give you one. A week ago last night Aunt Agatha had a party. Aunt Agatha and I live together here. It was quite a party. Oh, not like that—everybody went home sober, I assure you! But the whole crowd, friends of Agatha's, friends of mine, can tell you I was here the whole evening. . . . You aren't serious?"

"But I am," said Mendoza. "You don't have a job, Mr. Patterson?"

He laughed. "A job? What for? Dad left me plenty, and I'm just one of the world's drones. Aunt Agatha and I like each other, live our own lives, have fun. But this I don't get. You think it was some personal reason—on *Michele?*"

"We don't know, Mr. Patterson. Thanks very much," said Mendoza. One to cross off the list, with an alibi.

Landers and Piggott descended on the Ace TV Sales and Repair Service and demanded the manager. He was a tall rangy fellow named Haverkamp, and when Landers was halfway through his recital, a TV antenna sold to a Mr. Weiss on Leeward Avenue, about two weeks ago, he interrupted with an abrupt, "Buyer got any complaint?"

"No, no, it's the salesman we're interested in," said Landers. "His name and address. If you could—"

"Oh," said Haverkamp. "Oh. You more skip-tracers?"

"We're L.A.P.D." Landers showed him the badge again. "What do you mean?"

"That damn guy," said Haverkamp disgustedly. "I had enough of him up to here! He must owe everybody in town. He only come to work for me about two months back, he's a good talker, good salesman all right, sales he gets for me, sure. But about the first thing he asks me is not to give his address to nobody, he says his first wife is always givin' him a hard time, do I know if that's so or not—" he shrugged. "But anyways, there wasn't hardly a day goes by somebody wasn't in here askin' for him, an' seems he owed all of 'em money an' they're tryin' get him to pay off. What the hell, I don't need a dead-beat around, good salesman or not. I'm not that big a fool. Guy like that, he's all too liable to be tempted to stick his finger in the till, hey? So I fired him. Last week. And do you know, I had skip-tracers in here after him, and guys look like pro gamblers an' all—"

"So what's his name?" asked Landers.

"Bill Vincent."

"You had an address for him? Of course he may be long gone, but—"

"Yeah. Eleventh Street," said Haverkamp. "What do you want him for? The cops?"

"Well," said Landers, "we're not quite sure we want him at all." Haverkamp stared, and went to look up the address.

"It's wild," said Piggott.

"Sometimes a thing comes unstuck all of a sudden," said Landers.

They went up to the address on Eleventh Street, and it was a big old house with a sign in the window, *Room for Rent.* A motherly-looking woman with gray hair and friendly eyes answered the bell, and was adamant on refusing to answer any questions about Bill Vincent until they got it across that they were police, plainclothes police. "Oh!" she said. "Oh, well, then, you're all right to talk to. It's just, I feel sorry for Martha. I'm a fool, I suppose, but he's not a bad man, just unlucky—and he will go gambling. And Martha expecting the baby next month. Yes, they're still here—owe me four months' back rent but like I say I couldn't turn Martha out —no, they're not here now, they went to the doctor's, they'll be back by four. Oh, you're welcome." But she stared after them curiously, belatedly perhaps wondering about plainclothes cops coming.

"Check back with the office," said Landers, "and try here again then?"

"Might as well," agreed Piggott.

At the office, they ran into Lieutenant Goldberg of Robbery who was looking for Mendoza. "He's doing his own legwork these days?" asked Goldberg. "Well, I haven't got anything for him anyway. He sent down to ask me about known daylight burglars. What the hell does he think I am, a computer? Daylight burglars, nighttime burglars, violent burglars—legion these days and"—he sneezed, reached for Kleenex—"and any of the young punks at all might be given to random violence. They've got computers down in Records —tell him to ask there. Oh, and about those diamonds—missing from one of your corpses, and what the hell was a corpse on Central's beat doing covered with ten grand worth of diamonds?—they're on the hot list for the pawnbrokers, of course, but nothing's showed. We don't know all the fences in L.A.—though we think we may have dropped on a new one—and if the diamonds went to a fence you won't get a lead that"—he sneezed—"way."

"God bless you," said Piggott.

"Damn allergies," said Goldberg, and departed.

"At least," said Sergeant Lake, looking after him, "I don't have allergies. No, for once there's nothing new in."

He was wrong. The next minute tubby little Dr. Bainbridge marched in and asked, "The mastermind in? No? Hah! out working for a change, is he? You brain-trust boys are slipping these days."

"How so, doctor?" asked Landers.

Bainbridge snorted. "I haven't done a complete autopsy yet, but I didn't need to. Your damn report about her said suicide by hanging. Suicide by hanging be damned. Woman was hit with our old friend the blunt instrument, and her skull's fractured. She may have been strung up somewhere afterward but she was already dead. One Gerda Hanson."

"What the hell"—Landers stared at him. "She was—well, I will be damned. My God, and he sounded all broken up, the bereaved widower, his poor dear Gerda—I swear to God, this job eventually gets you afraid to trust anybody!"

"I just thought you'd like to know," said Bainbridge.

And Piggott said, "You know, Tom, we did say we'd send a car for Mrs. Wemberg—"

"Oh, hell," said Landers, harassed.

"Why are you asking all these questions? I don't have to answer you—I don't have to tell you anything! Why did you come here?"

Mendoza regarded Lester Gerard interestedly. Wanda had said the Gerards lived near the Stanyards—she didn't know them, she said, but years back he'd been Michele's first steady. The parents friends, pushing them together. Mendoza had found Gerard by the simple expedient of looking in the phone book. Geographically the house was near the Stanyards', but it was over the line into a much older residential area and it was an old Spanish stucco place, shabby, the front yard a jungle of overgrown planting.

And Lester Gerard seemed to be a very nervous fellow. He was perhaps twenty-two, about five-ten, a little overweight, nondescript —medium everything. He was wearing a baggy pair of slacks and a sloppy T-shirt, he needed a shave, and he hadn't sat down, but paced this old shabby living room shadowed to gloom by the jungle outside, and his eyes moved rapidly, and he chewed furiously at a hangnail on one thumb.

"I don't know what you want with me," he said fretfully.

"Michele Stanyard," said Mendoza patiently. "You used to go around with her, a while back."

Gerard shrugged pettishly. "That was—that never meant anything. Was anything. Just silly—I never—"

"When was the last time you saw her? Not went out with her, just saw her?"

"I don't know, I don't remember. Why should I?"

"She was murdered last week, you know," said Mendoza.

"I saw it in the paper," said Gerard, his back turned then. "I—I didn't *know* her. Not really. It was years and years ago I—I don't don't know what you want from *me*." But his eyes flickered from side to side slyly, and he chewed the thumb. Mendoza's interest quickened. Gerard an oddball, not looking just so stable. The pretty girl Michele, and Gerard? Well, some time back—five, six years, more? But, Michele's first boyfriend.

"Mr. Gerard—"

"What? What did you say? A week ago last night? A week ago Mon—" Gerard whirled. "That's when she was killed—" He looked around the room wildly. "I don't know anything about it, about anything, and I don't have to answer your questions—"

"Where were you that night, Mr. Gerard? Do you live here with your parents?"

"With Mother. I was here, that's all, right here. I won't talk to you any more!" He turned and ran out of the room fast and a door slammed on the other side of the house.

Well, well, thought Mendoza. *Muy interesante.* Gerard certainly unstable to say the least, whatever he might have been when Michele dated him. And if Michele hadn't seen him recently—if, on impulse, she'd phoned him— Look a little harder at Gerard.

He let himself out of the house just as a middle-aged woman got out of a car in the drive. She got a bag of groceries from the back seat, started toward the house, and stopped as she saw Mendoza. Her eyes widened. She set the bag of groceries down on the low cement wall round the front yard, as he came up to her. "And who might you be?"

Mendoza introduced himself, showed the badge. "Oh," she said. "Oh! Is—is Lester in any trouble? Police—"

"You're Mrs. Gerard?"

"Yes. Yes, I'm Mrs. Gerard." She might once have been pretty, but she hadn't bothered about the cosmetics, the professional hairstyling, in a long while. By the house, the middle-aged Dodge in the drive, the shabby wool dress she wore, he deduced, no money.

"I just had a few questions to ask your son, Mrs. Gerard—" He let that trail off deliberately, his tone doubtful, and her lined face crumpled and she put up a hand as if to ward off a blow.

"I've been so afraid—so afraid he'll—not like himself, oh, I don't know what to do—dropping out of college, and I don't know where he is half the time—I've been worried to death! Just—what was it you—" Her eyes were frightened.

"Mrs. Gerard, can you remember a week ago last night? Monday night last week. Do you remember if Lester was here with you?"

"A week ago Monday night," she said dully. "Yes. Yes, I do—because—he'd promised me—he'd stay home one evening at least—with me—the way he used to. And then—he didn't. He went out somewhere, I don't know where. Took the car. There was a phone call—about eight o'clock—and he just went out without saying—anything—"

Mendoza's interest in Lester Gerard sharpened to fever-pitch. And the woman watched with her terrified eyes as he thanked her abruptly and went down the walk to the long black Ferrari waiting there. Do a little research on Lester Gerard, he thought, and then a lot more questioning.

At four-fifteen Landers and Piggott arrived back at the rooming house on Eleventh Street. This time the motherly landlady was not quite so welcoming; she'd been having second thoughts about police coming.

"I ought to've asked you before, what on earth police want with Bill? I know he gets in debt, and gambling and all, but he wouldn't be in police trouble! What do you *want* with him?"

"Is he here, ma'am?" asked Piggott.

"I don't reckon I ought to say unless—well, yes, he's here," she said reluctantly. "Bill wouldn't do nothing real bad—" She led them up the stairs slowly, and rapped at the door at the head of the landing. "Martha!"

The door opened. A pretty blonde girl in her early twenties, heavy in pregnancy, looked at them dully. She had a pink chiffon peignoir wrapped around her, clutching it together modestly.

"Martha, it's a couple of policemen. They want to see Bill."

"*Policemen?*" said the girl. "Why, whatever for? Bill! Come here, honey—it's for you."

The man who came up behind her slowly and looked at them over her head wasn't quite so young—maybe thirty. He looked like the description they'd had from Haverkamp—the spiritual description, Landers thought Piggott might call it. He was goodlooking in a flamboyant way, the cheap clothes too colorful, the brilliantined hair and a foppish little moustache. He was fairly tall, but narrow-shouldered, and he looked at them with a rather sickly would-be-brash grin.

"Mr. Vincent—"

"That's me. You cops? What can I do for cops?" he asked cockily.

"Mr. Vincent," and Landers felt sorry for the blonde, "we'd like you to come downtown with us to answer some questions."

"*What?*" said Martha Vincent. "Why? Bill hasn't done anything!"

"I'm not goin' anyplace," said Vincent, looking very frightened. "Anything you got to ask, you can ask here." He put his arm around his wife.

"Have it your way," said Landers. "When you were still working for Mr. Haverkamp a couple of weeks ago, you sold a TV antenna to a Mr. Weiss on Leeward Avenue."

"D-did I? Yeah, I guess so. What about it?"

"Mr. Weiss paid you a hundred and ten dollars in cash. Not many people keep that much cash around, do they? Did you wonder if maybe there was more where that came from? Did you go back there a few days ago—really strapped for money now—maybe having cased the house and seen that Mr. and Mrs. Weiss were working in the backyard—"

Not a muscle moved in Vincent's face, but his eyes moved. By God, thought Landers, is this another jackpot? The idiotic citizen suddenly deciding he knew who, all this time after, and being right? It was ridiculous.

"And then you didn't get anything after all, did you? The woman came in and surprised you. And you—"

"You must be nuts," said the blonde. "Bill wouldn't—how come you think any such crazy—"

"Mr. Vincent," said Landers, "Mr. Weiss identifies you."

"Oh, my God," he said tiredly. His wife looked up at him blankly.

"Identifies you as the man who stabbed—"

"*Stabbed* somebody?" Martha Vincent laughed. "*Bill?* Oh, you got to be kidding!"

157

And Vincent turned and buried his face in one arm against the door-jamb, and began to beat the flat of his other hand senselessly against the wall. "Oh, God, oh, God," he said. "I was scared—I was just scared! That old man—the wad of cash. And everybody after me—and Martha—and losing the job and I—I thought, easy, both of them out back—and I'd just found that old trunk, I had the knife out to pry it—and then she came in and I was *scared!* I never even knew I'd touched her with the knife—I just wanted to get away, get away—"

And Landers still didn't believe it.

"Talk about jackpots," said Hackett, coming in to hear about that. "The citizens—you just never do know what they're going to come up with. But, another one cleaned up, and getting on for the end of another day."

They'd got a statement from Vincent, after reciting the little piece about his rights, and Piggott had taken him down to book him in. "What next?" said Hackett, yawning. "That thing on Luis' own doorstep still gets me. As it would any man with kids, my God. . . ."

Mendoza came home to a household still talking about that. "I just canna believe it," Mrs. MacTaggart was saying. "I canna get over it. That boy—"

"We think there were relatives," said Alison. "Máiri remembers her mentioning a sister back east. They'll—get the other boy, won't they? The relatives?"

"I should think so," said Mendoza inattentively. "Yes, *cara*, nine days' wonder, but I've got enough to worry about on my own beat without borrowing Wilcox Street's troubles. . . . That damn suicide that isn't, and the more I think about Gerard, how could Michele—"

"But such a thing, Luis! The whole block's been out all day talking about nothing else." The twins came to pounce on him, and Cedric wandered up and politely offered a hairy paw in greeting.

"Daddy, Daddy, come read *los cuentos!*"

"*Los cuentos* 'bout nellephants—Daddy—"

"And how can I read *los cuentos* if you monsters are strangling me?"

Alison extricated him. "Daddy'll come read to you in just a little while, *honestamente*. There, we're both doing it too. They'll have to get languages sorted out some time! But honestly, Luis—there've been reporters and more cops and a lab truck and I don't know what—"

"Yes, Barth knows his job," said Mendoza, stripping off his jacket. "I've had quite a day myself—I need a drink." He started for the kitchen, and El Señor appeared from nowhere to follow, demanding his share. "That suicide—¡ca!" he said, watching El Señor lap rye. "And Gerard—"

"I just canna take it *in*," said Máiri, shaking her silver curls. "And I'll be saying some special prayers for that poor boy."

"Luis, you promised to read to them—"

"Domesticities!" said Mendoza.

Hackett went home and told Angel about the murder on Luis' doorstep. "*That* awful—I saw it in tonight's paper, but I didn't—right across the *street* from them? What a *thing!* I'll bet Alison's tried to call—I've been out all day, what with one thing and—goodness, I must call Alison after dinner."

"Enough to make a man think," said Hackett, eyeing Mark Christopher lying full-length on the floor wielding crayons.

"Oh, don't be silly," said Angel. "We're bringing them up right, Art—the discipline and all. That is—" Sheila tottered up to him lifting appealing arms and he picked her up.

"How's my Sheila? You know, her hair *is* going to be curly—and sort of reddish like my mother's—"

"That is," said Angel, "always providing I can prevent you from spoiling her to death. And if I'm any judge, that Higgins is even worse. Honestly, men."

"What?" said Hackett.

Higgins went home and told Mary about the murder on Luis' doorstep. "For heaven's sake!" she said. "His own—! It's hard to believe. The things that happen these— And yes, I'm fine. You fuss, George."

"About you I fuss. And the kids. A family I never had before. Oh, I just remember my mother—"

Mary's gray eyes smiled up at him. "It just isn't natural, you acting diffident, that's all. Humble."

"Me?" said Higgins, surprised. And the kids came into the dinette where Mary was setting the table. Laura had a library book importantly open.

"George! I got Mother to get this out of the library—it's got all the names there *are* in it—it's a dictionary of names, see, George—and I found a just absolutely perfect name for a baby boy! Courtenay, isn't that a beautiful name, George? I wasn't sure if I liked it better than Gareth, but I decided just now—"

"It's a crazy name," said Steve. "Christabel. That's the one I pick. Christabel Eugenia."

"My God!" said Higgins. "Listen, Steve. With Higgins for a last name?"

"Well, I suppose she'll get married someday," said Steve. "I picked some others if you don't like that one. Ariadne—that's a nice one. Or Cassandra."

"You don't even know it's a girl!" said Laura impatiently. "And I picked some others too, so you and Mother have a choice, George," she added virtuously. "Conrad is *sort* of nice—or Desmond. And—"

"You two!" said Mary. "I've decided too, and it's my baby after all. If it's a boy he'll be David George."

"And I do guess," said Higgins, "if that homicide on Luis' doorstep says anything to me, it says this and that about discipline and authority. And proper respect for your elders and betters, you kids. This isn't your baby, you know."

"Well, but, George—" began Laura.

"And if it's a girl she's going to be named after my mother. Margaret Emily. And *that's* final," said Higgins sternly.

"Margaret Emily," said Mary. "It's nice—I like it, George. I like it very much—a nice old-fashioned name. So that's settled, and we'll hear no more about it."

"Christabel's a lot *classier* sounding name," said Steve mournfully.

THIRTEEN

Wednesday morning, and Glasser off. As Landers came into the office, Palliser was telling Grace about the homicide on Mendoza's own doorstep, and Grace was exclaiming incredulously. They had both just greeted Landers when Sergeant Lake turned from the switchboard and said that was the D.A.'s office, they were yelling for the officers who had handled the Yocum case, a conference in order.

Palliser looked resigned and Grace grim. "So tell the boss where we are," said Palliser. "That's us—come on, Jase."

Landers said, "Morning," to Piggott as he came in, and looked into Mendoza's office. Mendoza was saying to Hackett and Higgins, "*Condenación*, all up in the air you can say—not one solid fact, damn it, or at least damn few. All I say is, that motley crew of Eileen's will be well dried out and sobered up and it won't do any harm to question them again— Oh, Tom."

"If you're trying to rope me in," said Landers, "I thought I'd better look at that Hanson thing, Lieutenant."

"Just what you will be looking at." Mendoza looked annoyed. He was smoking rapidly; he was dapper as always in charcoal-gray dacron, snowy shirt, silk tie; and evidently he intended to get out and around himself, for the perennial wide-brimmed black Homburg—he must, thought Landers, have them specially made now—waited on the desk. "The autopsy report on that's in. Here it is. That damned thing. Of course it's the husband, ninety percent sure. Had his eye on another woman or just wanted to be rid of this one. Go and look. I think we may have a real lead on Michele—we'll be on that."

Landers took the report and shared it with Piggott. Who said,

"You know I've got to cover that Weiss inquest at ten o'clock. That was an odd one, that Vincent."

The autopsy report said that Gerda Hanson (and by the description of the body she hadn't been a glamorous wife—overweight, arthritic) had died of a fractured skull inflicted between one and three P.M. last Monday afternoon. The contusions on the throat were postmortem.

"The husband, most likely, all right," said Landers. "This job makes us all cynics. Let's go and ask some questions. . . . I wonder if he has got a lead on Michele. That is the strangest thing we've had in a while."

Jan Hanson and his wife had lived in an apartment on Bimini Street. They drove over there in Landers' car and went in. Two apartments down, two up: no manager living on the premises. The front door of the right-hand apartment downstairs was open, and John Elderby was sitting by the window in there smoking a cigar and reading a newspaper. He got up when Landers rang the door-bell.

"Oh," he said to the badge. "Anything I can do—more about poor Mrs. Hanson? I suppose you got a lot of red tape these days too."

"Yes, Mr. Elderby. Did you know Mr. and Mrs. Hanson well?"

"Well—just like other tenants, you know. Usually see him come and go—my door's usually open. Nice quiet people, acourse she didn't hardly go out at all. Had the arthritis and all, poor lady."

"Well," said Landers, "last Monday afternoon, Mr. Elderby. Mr. Hanson came home about six-thirty, you saw him start upstairs, and in a very short time he came running back down, you went up with him and helped him break in the bathroom there. Yes." Obviously Hanson hadn't done it then, by the autopsy. She'd been dead by at least three o'clock. "The door was locked, but was the key in it, inside?" Had he noticed?

"Nope," he said. "It was on the bathroom floor."

"Yes," said Landers. The lab report had noted that.

"Acourse we had to break the door in. It musta been in the lock inside and fell out when we—" Elderby looked slightly puzzled. "Why you asking? Maybe Mr. Hanson could say if it was in the door before, he tried the door and all before comin' down for me. He's home, didn't go to work this mornin', still all broke up, you know. You could ask him."

Landers considered. He didn't want to tackle Hanson yet. Get some more facts, if possible, first. "Mr. Elderby, do you mind if we look at your bathroom?"

Elderby looked astonished. "Well, I don't *mind*—but what in tarnation—"

They went in and looked. Apartments in the same building tended to sameness. And the door to Elderby's bathroom had a gap between its bottom and the floor a good inch deep. Landers looked at Piggott, who said, "Very easy. Lock the door on the outside and shove the key under the door. No locked-room puzzle, Tom."

"No," said Landers. "There won't be any more lab evidence to get now. And even if they picked up prints, well, he lives there too."

"Sure," said Piggott.

"What in time are you fellows talking about?" asked Elderby.

"Thanks so much, Mr. Elderby," said Landers. They went out to the sidewalk. "Let's go see his pharmacy."

That was on Virgil Avenue. It was more than a pharmacy—Hanson's European word—it was a modestly thriving independent drugstore, with all the sundries a drugstore carries, and besides three customers at the moment there was an elderly man in a white jacket behind the counter labeled *Prescriptions*, and a gray-haired fat woman in a blue rayon smock behind the cosmetics counter. She was waiting on a young woman sampling cologne. Landers and Piggott went up to the man, introduced themselves.

"Oh, yes, sir. About poor Mrs. Hanson? We were so shocked—a terrible thing. My name's Parsons, sir."

"Do you work here full time, Mr. Parsons?"

"Oh, no, sir. I just spell Mr. Hanson as a pharmacist. Tuesdays and Thursdays and Sunday afternoons. I'm retired really, live with my daughter Anna. We were all shocked about Mrs. Hanson—suicide—the poor woman hadn't been well, I understand—and poor Mr. Hanson, such a blow it's been to him."

"You weren't here on Monday, then?"

"No, sir, I wasn't. I didn't hear about it till the next day. Why, Mr. Hanson had been at our place just the night before—he comes most Sunday nights to play chess with me, you see—the one little diversion he allowed himself, of course she needed some waiting on—"

Landers thanked him, choked him off politely, and approached the woman as the customer went out. She said all the same things Parsons had said. "So devoted to his wife, such a fine man, Mr.

Hanson. What? Oh, my name is Philpotts. Thomasina Philpotts. Mrs. What? Well, I'm here all the time, yes. I'm in charge of all the cosmetics and cologne and all like that. Yes, I was here on Monday, why?"

"Was Mr. Hanson here all day?" asked Landers.

"Why, yes, he was. I thought you knew—it wasn't till he went home about six-thirty that he found her. Dreadful. The poor man—"

"He must have gone to lunch?" said Piggott.

"Oh, he usually does, yes, up to the luncheonette right up the block, but he was working on his tax forms and he didn't, Monday. He asked me to bring him a sandwich when I went to lunch—that was twelve to one, but I didn't take the full hour, I was back by twenty to. No, he was here all day," said Mrs. Philpotts brightly. "Why?"

"Er—Mrs. Philpotts. Between one and three that afternoon, you were here? All the time?"

"Yes, I just said so. We were quite busy, as I recall. There were several regular customers with prescriptions, and—"

"You're sure of that?" said Landers. "That Mr. Hanson was right here then? You could swear to it?"

She was indignant. "Of course I'm sure of it! Why? Of course he was here! Ever since nine that morning. And so was I, except for about half an hour, forty minutes, when I went for lunch—I knew he was busy with those tax things, I came back right away to save him having to wait on people. Why?"

"Well, thank you," said Landers. Outside, he looked at Piggott. "She sounds straight. Unless she's a great actress. So, not Hanson? Who?"

"It looks like a little mystery, Tom," said Piggott, looking at his watch. "I'll leave you to it for a while—I've got to attend that inquest."

Landers drove him back to headquarters, wondering. Mrs. Philpotts looked and sounded like an honest woman. Dropping Piggott, he went back and talked with her some more, putting out a little charm; and she unbent. It emerged that she had a husband, two daughters and four grandchildren—she showed him snapshots of all of them—and he really didn't think she was either conspiring with Hanson or bribed to back up the alibi. It was an honest to God alibi. The little mystery.

If not Hanson, who?

Hackett emerged from the jail on Alameda at ten-thirty feeling frustrated. "All I say is," Mendoza had argued, "they're all cold sober, sitting there waiting for the indictment on the Narco charge. There's a better chance we'd get the truth out of them now. They ought to be talked to again. Go and see what you get, Art."

Hackett had talked to them. All of them separately—Eileen Rodney and her crew of kids that had opted out of the social scene via dope. Because it was still very much up in the air about Michele, and she could have wound up there that night.

Now, he didn't think so. A very sober and surly Eileen had told him wearily that she hadn't seen the little creep in a week or so before then. And Tommy—all of them now looked strangely clean, and the boys' hair had been cut, probably under protest—Tommy had said with dreary frankness, "Look, man, we had a li'l pot party that night, sure, an' like if you'd said eleven o'clock, midnight, sure, maybe nobody'd remember who was there, what doin'. But eight o'clock you say. And then, people just startin' to drop in, see, nobody high on anythin', we was just gettin' started. That kid wasn't there. I don't remember the phone rang at all."

"Are you sure of the night? Monday night a week ago?" This kind, what did days mean to them?

"I'm sure. Sure it was. Reason I know," said Tommy, "Buck was there. Buck Hendry. He just got out that mornin', I run into him and invite him come up, see? And he came. That night. He'd just got out that mornin'—"

"Out of where?"

"Here," said Tommy, surprised. "He got thirty days, see, an' he'd just got out." He eyed Hackett resentfully. "That's how I know what day. He said he'd just got out, an' he oughta know."

"So he had," said Hackett, and sent him back to his cell and asked to look at some records. Sure enough, one Samuel Clarence Hendry had been released that Monday, after serving a thirty-day sentence for possession of marijuana.

Thirty days, thought Hackett. The slap on the wrist. But that did, in a way, substantiate Tommy's tale. Unless they were all lying, which Hackett didn't think was likely. Or even possible: given this kind, their minds befuddled with the habitual alcohol, the drugs, could they remember to tell the same lie? So, did that clear Eileen and her crowd out of it?

Hackett thought about Luis' perennial maxim for astute detection: the idiot boy and the lost horse. What the hell *had* happened to Michele Stanyard that night? If he were Michele, the pretty sheltered young thing, deciding to ditch a fiancé temporarily, where—?

Maybe he hadn't enough imagination.

Nobody was at home at the Gerard place, so as the next bit of routine Mendoza and Higgins presented themselves at the Beverly Hills Police Department. It was an old but dignified building downtown, and a Captain Mundy gave them chairs in his office and asked, "How can we help the big-city boys, Lieutenant?"

"We're interested," said Mendoza, "in a Lester Gerard of your fair city. Does the name ring any bells? Is he in your records anywhere?"

"It rings a very faint bell," said Mundy, frowning, "but I can't—just a minute." He got up, went to the door and said, "Sergeant." Another man came in, a chubby big man with a placid, rather stupid-looking face. "Sergeant Steinberg. Our local deadeye. He never forgets anything."

"I forgot our wedding anniversary two years ago," said Steinberg. "I'm still getting reminded of it."

"Joe, why does the name Lester Gerard ring a very tiny bell in my head?"

Steinberg sniffed. "The Topaz Room."

"The—oh, is he?" asked Mundy. "One of those?"

"Never been charged," said Steinberg. "Frisked there, nearly every time we pull a raid."

"Oh," said Mundy.

"The Topaz Room?" said Mendoza.

"Local fag hangout. We don't like these places around—try to discourage 'em," said Mundy. "Pull the unexpected raids every so often, act a little tough, maybe some day we'll put it out of business. It's run by one Angelo Fantino. Occasionally we find a customer with some stuff on him—Mary Jane usually—but that doesn't involve Fantino, unfortunately."

"Oh, is that so?" said Higgins. "So he's a known fag. Since when?"

Steinberg said, "Seem to remember we've spotted him there all the way back to four years or so when the place opened."

"*¡Qué interesante es!*" said Mendoza. "You know, George, she wouldn't have known that—Michele—obviously. He wasn't, or not so definitely, when he dated her years back. Under family pressure?

166

But, George, being one like that, the ambivalent attitude to women, if she did call him that night—that kind unstable anyway—"

"Now wait just a minute, Luis—"

"—might have been just the kind to—"

"But, Luis, would he have gone to meet her?" asked Higgins reasonably. "Suppose she did call him. From way down there in L.A. For some reason, called him—and we've just been told that he's been running with homos at least four years so it's at least that long, probably more, since she's dated him or maybe even seen him—called and said, I'm ditching my date, come get me. *Would* he have? He wouldn't have been less interested."

"*¡Diez millones de demonios!*" said Mendoza. The Beverly Hills cops were listening interestedly. "But, damn it, George, his mother said he got a phone call about the right time and took off—"

"There are a lot of other people in L.A. County besides Michele Stanyard," said Higgins. "I just say you're reading too much into it."

"If it's any help to you," said Steinberg, "I can give you some names of other fags he seems to pal with. We try to keep an eye on 'em. There's Don Merchant and Eddy Corning—hang around that place a good deal. Eddy is one of Gerard's close pals—comes all the way from Pasadena. Don lives in Malibu."

"It's just unlikely," said Higgins, "now we hear he is a fag."

"We've got to check it out. I know it is, but damn it, the whole case is unlikely too," said Mendoza.

"This is that Stanyard thing?" asked Mundy. "You haven't got anywhere on it?"

"It is all up in the air," said Mendoza. "Well, let's have the addresses. The routine has to be done."

Piggott wandered into Federico's just as Landers was sitting down, and joined him. Landers was talking to himself about Hanson. "I just can't figure it," he said. Hackett came up to the table and sat down, looking glum. "I've now got it established that it couldn't have been Hanson who pulled off the actual murder."

"That pseudo-suicide," said Hackett. "I'll have the steak sandwich, Adam."

"He's o-u-t out," said Landers. "You can bring me a Scotch and water and the small steak. You shouldn't have the sandwich, Art—all the bread. Damn it, he's absolutely clear. It's a neighborhood store—I went asking, took some names from his prescription list, and I've talked to four customers who were in that drugstore on

Monday afternoon at one-twenty, two o'clock, two-fifteen and a quarter to three. We went into detail on the times and that's pinned down pretty sure. Now the apartment is sixteen blocks from the drugstore, through traffic. A man couldn't walk it in under half an hour at least, and he wouldn't be such a fool as to take his car—never any parking places along a narrow old street like that and if he drove into the drive, his garage, he'd be seen. And when he got there, he'd have to bang her on the head, and then somehow hoist her up hanging from the shower-rod, pull the business with the door, and get back to the store. It'd have taken him at the very least an hour, and I think longer. He couldn't have done it. He didn't do it. So who did? Set up the phony suicide? Who had any reason to?"

"She wasn't anybody," said Piggott. "A nonentity. The fat, deaf old wife of a smalltime druggist. No money. No—"

"Well, we don't know that," said Landers thoughtfully. "I wonder if she had. And then there's another thing, Matt. Yes, old and fat and deaf and arthritic. But he's quite a goodlooking fellow—virile-looking. That blond hair. He looks younger than he is, maybe. Maybe—"

"The other woman," said Hackett. "That could be too, Tom."

"But even if there was," said Landers, exasperated, "how could he have done it? It's impossible. Nobody else would do it for him out of sympathy—and you don't tell me a woman did it—she weighed a hundred and eighty—and I doubt very much whether Hanson's got the kind of money to pay a hired dropper—even if he knew how to find one." He swallowed Scotch and water moodily.

"It's a funny one," agreed Hackett. "I wonder what Luis and George are getting—if anything. That's a damned funny one too, Michele. Shapeless. The only really solid facts, there she was in her green lace evening dress, dead. Hardly a mark on her, the diamonds gone, and no leads whatever. . . . I'm back to thinking about Trulock, because I think Eileen and that crowd are out of the running."

"I think," said Piggott, "we should just lay both the queer things before the Lord and ask for a little help on it."

"The Lord," said Landers, "helps those who help themselves, Matt."

They went on kicking it around over lunch, and had just divided the tip and got up, at one-fifteen, when Palliser and Grace came in. They were both looking annoyed and wilted. Palliser had taken his tie off, and Grace's was under one ear, unprecedented for the fastidious Grace.

"What wringer have you been through?" asked Hackett.

Grace snarled and sat down. "Adam, I'll have a double Scotch. Quick."

Palliser sat down. "I'll have some aspirin if you've got any. We've had a session, Art, with the D.A. and—"

It seemed that one of the more militant black organizations had taken up the Yocums' case and hired a battery of high-powered attorneys who were making various charges of discrimination and violated rights and intimidation, and trying to get the charge reduced or wiped out entirely.

"Annoying," said Hackett, and both Palliser and Grace snarled.

"Don't speak to me," said Grace. "Especially not if you're going to try to be funny with understatements. There isn't a word in the Thesaurus for what it is." He took up his drink.

"But I don't see how they can do it, Jase," said Palliser. "The inquest brought it in first degree homicide. It *was* rat-poison, after all. We've got a good case—the D.A. said he wished to hell it was a better one, but—"

"I am taking no bets," said Grace.

"Well, we'll hold some good thoughts on it," said Hackett.

"Damn it, the routine," said Landers, on the sidewalk outside Hanson's drugstore. They'd come back to arrange for Mrs. Philpotts to come down to the office and make a formal statement—if they ever got anywhere on this, the D.A. liked the formal statements—and on stepping in, Landers had spotted Hanson behind the pharmacy counter, Hanson grave and urbane and white-jacketed. He wasn't by any means ready to tackle Hanson on this, and he could hope that Mrs. Philpotts hadn't said much to him about what they'd asked her. He came out to the street again. "Parsons said he usually spells him just Tuesdays, Thursdays and Sunday afternoons. Hanson playing the grief-stricken husband—Parsons completely sold on him. Who the hell, Matt? Who could have set it up? And where else do we look on it?"

Higgins stopped for lunch in Glendale and got over to Pasadena police headquarters at one-thirty. They had, with the blessings of Captain Mundy, gone to question Fantino, the proprietor of that fag hangout, and wasted some time on it, getting exactly nothing.

So then they'd found that Don Merchant, in a ramshackle beach cottage up in Malibu, and wasted more time getting nothing from him. They knew he knew Gerard, he couldn't deny that, but according to him he hadn't seen Gerard in a while, didn't know where he'd been or what he'd been doing.

So Mendoza drove them back to headquarters, and Higgins started for Pasadena in his own car, to find Eddy Corning. Which would probably be another waste of time, but the routine had to be done.

The address he had for Eddy was on Queensberry Street. It was a little old frame house. The woman who answered the door was gray and tired-looking and middle-aged, in a shabby house-dress and ancient bedroom slippers. She looked frightened at the looming craggy-featured Higgins there on her front porch, and at his proffered badge. She said in a thin voice, "Eddy? He's not here. He's in jail. They got Eddy in jail." And then she began to cry and shut the door in his face. And that was why he ended up at Pasadena police headquarters.

He was welcomed as a diversion by the desk-man. "What can we do for L.A., Sergeant?" Higgins asked for somebody familiar with the Vice situation. He was taken upstairs and introduced to a Lieutenant Waterford and two sergeants, Klein and Purcell.

"Eddy Corning," he said. "I understand you've got him in your jail. What for, when, and who else with him maybe?"

Waterford looked surprised. "You said you're Central Homicide? What's your interest in this cheap little fag, Sergeant?"

"We are," said Higgins with a sigh, "busy at the routine. Clearing up as we go along. He just showed as connected to a possible suspect, though I think he's about as unlikely as you can get, but we have to look."

"Well," said Klein, "Eddy has been on our books for some time. Just a fag. At the couple of known fag hangouts, picked up once in a while, the places raided. He's got a small pedigree—D. and D., petty theft. Funnily enough he hasn't been spotted at any of those places for about, oh, six months—"

"No. He found a new pal, maybe a couple of them, down in Beverly Hills," said Higgins. "He's been spotted there at the fag place."

"Well, do tell," said Klein. "Anyway, we dropped on Eddy kind of unexpectedly about ten days ago. Traffic got a 415 call to this place, and it was quite a little donnybrook, Eddy and another one named Katz and a local pusher—"

"Who was loose on a leash in the hope he'd lead you to the supplier," nodded Higgins. "Eddy a user?"

"Not that we knew. Maybe he'd just taken it up. Far as we could make out, there'd been an argument going on for some time over the price—and they all three had the stuff on them, Mary Jane, so we brought them in. The other guy who showed up, no—he was clean, we let him go."

"What other guy?"

"One that walked in just after the squad-car got there. Friend of Eddy's," said Purcell. "We frisked 'em and so on—I went out on it when I heard the pusher was there—but he hadn't anything on him, he hadn't been mixed up in the brawl."

"What was his name? I'm taking bets," said Higgins.

"I took it down," and Purcell reached for his notebook. "Lester Gerard. He said Eddy'd called him, said he was in trouble, needed some bread, so like a good pal he—"

"Oh, yes," said Higgins sadly. "Give me some times." They had to do a little looking, but police records are precise. The squad-car had got the call at nine-ten, and arrived at the disturbance at nine-thirteen, and it had, of course, been that Monday night a week back. The night Michele had been murdered. Just after the squad-car men broke up the fight, Gerard had walked in, call it nine-fifteen. "Yes," said Higgins, "so that was his eight o'clock call. Eddy. It took him that long to drive up here. So, just as I thought, Gerard hadn't one damned thing to do with Michele Stanyard, and thank you so much for pointing it out." He got up.

"That's being a tough one?" asked Waterford.

"There's nothing *to* it," said Higgins. "One of those things with no handle to get hold of. She was in the restaurant—boom—she vanished away. Not a single lead. Except, of course, Trulock. And I'm beginning to think maybe we ought to look at Trulock all over again. Well, thanks."

Landers, after looking all around the problem and seeing no way to get anything solid on it at all without taking the bull by the horns, did just that at three-thirty that afternoon. Piggot had been saying it was the only thing to do since they'd had lunch.

They went into the drugstore—it could be a little goldmine for Hanson, thought Landers—and found Mrs. Philpotts waiting on a woman buying face powder and Hanson just handing a prescription bottle to an elderly man at that counter.

"There you are, Mr. Andrews—fifteen makes seven, eight, nine and ten," as he counted out bills. He looked at Landers and Piggott, recognizing them for what they were, and his expression fell into sadness. "You want to see me, gentlemen? It is more of the—red tape? This is all very sad for me, but one must keep up. The other officer, he did not say when I might have the—to make the arrangements—"

"Well, Mr. Hanson," said Landers deliberately, "right now we're wondering just who might have had reason to murder your wife." He spoke loud enough for Mrs. Philpotts to hear; she looked up and stared.

Hanson went gray-white. He stammered, "To m-murder—to—"

"Because she was murdered, you know," said Landers. "Deliberately murdered, Mr. Hanson. She didn't die of hanging—she was hit on the head and her skull fractured, and that's what she died of. Then somebody put the clothesline around her neck and hung her up on the shower-rod. Our police surgeon—" he stopped.

For Hanson was, it seemed, literally swelling. His face turned an alarming crimson and he said chokingly, "*Verdammt Sudetener!* This idiot—this *Blodsinniger*—he can't even do that efficiently—he—" Landers thought he'd have a stroke then and there. He raised impotent fists, nearly strangling on his fury. "This *verdammt Pfuscher*—I *tell* him what to do, just how to do it—*mein Gott*, even a simple thing like—"

Landers and Piggott looked at each other. And Landers said sharply, "Who, Hanson? Who?"

"*Gott*—a simple little thing like this is—*es ist Wahnsinn!* This Rudi, *mein Gott*—Rudi Schultz—but he shall pay! You shall have him to hang! He is a fool, but I had thought he could accomplish such a simple—" Hanson grabbed Landers' arm; his face worked convulsively, he was gibbering with rage. "*Ach*, he shall pay for his idiocy—this—this—I will tell you—"

He told them this and that before he collapsed, and they called an ambulance. The interns said, not a stroke, a simple faint, but his blood pressure was shocking. They took him to the General for observation. And Landers and Piggott went to pick up Rudi Schultz.

Schultz worked at a service station on Vermont Avenue. He was an ingenuous young fellow about twenty-five, from a little town in southern Germany. And he was, it emerged, in the country illegally. An uncle of his back home, knowing he'd jumped ship in San Francisco, knowing Hanson from years back in the old country, had asked Hanson to help Rudi, find him a job. And so when Hanson wanted a little job of murder done, with a nice safe alibi for himself, there was Rudi to hand. The threat to hold over him—Hanson could get Rudi deported.

They brought him back to the office and asked him questions. He wrinkled his broad brow and answered them after painful thought.

"I think there is another woman he wishes marry with," he said. But that was all he knew of the reason—any reason. "He says, he will in her coffee put something to make her sleep. Always the coffee he makes before he goes to work. But she is not asleep." He looked at them stolidly. "And me, I'm strong, *ja*, but she's a big fat woman—she fights me, what to do? I got to quiet make her, so I can do like he says, put the rope on. I hit her with my wrench. It is my back pocket in, I come there from my job when I go to have dinner, half after twelve. Is all. I think, O.K."

"How did you get into the apartment, Rudi?" asked Landers. This too was one for the books.

"How? Oh, he has the key give me. All he says to do, I do. About the key, too—the door to the bathroom I lock and the key put the door under. Everything he tell me, I remember," said Rudi with naive pride.

"My God," said Landers. "My God, Matt. He didn't see anything wrong with it at all? Killing a woman? Just like that?"

"The devil," said Piggott, "is busy these days, Tom. Of course, he's not very bright—Rudi, that is—the devil, Tom, is all too bright —and not very what you might call sensitive. But all the same—"

"Yes, all the same," said Landers. "My God. And Hanson just coming apart like that—with luck we'll get 'em both, Conspiracy to commit. What a thing."

"We seem to be getting the offbeat things," said Piggott.

Piggott went to choir practise after he'd had dinner, and told Prudence Russell all about the offbeat homicide across the street from the Lieutenant's house. "For heaven's sake!" said Prudence. "What an awful—"

"Enough to make you wonder about getting married at all," said Piggott. "Producing offspring."

173

"Oh, well, really, Matt," said Prudence. "I mean, if you bring them up right—that's silly to say, just because—" She bit her lip, looking at thin dark pessimistic Piggott.

Mendoza heard about the high-powered attorneys on the Yocum thing and did a little cussing about that, but he went home talking more to himself about Michele Stanyard.

"Because as a rule *something* shows up eventually," he said to Alison as he shrugged out of his jacket. "*Some* kind of lead. Oh, hell, some we have to throw in Pending, but a thing like this—beautiful socialite—hardly the anonymous knifing over on the Row—"

"Yes, *amante*. Something will," said Alison. "Don't fuss so, Luis, you'll be getting high blood pressure. . . . Mrs. Spencer's sister is here, poor woman. She came to ask us about—and all we could tell her, of course—"

"It doesn't make sense," said Mendoza irritably. "Vanishing from that nice respectable restaurant—and not one solid lead on it at all, in ten days!" He had seen Hackett's and Higgins' reports by then.

"For goodness' sake," said Alison, "leave the job downtown, Luis!"

"The mystery we do so seldom get. The odd little mystery—just what the hell did happen to Michele?"

"You and your 'satiable curiosity,'" said Alison. "Dinner in ten minutes."

FOURTEEN

Thursday morning, and Hackett was off. The rain had stopped two days ago and today was sunny and warmer. There was a report signed by Galeano on Mendoza's desk—just as the Traffic shift was changing, at six this morning, a body had been found in the gutter along Beverly Boulevard between Rampart and Coronado. Galeano had left it for the day men.

When Landers came in, Mendoza handed him that one. "At least you untangled the pseudo-suicide, Tom. Yes, I saw your report."

"He just came apart—it was almost funny," said Landers. "But the other one, my God, just as casual as if he'd been talking about a picnic. And I hope those warrants come through today— What's this?"

"New corpse. Go see what it looks like."

Higgins and Palliser came in together, and Higgins sat down beside Mendoza's desk, lit a cigarette, and said, "Luis, I have the feeling we go back to the beginning on Michele."

"The beginning," said Mendoza, "being Paul Trulock." He swiveled around and stared out at the nice sunny day.

"You saw what turned up on Gerard. He's nothing—he hasn't a damn thing to do with it. It was far-fetched to think she'd phone him, anyway. Maybe she didn't phone anybody."

"After all," said Palliser, "Trulock was there. I mean, just because—"

"Yes, I had that little thought too," said Mendoza. "You mean—"

"That's how he got to be a Lieutenant, John. Waits till some bright junior says something profound, and then says he already thought of that."

"¡Ay de mí!" Mendoza laughed. "What you were going to say

175

is, just because I've got a dime in my pocket, it doesn't mean I have to make a phone call."

"That was it," said Higgins. "We thought she hadn't any money on her, so we said she couldn't have intended to ditch Trulock. Then we heard she had some money—that Mexican newsboy—so we galloped off in all directions on the premise that because she had money on her, and could have made a phone call, or taken a bus somewhere, she did."

"*Pues sí*," said Mendoza. "I see it, George. But Trulock—"

"It's possible," said Palliser, "that it was pretty simple, just as you said before we heard about the money. There were people coming and going—that cashier, Margot Guillaume, couldn't be sure Michele didn't just come out of the ladies' room and go out to join Trulock."

"All right," said Mendoza, and swiveled back. "Let's go back and see what we know, definitely. They had a little spat over dinner, according to Trulock. It could have been a big spat. Over, he says, Eileen the improper friend for Michele. In passing, why didn't we think about that? It might have been about something else—we don't know. Though the waitress says she didn't see any signs of argument, so probably, like nice well-bred high-class people, they weren't letting it show. Which maybe says it wasn't really much of a spat? Anyway, they leave the table. Michele heads for the ladies' room, and Madame Gallard saw her go in. Nobody in there then, says Gallard, who's just come out. Trulock gets change from the cashier about the same time, goes back and leaves a tip. Comes back to the anteroom—or the area between the doors, or both— and waits. Michele went into *Ladies* at about twenty to eight. We've only got approximate times. At about five to eight, give or take a little, the Chavez boy saw her presumably coming out of *Ladies*, and her bag was open and she dropped some money on the floor."

"Which does not say," said Higgins, "that she was getting out any money. For any reason. Those evening bags aren't very big. She'd probably be putting away her lipstick, powder puff, etcetera. The money fell out."

"Yes. Why was she carrying a wad of money, George? On a date with her fiancé?"

"What's in your mind now?"

"Nothing. I just wondered. Again in passing. Just as you say, people coming and going, the Guillaume woman couldn't swear Michele didn't just join Trulock and go out."

"Which leaves it up in the air again. I just say, it's a little simpler story if it was Trulock, and the homicides are very seldom as complicated in real life as in books and on TV," said Higgins.

"Granted, granted," said Mendoza. He made a steeple of his long hands and rested his chin on it. "As I said at the time, very simple, if so. They went on arguing, he lost his temper, and grabbed hold of her to shake her, and hey presto, he's left with a corpse. And the rest of it. What do you suggest we do about it, George? If so?"

"What? Well—"

"He's a shrewd young fellow," said Mendoza. "If that was how it happened, George, we'll never nail him unless he swears out a confession in front of a notary public. There's nothing to connect him. If he did it, he covered it up just fine."

"Unless we could break him down," said Higgins. "Get him to admit it."

"*Pues sí.* I don't think we would. And I don't, somehow, think that was the way it happened," said Mendoza, sounding dissatisfied.

"A hunch," said Higgins. "One of your duds." He sounded exasperated.

"I don't think so," said Mendoza. "He was so annoyed, George. Sounding genuinely annoyed. As well as concerned. Michele vanishing from *Ladies.*"

"You and your nuances," said Higgins. "I still think we ought to lean on him some more."

"Go and lean on him then," said Mendoza. "You're just the boy to do it right—the big tough cop. See what you get."

"You always say," said Palliser, "the simple explanation is more apt to be the right one."

"So it is," said Mendoza. "But there's a saying that it's the exception that proves the rule. Archaic use of the word—proves. As in automobile proving runs—meaning, tests the rule."

Sergeant Lake looked in. "Traffic call. D.O.A. over on Occidental. There's an ambulance there, they tried to save the kid, no go."

"Oh, damn," said Higgins.

"The routine does go on, George."

The new body looked like being another little mystery, and after getting what the squad-car's report and the General Hospital could tell him, Landers came back to the office and roped Jason Grace in on it.

The body was identified. There had been a billfold still on it, holding plenty of I.D. The body was that of Francis DeLuccio, of an address on Sycamore Drive in Hollywood. There were several credit cards in the billfold, an up-to-date driver's license, membership cards in the Elks, Lions, Rotary and Kiwanis, and some snapshots probably of his family—a darkhaired woman, some kids about nine or ten. The body had been wearing some very good and expensive clothes, a custom-tailored suit, handmade shoes. It had been lying on the sidewalk up against the building there, and there was, said the hospital, a bullet in its head.

"What was anybody doing down there in the middle of the night?" asked Landers. The estimated time of death was between two and four A.M.

"Late poker party," suggested Grace.

"Well, let's go ask questions. My car? Did I tell you about that Hanson thing? My God, the way he just fell apart—"

"I heard something. We just seem to be getting the offbeat ones lately," said Grace. "Did I tell you about those Goddamned shysters pressuring us on the Yocum thing? And I'd take no bets they don't get away with it, either. My God—the Yocums, about one step ahead of Neanderthal, the rat-poison, *five* kids, and it's spread all over the papers, simple rural family, accidental death, terrible tragedy, and these brutal Fascist cops—"

"You'll get high blood pressure," said Landers. "I know, I know."

"But I only left him a minute," she said to Higgins. "Only a minute. I never leave him long. I'm careful."

"Yes, Mrs. Ganacia," said Higgins.

She looked up at him piteously, a very pretty girl, the clear olive skin, big dark eyes, black hair in a neat gamin cut. She wasn't twenty, he thought. "I'm careful," she told him. "You have to take care of a baby. He's only ten months old, you know. He *was*—oh, my God—such a strong healthy baby."

"Yes, Mrs. Ganacia." The squad-car men stood by silently. But I hate these things, thought Higgins, why do these things have to happen? He thought about Mary; about Steve saying so earnestly, Gee, I hope it's a girl; of the kids arguing about names. A baby. Lively, demanding attention, annoying, time-consuming—and vulnerable.

178

"It was only a minute," she said. "I had his formula on the stove, I just went to check that. I didn't—didn't think about the new dress —on the bed—"

The new dress in its neat plastic bag. The baby crawling, playing with the plastic bag, getting the bag over its head— One of the squad-car men had tried mouth-to-mouth resuscitation, but it hadn't been any use. The ambulance had tried oxygen. N.G.

"She gave me her mother's phone number, sir," said one of the uniformed men. "I called her, she's coming right away."

"Mrs. Ganacia, if you'll tell me where your husband works," said Higgins, "we'll get him here—"

Her face twisted and her eyes went blank and she turned writhingly away from him as though he'd stabbed her to the heart, and he hated these things, and she said, "Tony—was killed—in Vietnam —five months ago."

Higgins put his notebook away.

"But I don't understand it!" said Rosemary DeLuccio. She looked at Landers and Grace a little wildly. "It—it isn't—anything that could *happen.* I told you—" She gestured, and put her head in one palm.

She had told them things. She wasn't the kind to go to pieces, even at such drastic news. A handsome rather than pretty woman in the mid-thirties, which had been her husband's age. And this house on Sycamore Drive said money, said success, said people of taste; if this living room was very modern in décor, it was also very neat and clean.

Francis DeLuccio had been co-owner of a chain of discount stores. Well-known stores. He had, obviously, made a lot of money via the satisfied customers. His partner was one Herbert Ochsenstein, and at the moment he was back in Chicago negotiating a wholesale purchase of some kind.

A business of that kind—both Landers and Grace were familiar with the stores—dealt in anything and everything. The partners, relying on a very small percentage of profit but enormous volume, bought merchandise in carload lots—from companies gone bankrupt, companies behind on payments, that kind of thing, and sold at discount prices. Anything from kitchen chairs to cosmetics, wallboard to lamps and carpets and toys.

"I told you," she said. "Frank shot—it's a nightmare, nothing like that could happen—I *told* you. He went out after dinner last night, yes. He said he was going to meet a Mr. Potter, it was about a big shipment of—of steel office desks, there might be a terrific profit in it. It was somewhere in Hollywood—he said he'd probably be home about ten. But he didn't come and didn't come and—he was a careful driver but I thought—and I called the police but they—"

"He was driving," said Landers. "What's his car?"

"A two-door Cadillac, two years old," she said automatically. "White. I don't know the license—"

Grace said in his soft voice, "Mr. Potter? Did he tell you his first name? Mention where they were meeting?"

She looked up blindly at his brown face and grave dark eyes. "I don't know," she said. "There might—be something about it—in his desk. In the study. You can look—"

Higgins had typed up a report on the baby, and finding Palliser in, vented his feelings on that. Palliser listened absently. "You do look so much like the big tough cop in the murder mysteries thirty years back," he said, putting out his cigarette. "And the boss did say—I've been thinking about it, and the more I think—"

"About what?" said Higgins.

"Trulock," said Palliser. "It is really the easiest explanation, isn't it? On Michele."

"It damn well is."

"Let's go lean on him," said Palliser.

They were leaning on Trulock now, in his cubicle of an office in the handsome new building of that very reputable law firm; and so far from intimidating him, they had made him mad.

He was pacing the confines of the little office; he drove fingers through his dark hair, and he said savagely to the two men from Homicide, "So *I* did it. You can't find out who did it or what happened or anything about it, so you get the notion in your stupid heads I must be it! You can't *prove* what I told you is so—that's the word you used, isn't it, prove—so it must be a lie! Goddamn it, I always heard we had some brainy cops in L.A., but if this is a sample—"

"Sit down, Trulock," said Higgins. "Calm down. We like to think we're halfway smart, sure. We usually get at the truth in the end, Trulock. Separate it from the cock-and-bull stories."

"So you think I told you a—"

"Nobody said that, Mr. Trulock," said Palliser gently. The time-honored technique: tough, threatening cop and nice polite cop.

"But what you have told us just isn't so plausible, when you think it over. Everything we've heard about Michele Stanyard says she wasn't—well, a very strong character, shall we say? Somebody said she was 'always a follower,' which I guess sums it up. Yet you told us you thought she might have been angry enough at you that night to walk out on you, and that was why you didn't call the police at once. You—"

"Well, for God's sake," said Trulock, "you don't have to be a strong character to lose your temper! When she didn't come—when—damn it, sometimes she sulked a little. Over it in half an hour, but— And everything I told you is the exact damn truth! I thought you were supposed to be good, this force. You haven't found out *anything* on it? Not one damn thing? So you need a damn scapegoat and—saying *I*—"

The door opened and a glamorous-looking blonde peeped in shyly. "Mr. Paul," she said apologetically. "Your father has a client with him, if you'd keep your voice down—"

"Oh, all right, sorry, Dotty. But Goddamn it—" Trulock whirled on Higgins and Palliser. "Of all the crazy—I'll swear on a stack of Bibles, everything I told you—"

Mendoza was just leaving for lunch when Sergeant Lake put through an outside call. It was that Fed, Claude Serio. "We've been kind of busy, but I thought I'd check back on that case. First supposed a kidnaping. I assume, hearing nothing from you, that it wasn't. Got anything on it?"

"*Absolutamente* nothing," said Mendoza sadly. "And while the high-class moneyed citizens from Beverly Hills haven't been doing so yet, Serio, I have the feeling that when they recover from their first grief they're going to be—mmh—nipping at my heels, haven't you found the villain yet? It's very funny something hasn't showed, and what my wife calls my 'satiable curiosity' is bothering me."

"Well, you boys are usually sharp at getting there," said Serio.

"Even the L.A.P.D.," said Mendoza, "can't make bricks without straw."

He went up to Federico's and met Higgins and Palliser just sitting down. "Evidently that new thing is keeping Tom and Jase busy," he told them. "Tom called in half an hour ago and said they were heading for Van Nuys. Didn't say why. At least it isn't raining. The steak sandwich, Adam."

"Yes, sir, well done. Gentlemen?"

"I'll have a Scotch and water and the steak sandwich," said Higgins. "You're absolutely right about Trulock, Luis. We've had a session with him. If he is X—if it happened like that, and by God I'd like to think it did—we'll never prove it on him. How could we, as long as he keeps saying *She never met me, I never saw her again?* And he'll keep on saying it till hell freezes over—he's a lawyer, he can see that as well as we can."

"And just suppose," said Mendoza, "*por casualidad,* that he keeps on saying so because it's the truth?"

"Then what the hell *did* happen to her?" asked Palliser almost violently. "All right. She might have meant to run out on him. In a fit of the sulks. She might have phoned somebody. We haven't asked every living soul she knew whether she had. Do we go and do that? And if she phoned X, come and get me, we ask and X says no and where are we? It's just like Art says, no handle to get hold of."

"The diamonds," said Mendoza meditatively. "I'm thinking about the diamonds. We're supposing for the moment it was a private, personal kill? Even if unintended, some personal motive for somebody to get mad at her? Somebody she knew. Somebody, barring Eileen and her crowd, and I really think they're out of the running, who hadn't any real use for the diamonds—they were taken to make it look like robbery and assault."

"Well?" Higgins sampled his drink.

"Well, in that case, X will hang on to the diamonds for dear life. Anybody Michele knew personally is very unlikely to know a real fence, get rid of them that way. But that many diamonds might be a little awkward to keep secret."

"I don't see that—"

"No handle," said Mendoza. "And it is so tempting to think, Trulock. But—I just have the feeling that we're reading too many ramifications into it, boys."

"That, from you!" said Higgins.

"No, but it usually is simple, isn't it? The deliberate or unintended homicide. Look at some of what we've been coping with just lately." Mendoza emitted a long stream of blue smoke. "Hanson. Ordering the pseudo-suicide. Coming apart as soon as it's shown to be pseudo. That Weiss thing—poor devil Vincent losing his head, scared. That Darley thing—she stopped the kid from watching his favorite TV shows. Even the Spencer thing—on my own doorstep. Mom wouldn't let him have the car that night."

"Well?" said Higgins again.

"I just have the feeling," said Mendoza, "that it's such a simple explanation nobody's thought of it."

He hadn't been back in his office half an hour when Sergeant Lake put through an inside call. "Mendoza."

"Me," said Lieutenant Goldberg. "You sent down a description and appraisal of some diamonds. About ten grand worth. A four-and-a-half-carat solitaire ring and a diamond and emerald necklace. And what one of your corpses down here was doing with—"

"¡Válgame Dios! Don't tell me—"

"They've just turned up," said Goldberg. "We dropped on a fence an hour ago—I haven't had lunch yet—and we're going through the stuff he had on hand. Lucky he hadn't got round to breaking up the necklace yet. . . . Yes, my office."

"¡Allá voy!" said Mendoza. "I'm on my way!"

Higgins and Palliser were still there, no new call in, so he took them along with him, down to Burglary.

"Pretty things," said Goldberg. The solitaire ring and the necklace were lying on his desk; he touched them. "A lot classier stuff than this particular fence usually would get in, and I bet he dickered over them."

"So, give!" said Mendoza. It was Michele's necklace all right, the old-fashioned design, some sixty delicate little flowers strung together on a chain.

"One Joel Wechsler, Grand Avenue," said Goldberg, blowing his nose. "We've had an eye on him for some time. He's done time for fencing before. I'd had a tail on a pro burglar not long out of Quentin, and just last night we got the lab evidence on him—prints off a local job—and by that time he was already with Wechsler." He sneezed. "Ostensibly a second-hand furniture store, Wechsler's place. So we picked 'em both up, having an excuse to get into the store. Now we're busy inventorying everything there." He sneezed again and reached for Kleenex.

"All right, who'd he get the diamonds from?" asked Higgins eagerly.

"I haven't asked him," said Goldberg. "It's a Homicide case," and he grinned up at them. "You can go and ask. There aren't any records in the store, of course."

"¡Muchas gracias!" said Mendoza. "We may get some answers on this thing now."

They went straight down to the jail, and asked to see Wechsler. He was a big fat fellow about fifty, still unshaven and looking unkempt in the loose jail clothes. He went on saying I don't know and Why should I tell you anything, in a dispirited way, until Mendoza said firmly, "Listen to me, Wechsler! We're from Homicide and that lot of diamonds you bought is hooked up to a murder—do you want to be roped in on it?"

Wechsler licked his lips. "M-murder?" he said. "I didn't have anything to do with—no, no, you don't rope me in on a thing like that! I didn't know—"

"So, who brought you the solitaire ring, that necklace?" demanded Mendoza.

"It was beautiful stuff," said Wechsler. "Lovely. I—I used to have my own jewelry store, you know, I know the trade. Stones. I don't see pieces like that much now—down here." His mouth was bitter. "I gave him thirty-four hundred, and I don't usually have money like that on hand either, but I'd just made a deal— Never mind."

"Who?" asked Mendoza.

Wechsler looked up at him. "Roberto Diaz," he said. "That young fellow calls himself a boxer. Well, he's had a few pro fights—middleweight he is—nothing big yet, but he's pretty good—got the hell of a good left. But a smasher, you know? No science, just a bullheaded smasher. He calls himself the Mexico City Kid, but I don't think he's ever been out of California—local boy."

They looked at each other blankly. "Do you know where he lives?"

"No, no. The only reason I know him at all, my place is on Grand and he hangs around Bernie's gym up the street—trains there, I guess. Also the pool-hall on that corner. I've seen him in the ring a couple of times. I don't think he knew I knew him, and I've got no idea who told him I'd—buy under the counter. No, he never came in before with anything."

"When did he bring it in?"

"Last Saturday night. I hadn't broken up the necklace yet because I wasn't sure where—I'd put out some feelers on it, but I don't usually handle that class of—"

"Did he say anything about where he got it?"

"Now, would he?" asked Wechsler wearily. "Of course not. Came in, plunked it down, and I saw it was good stuff. I offered him three grand, we dickered around and I ended up giving him thirty-four hundred. And that's all I know about it."

At Bernie's gym on Grand Avenue, the little wizened ex-light-weight who was Bernie said, "Bobby Diaz? You maybe got a proposition for him? A real fighter, that boy—make the big time some day—"

"Maybe," said Mendoza. "Where do we find him?"

"He lives on Magdalena. I get you the address."

"But what the hell," said Higgins, "does Diaz the pro boxer have to do with Michele? For God's sake?"

"Paciencia," said Mendoza.

And they found Diaz out in front of the old house on Magdalena Street where he rented a room, and that was not very far from the alley where Michele had been left. He was busily polishing up an old Ford Galaxie sedan. He was stripped to the waist, so they could see all his muscles: a stocky, hard-bodied young man in the early twenties. He didn't look as if he was overburdened with brains, and they would probably have got the story out of him sooner or later via the questioning in depth; but fate took a little hand in the proceedings.

Diaz was still gazing in awed admiration at the sleek black Ferrari when they came up to him and Mendoza said, "Roberto Diaz?"

"Yeah, that's me. Say, mister, that's some car you got—"

Mendoza reached for his badge; and just then a boy's clear voice rang out behind him. "Hey, Roberto! Rita says tell you she's gonna be off early, you pick her up at five—"

Mendoza whirled. And the boy, spotting him, lost his balance and tumbled from the old bicycle with its saddlebags of newspapers, and sprawled, and got up to run. Palliser caught him.

"Manuel Chavez," said Mendoza. And his mind made one leap, and he said with a little gasp, *"¡Yo caigo en ello! Dios*—but, *sin duda,* you told us and we swallowed it whole without one question—"

The boy squirmed in Palliser's grasp, and his eyes were frightened.

"Hey," said Diaz, "you got no call hurt the kid. Who are you guys?"

Higgins showed him the badge and he froze.

And Mendoza said, *"Condenación.* A juvenile. Have to contact the parents before we—"

"He ain't got none," said Diaz stupidly. "What—you *cops*—"

"There's only Rita—Rita won't let you hurt me, you bastards—"

So they wanted to talk to Rita too.

"You gotta get things how you can," said the boy. "Rita always says." He was dirty and ragged, but his dark eyes were intelligent

185

on the Homicide men: a bright boy, and he was talking because he'd seen sense in what they told him. It was all hooked up, connected now, and Manuel and Rita and Diaz were linked in whether they talked or not. "I go in Mr. Robineau's alla time—people buy, feel sorry for me." He grinned; he was wholly at ease now he saw they weren't going to lay a finger on him. "A lotta rich people go there, and I seen that girl and her fella before. And I hear what that lady in front says to Mr. Robineau about her di'mond ring— the girl's. It's worth a lotta money, thousands of dollars. So I see 'em go in that night"—he gestured—"and I think, Rita'll know some way to get it. Rita's smart."

Rita was nineteen, his sister and only relative. She worked at a Woolworth lunch-counter uptown, and they lived in two rooms on St. John Street, four blocks from Diaz.

And Diaz was Rita's steady boyfriend.

"And she did?" asked Mendoza.

"Sure. She's smart," said Manuel. "I went home and told her about it—" It was only another four blocks from the restaurant, of course. "And she called Roberto. She figured out right away how to do. She told Roberto just how to do, wait in the parking lot, see. Then she went in the restaurant—Rita, she's pretty, and she put her best dress on, nobody noticed, there was people goin' and comin'— and she went down to that side door there, wait. She said, prob'ly the girl'd go in *Ladies* when they left."

"As she did," said Mendoza. So very simple indeed.

"Sure. Rita told us how she'd do. Pretend to be sick, goin' to faint maybe, an' ask the girl help her out where her husband's waitin' in the lot. I was supposed to wait in the hall there, tell her if anybody else was comin' into *Ladies,* but nobody did. No other lady. One came out just when the girl went in, an' I give the sign to Rita. Pretty soon I saw 'em come out, Rita pretendin' be sick an' the girl helpin' her—out that side door Rita takes her—"

It was all frighteningly simple.

"Listen," said Diaz passionately, "I didn't mean *that!* My God, I never—Rita says, just keep the girl quiet till we get the jewelry off her, that's all—they come out, an' I just took hold o' the girl, shut her up—but my God, we get down to my car, she was—she was— I didn't know what the hell to do, but Rita, she said just leave her some place and nobody'd ever find out—my God, you got to believe I never meant—"

And Rita, who was much the strongest character of the three, looked at them with smouldering dark eyes and said exactly nothing. But they found Michele's black velvet evening bag and the black velvet jacket in her bedroom. With Michele's initialed compact in the bag.

"And Manuel," said Mendoza sardonically, "is one smart boy. Sharp enough to cut himself. *Pues sí.* He was there that night I was poking around in Le Renard Bleu. Talking to myself about Michele —talking to Robineau. He heard me say I was convinced, if she hadn't had any money on her, whatever happened to her had happened right there. As of course it had. And if we went sniffing around right there— One very bright boy indeed. The chain-lightning mind. He hears that, and he looks at me wide-eyed and says, But, mister, she did have some money. And I take him as the providential witness —my God!" Mendoza laughed.

"My God, of course," said Palliser. "I see—just because you said that—too damn bright a boy, you ask me. What's going to become of him?"

"He's what, twelve?" said Higgins. They were sitting around Mendoza's office after the preliminary routine had been done: Manuel in Juvenile Hall, Rita and Diaz in jail, the warrants applied for. "Twelve—spotting the mark for Rita and Roberto. Probation, and the foster homes for Manuel. My God."

"Yes," said Mendoza. "Anybody's guess how Manuel will turn out, George. But didn't I say it was the simple thing? It usually is." He gave a long sigh. "Now, at least, we know. About Michele. And I can go tell the high-class parents that X is caught. Though, as to punishment—"

"Well, yes," said Palliser. "They'll probably charge him with second degree—no intent—and he'll be out within five years."

"We're only paid to find them," said Higgins heavily. "I think I'll call Art to tell him—he'll be interested. . . . That new thing must be tough, Tom and Grace out on it all day. . . . But what a silly thing this was, Luis—Michele. What an unnecessary thing. The nice girl—"

"Homicides," said Mendoza, "so often are, George." It was six-fifteen; the preliminary routine had taken a while. "At least my 'satiable curiosity' is satisfied—until the next little mystery comes along." He stood up from his desk and reached for the wide-brimmed Homburg. He said, "The new one—yes, possibly a new mystery, by what Tom said—but, sufficient is the evil unto the day. See you, boys," and he started for home, for Alison, the twins, the cats, and their shaggy dog Cedric.

Tomorrow was also a day.